The Grace Murders: Caspar's Run

By
Karen Michaud

~~~

This story was a Nanowrimo 2012 entry. Thank you to the Nanowrimo team and all the volunteers who make Nanowrimo possible. Thank you, everyone who cheered me on: friends, family, and all the on-line Nanowrimo enthusiasts on Google+ who make the event so fun.

~~~

License Notes:

~~~

Cover art: The woman chained to Death is by Karin Boye circa 1916-1918; autopsy engraving by John Bell circa 1810. Cover layout by Karen Michaud.

~~~

[1. Paranormal—Fiction. 2. Romance—Fiction.
3. Horror—Fiction. 4. Suspense—Fiction.
5. The Great Depression—Fiction.]

First Edition, November 2012

~~~

About the translations: The French in this story is Quebecois French. Much of it is swear words, and these do not translate readily in a manner that would mean anything to an English reader. I translated them to the nearest equivalent that an English speaking person would use. The most disrespectful French swear words involve religious symbols. Sexual-based profanities, such as the ever prevalent four letter word, often mean little to a French-speaking Quebec citizen. Incorrect spelling is intentional for the French swearing in this novel. The misspellings reflect the patois of the people and also their way of avoiding proper pronunciation of a religious word.

Other characters in the story speak Swedish or Italian. For the French, I live in a bilingual family and am familiar with the Quebecois dialect, but for the Swedish and Italian, I did my best to research these languages and check their translations off against different on-line translators, Google and Bing primarily. I'm always open to feedback. If a Swedish or Italian-speaking reader should wish to correct any of my blunders, please feel to contact me on one of my blogs.

Rather than force a reader to look elsewhere on the page for the English translations, I placed them in the same paragraph near the sentences with the French, Swedish or Italian. Just look for italic font. The last chapter has the translations afterward, however, since the point of view character of the final section does not, as of this book, understand Swedish and I wanted the reader to feel her bewilderment.

For the research of the Great Depression and the years prior, I used Wikipedia. Wikipedia has no advertisement other than when the yearly fund-raising comes up. The site is kept free through donations. Please donate to the Wikipedia Foundation and help keep this superlative site free and available.

~~~

~~~

Parent advisory and content warning: This novel has teenaged characters central to the plot, but the story content is not intended for a young readership. This novel contains profanity, sexual situations and violence. The sexual content is not graphic, but it is unambiguous and sometimes combined with conversations concerning violence or with a character's evil intentions. Sensitive readers should refrain from reading this novel.

~~~

Two extra notes: When Godefroy mentions eleven labours in Chapter Twelve, he's referring to the Twelve Labours of Hercules, and in Chapter Five, Farideh is reading from The Land of Oz by L. Frank Baum.

~~~

Chapter One

"Godefroy," Edvard whispered.

"Ja." Godefroy slithered deeper under cover. Their remaining targets had arrived and almost too late. The sun barely lit the wooded shore. Edvard was unlikely to get all his shots fired now. If anything, the family might win a few years of grace if Edvard managed a kill or two. Murdering criminals never offered them much.

They could have killed the three men who had arrived with the truck a few minutes ago rather than wait for the smugglers on the lake, but Godefroy hadn't wanted to haul oars in a boat chase after, though Edvard had expressed an interest in sniping the boatmen from the canoe.

The boat slowed. The oars rose out of the water and were stowed. The leader caught a rope tossed from shore and wound the end around a cleat. The men waiting for the load hauled the vessel toward a rickety dock that had seen better days. Edvard nosed the Lee-Enfield slightly left.

Godefroy glanced to his rear. He'd heard a faint snap. "Edvard. Jag horde ett ljud." *I heard a noise.*

"Ja," Edvard breathed. *Yes.* He squeezed the trigger, and someone at the lake died. Shouts of alarm in French, English and Italian sounded.

"Godefroy! Du är inte ute. Slösa inte detta." *You aren't looking. Don't waste this.*

Godefroy cast his gaze back at the lake to spot one body sprawled on the dock, but then his attention reverted to the dim spaces between trees. Edvard squeezed the trigger again. Another man died by the lake, but now there were shouts within the forest as well.

"This way! This way!"

Godefroy lifted to a crouch. Down at the lake, men scattered away from the shore. A second body floated in the water near the base of the dock. "Edvard! Vi går nu!" *We go now!*

"Ja." Edvard pulled the rifle back and hefted off his belly. He and his brother charged north, toward the canoe they'd hidden along the lake shore beneath scrub.

"I see them!"

A shot sounded. The bullet thwacked into a tree near Godefroy's head. He stumbled and put a hand to his ear. He pulled it away covered in blood. He'd scraped his ear against a broken branch when he'd flinched. "Gud i himlen!" *God in heaven!*

Edvard turned and shot the pursuer, his motions quick and easy. "Flytta." *Move.*

Godefroy snapped the dead branch from the tree and rushed onward. Back at the dock, gunfire and angry shouts sounded. Here in the woods, a man cursed somewhere not distant enough. Another shot fired. Godefroy didn't know where the bullet hit, because he didn't hear the strike. Likely it had sunk into moss somewhere in advance of them. He sprinted and dodged around trees with Edvard thumping the uneven ground to his rear.

No sound of pursuit or shots were fired for minutes after, and Godefroy hoped they were in the clear, that their pursuers had turned back to help their cohorts arrest smugglers rather than chase dangerous men who had shot two criminals. He and his brother arrived at the canoe, barely able to see now. They hauled the scrub away and shoved the canoe down the slope to the lake.

"Få i. Få paddeln," Edvard urged his brother. *Get in. Get the paddle.*

"Ja, ja."

Godefroy crawled in while Edvard continued pushing further into the water. Godefroy grabbed a paddle. A shot sounded. His brother grunted and stumbled away from the stern. Blood spread from his right side and clouded the water.

"Edvard!" Godefroy lunged forward and avoided a shot that breezed past his head. The canoe floated further away from his brother. Godefroy stretched an arm, but couldn't reach him. They were already yards away. He started to offer the oar.

"Nej! Gå! Gå!" *No! Go! Go!*

"Nej!"

"Gå! Du vet jag är dömd redan!" *You know I am doomed already.* Edvard tossed the rifle. It sailed the air and landed in the canoe. "Gå!"

2

A third and fourth shot sounded. The third splattered water. The fourth hit the bow and splintered wood.

"Gå!" Edvard shouted again. He pulled a pistol from the holster hidden within his coat and fired at the shooter, who hid in a tangle of deadwood a little south. Godefroy hauled on the oar while Edvard edged from the water. "Ta väl hand om Caspar," Edvard said. *Take good care of Caspar.*

"Ja," Godefroy replied, already weeping. "Döda några i fängelse om du bor." *Kill a few in jail if you live.*

"Ja, ja! Inte att det kommer att hjälpa. Skynda dig!" *Yes, yes! Not that it will help. Hurry up!*

Godefroy dug in with his heels and pulled the oar through water. The canoe turned and shot away from shore. Another shot whizzed past his body. He ignored the near strike and focused on escape. His brother had already said it: Edvard was doomed. Caspar would be doomed next, but not for many years to come if Godefroy could help it; and if God granted any grace to their cursed family, then some extra kills in prison would keep the curse from Caspar for a few years at least, even without a witness.

"Käre Gud, låt pojken har sin barndom på minst," he breathed. *Dear God, let the boy have his childhood at least.*

On the shore, more shots were fired. Edvard had dragged himself behind a boulder. Godefroy could barely see him.

"Gud vara med er, min bror," Godefroy whispered, though in his heart he felt God had abandoned his family a millennium ago. *God be with you, my brother.*

Chapter Two

July 27, 1929. Coney Island, New York.

For summer holiday, Farideh Tremblay's family visited New York, and that meant Coney Island, Surf Avenue, a hotdog eating contest, a lapse in the alertness of parenting eyes and a confrontation with fate, despite that Farideh's mother had forbidden fortune telling and any other occult nonsense from her daughters' lives.

Farideh and her sister didn't participate in the hotdog eating contest, but they did watch. Ara vomited on the boardwalk after a competitor burped chewed hotdog out his nose. Farideh vomited after eating one too many balls of fairy floss. This was long after the burping incident of course; Farideh was much tougher than her sister, and she was less messy about it too. She threw up in someone's sand bucket and ran away after.

The fortune telling almost didn't occur, not until Farideh had the bad luck to happen across her nemesis, Sylvie Muise, on Surf Avenue. Sylvie as usual was dressed to the nines, every brunette ringlet artfully pinned to dance in the sea breeze without bouncing into her face. She wore everything a girl shouldn't wear to Coney Island: white Mary Janes that were useless in sand, a pristine white dress that would catch every accidental drop of food and cherish the stain for eternity. The Peter Pan collar didn't move at all in the wind. Neither did the huge white bow in her hair. Farideh thought it might have been starched directly to her head.

It didn't matter that Sylvie Muise was on summer holiday, that she was twelve, that her entourage of shoe-kissing curly girls weren't present. Sylvie lived to dominate the crowd, any crowd, even Coney Island too-hot and too-much hotdog crowd. She particularly lived to dominate the Tremblay twins, who had the nerve to be a mix of Canadian and Persian, therefore possessed of unusual vibrant blue eyes in faces that some referred to as dark and exotic. Sylvie called Farideh and Ara the sallow twins.

Sallow. Farideh hated the word sallow. She also hated the word olive, and olives in general. She didn't like the word tan much either. She especially hated black and nigger, but Sylvie hadn't dared call them the nigger twins after Sister Thérèse heard her say it. Sylvie had been sent to the front of the class, not as a reward this time, but to write 'I must not demean my fellow classmates, for it demeans me before God,' over and over until she'd whined that her arms were tired, and then Sister Thérèse had made her write 'I must not whine over my lot in life. It makes me weak and ineffectual.'

That had been a good day. Even one of the curly girls couldn't suppress a giggle over Sylvie's outraged, *ineffectual* snivelling. This had meant instant ejection from Sylvie's entourage, but it had also meant a new friend for Farideh, because Daniella, the giggler, had joined the Tremblay entourage and confessed it to be much funner. She especially liked the belly dancing tea parties.

But that was back home in Toronto, Canada, and this was here on Coney Island, and though Farideh adored Sister Thérèse and wished she could have brought the nun on holidays, Sister Thérèse wasn't here to protect them now. Farideh just had to hope the presence of both sets of parents would.

"Muise," Farideh's father said, hand reaching out for a shake.

Mr. Muise clasped it. "Tremblay."

The hands unclasped, and the two men commenced discussions about stock options, at which point Farideh at last understood the import of New York as a holiday choice. Her father's two disappearances during business hours had been work related. Today was Saturday, and her father hadn't been able to ditch a family outing, but he was working all the same, here on the busy pedestrian sidewalk of Surf Avenue when they were long overdue to return to the hotel, wash up and go down to the dining room for supper. Farideh had the grim realisation supper might include the Muises as dinner guests.

Farideh's mother must have noticed the angry stiffness of her daughter's features, because a hand settled lightly on one shoulder and gave a gentle squeeze. "Mrs. Muise, how are you?" her mother said.

"Dinah, I'm fine, thank you. And you?"

Her mother's name was Deena. Yes, a Persian alternative of Dinah, but still not Dinah. And Mrs. Muise should have been polite enough to call her Mrs. Tremblay. Mrs. Muise had been staring fixedly at Farideh's mother since the 'chance' meeting, distaste evident in the frigid stillness of her expression and the impolite use of an incorrect first name. Farideh finally understood from where

6

Sylvie's prejudice had originated, and judging by that smug smile, Sylvie had enjoyed the nasty social gunfire her mother had shot.

"Maman? Je peux aller chez Madame Vazeem?" *Can I go to Madame Vazeem's?*

"Sylvie, darling, we must speak English before your father's business associates. They aren't French," Mrs. Muise said.

"We're trilingual, Marie-Joseph," Deena said, smiling pleasantly. Farideh was amazed to see not a speck of distaste or anger in the smile, but that was a fine shot back at the French bigot. Unless Sylvie's mother wished to be referred to as Mrs. Muise or something other than Marie-Joseph, then Marie-Joseph was stuck with a girl boy name for the evening. "French, English and Persian," Deena continued. "There's no need to worry over speaking English or French."

"Don't forget German," Ara said. "And … Spanish? Right?"

"Yes, my beauty. German and Spanish too, but as a family, only English, French and Persian," Deena said, giving Ara a quick kiss on the top of her head and passing a hand part way down the thick French braid. Their mothered adored French braids. She said it gave them a girlish but cultured appearance, and it was better for the health of their hair. No burned-in curls for them.

"Oh, this is right. Fairy's maman worked as a spy during the war," Sylvie gushed with an artful cant to her head and the sickest sweet smile possible. Farideh wanted to vomit again. On that white dress.

"Translator," Deena corrected lightly. "It's how I met Mr. Tremblay. He needed help with German."

Spy. Her mother had been a spy. Truly. But translator was the official story. Beauty and a skill for belly dancing could get a girl close enough to arrogant and stupid men for the purpose of acquiring interesting information—that and the ability to play at being an oblivious, uneducated woman of no value who spoke neither English, French or German. Deena had perfected the art of smiling with abandon at anything like everything made her happy. Sometimes Farideh wondered if everything did.

It was a secret, the spy work, even from Farideh and Ara. Farideh's mother didn't know that she knew. Ara still didn't know either. Farideh had kept hush after sneaking into her mother's room to filch the war diary for a quick peek. The quick peek had become a multi-visit stealth operation and a lot of things learned, things she probably shouldn't have learned—not about spying, but about her mother and father and the skills Deena had shown David Tremblay during the war, skills that had little to do with warfare.

Since these skills had resulted in a marriage and the arrival of herself and Ara, Farideh didn't like to complain, even in her head, but that her mother had been a high class courtesan prior to the outbreak of the war still sometimes bothered her. She hadn't informed Ara of these facts simply because Ara had always been the more innocent and honest twin and therefore unable to keep a secret. Farideh liked to protect her sister from hurtful things. Today she'd spend the rest of the afternoon and evening protecting Ara from Sylvie, who could smell a secret a mile away.

But everyone joked that Deena Tremblay had been a spy during the war. Most considered it unlikely and therefore funny. Sylvie might have caught a whiff of the truth, but she was guessing like anyone else. The other secret, the courtesan secret, would be more damaging to the family by far if it came into the light.

Farideh had overheard whispering—in the schoolyard, at functions—that suggested her father's peers suspected her mother's history was less than socially proper, but no one had been able to prove it. Her father had upset his own family marrying down and without warning. He'd simply arrived home from war with a woman of questionable ancestry, a diamond engagement ring and matching wedding band on her ring finger, and a set of tiny daughters in his arms. Deena's cultured charm had eventually won the elder Tremblay's over, but others, like Mrs. Muise, still fired the occasional unpleasant volley to see if they could rattle David Tremblay's foreign wife, the exotic beauty with too dark skin and unusual blue eyes. So far, no one had.

"Fairy?" Deena said. "Why that's a lovely nickname, Farideh. How sweet of Sylvie to choose it. Such potent creatures, fairies. Did you know your father saw one? He says it stole his pocket watch and put it inside his shoe the next day."

Farideh tried but could not suppress a smile. She'd taken the pocket watch when she was five and used it during a tea party with Ara and Mr. Poofs, Ara's invisible friend. Somehow, they and Mr. Poofs had gotten lost in her father's walk-in closet, which had been a dark forest at the time, and the pocket watch, which had been a talisman of protection, had dropped into a shoe during a battle with a ferocious child-eating ogre. They'd run screaming out of the closet

8

directly after and 'forgotten' they'd had the pocket watch, perhaps because Mr. Poofs had warned them Papa was feeling irritable over finding it missing from the top of his dresser.

"Maman, really. I want to visit Madame Vazeem's," Sylvie said in an obvious attempt to distract. She tugged the sleeve of her mother's cashmere sweater impatiently.

Farideh's smile brightened. Her mother had just cleansed the insult from Sylvie's choice of nickname, and Sylvie didn't like it one bit, because she barely refrained from scowling. The one thing she repeated most often to her curly girls: 'Never frown no matter what. You don't want wrinkles, do you?'

"Perhaps in a bit, my darling," Mrs. Muise said.

"Maman!"

"Oh, very well! Martha will take you." Mrs. Muise gave an exasperated wave to a sturdy woman in serviceable clothes who stood a few feet behind them. "Really. And I wanted to visit too, Sylvie," Mrs. Muise said. Her gaze narrowed on her husband rather than her daughter. Apparently he was to shoulder the blame for the disaccord.

"Hello," Deena said to the woman who stepped up to accompany Sylvie.

"This is Martha, our Scottish nanny," Mrs. Muise said.

Deena smiled and offered her hand.

Martha shook it. "Ma'am," she said.

Mrs. Muise set a hand on her husband's suit sleeve. "Richard, darling. Let's have that coffee you promised. Whatever you want to discuss with David can wait a few minutes while we relocate to this lovely café. The danishes smell delicious."

"Why don't you go along with Sylvie, darling?" Richard Muise suggested.

"My feet are tired." Mrs. Muise rolled her eyes in Deena's direction. Farideh found that interesting. Marie-Joseph Muise might dislike Deena Tremblay's excess of colour, but she still sided with the women over the men.

"Yes, of course," Mr. Muise said. "Run along, then, Sylvie."

"Papa, I need more money."

"No, you don't, young lady," the Scottish nanny inserted. "Your father gave us plenty for this outing, and there'll be no nonsense from you about it."

Sylvie's lower lip bulged.

"Isn't she lovely?" Mrs. Muise said. "Scottish nannies take no nonsense from children whatsoever. Martha is the best from the agency. Three of my acquaintances tried to have her first, but she's with us."

Ah. It was a status thing, having a woman who would fearlessly say no to the petulant pouting beastie of the Muise household, and for once Farideh was happy with high society. Fashionable standards had finally worked against Sylvie.

"How perfect!" Deena said. "It's never too soon to have such a woman about. They're ideal companions once the girls become a certain age."

"Exactly so," Mr. Muise said, giving Deena a warm look.

Farideh's father neatly offered his arm to his wife. She wrapped her fingers around it, her happy, oblivious smile now directed at him.

Mr. Muise quickly hid his disappointment by doing the same for his wife. "Shall we?" he said. "You'll join us of course, David."

"We'd love to," David said. "Come along, girls." Farideh noted that he'd pasted on one of his perfected smiles, the polite one with a dash of toothy warning. He had it directed at Mr. Muise. Farideh had seen it directed at Mr. Muise before. Her father never failed to complain, after a social outing, that Muise was a philandering back stabber with a habit of sniffing after another man's wife.

"Oh, but your girls must accompany Sylvie," Mrs. Muise said. "Martha is fully prepared to watch over three girls. Aren't you, Martha? Martha has the stamina of an Amazon. Don't you, Martha?"

"Yes, ma'am," Martha said firmly.

Farideh's mother hesitated.

"Oh, it's all right," David said. "They'll have a Scottish nanny. Perhaps we'll hire one, hmm? Let's have a coffee and danish."

"Very well," Deena said. She looked at Farideh.

"We'll be very good," Farideh promised, which meant: 'I'll look out for Ara. Don't worry.'

Deena smiled and turned with her husband toward the coffee shop.

"Off we go, then, girls," Martha said brusquely. Sylvie and the nanny commenced walking down the avenue, but Farideh and Ara paused long enough to see their father escort their mother into the little shop of heavenly smells. The twins liked watching their mother walk. She had an elegant, languid stride, even when wearing sturdy shoes for a day-long outing.

10

Their mother's sturdy shoes were the most expensive sort and therefore lovely, but the walk, the mild cultured sway; Farideh thought it was the epitome of sophistication and so did Ara. They'd been practicing the walk now for two years. Ara had it down flat, but not Farideh. Ara said her sister still walked like she intended to tromp someone into a puddle, maybe not now, but eventually.

"You have natural grace with presence," her mother had said when she'd complained that Ara was being mean and fussy—Ara was never mean and fussy—and by that, her mother meant Farideh did have the elegant part down, but with a clip to her strides that betrayed her impatient nature. Farideh wanted the disarming languidness of her mother's walk. A girl had to be able to disarm. One couldn't survive in the world of men without being disarming, as her mother had written in her diary. Charming had its uses, but disarming had more.

"Girls!" the Scottish nanny snapped.

"Yes, ma'am," Farideh said, and she and her sister turned to enter the Sylvie Muise parade.

"I like the way she talks," Ara said.

Farideh knew she meant the nanny's Scottish accent. "Me too."

"I'm amazed Sylvie's dress is still white," Ara added.

Farideh grinned. "Me too."

"And especially amazed at her shoes."

Farideh suppressed a laugh.

"I think it's talcum powder."

"What do you mean?"

"Well, if she powders her shoes before she walks out, won't the talc protect the silk from dirt? She'd only have to brush them off and dust them again occasionally."

"Could be," Farideh admitted. "Bad idea if it's wet out. Bad idea for a beach walk."

"I don't think she went to the beach," Ara said. "Sylvie is a shopping sort of girl. I wonder what Madame Vazeem sells?"

"She sounds like a frippery shop."

"Oh, I love fripperies."

"Girls! Keep up!" Martha barked.

"Yes, ma'am," Ara said.

"You shall have to walk more like me," Farideh said.

"Yes, there's no help for it. The 'walk' is sadly inappropriate for hurried school girls."

Farideh laughed. Ara had just quoted their father, who scowled every time he caught them practicing. Ara didn't understand why he disapproved, but Farideh did. What their father wanted in a wife, he didn't want to see in his daughters. Poor Papa. He was going to have a difficult time when they began seeing boys.

Sylvie decided to wait for them and tarried near a flower shop, which of course set her pristine outfit off to perfection. She looked the absolute innocent babe, and not a few passersby smiled at her.

"Sylvie?" Ara called as they arrived.

"Yes?"

"What does Madame Vazeem sell?"

"She doesn't sell anything, silly. Don't you know anything?" Sylvie's expression transformed from sweet to scathing. "Madame Vazeem is the most famous tarot reader in all of Coney Island, and she has a crystal ball too."

The twins halted in unison. "She's a fortune teller?" Farideh said.

"Yes, stupid," Sylvie said.

"That will do, young lady," the nanny said. "You will remember your manners."

"We're not allowed to see fortune tellers," Ara said. "We must return to our parents."

"Of all the nonsense," the nanny said. "You will let your parents have their coffee in peace, girls. Now, onward." She gave them a light push in the direction they'd been walking.

Farideh grabbed her sister's arm and dug in her heels. "We really don't have permission. If you must take us, we'll have to wait outside the shop until you're done inside."

"I will not have girls in my charge standing outside a shop," Martha said with a warning squint. "Now, you will move along, or I shall walk you forcibly."

They moved, following directly behind a smug Sylvie this time, with the nanny guarding their rear. Hired by the Muises and therefore concerned only with Muise goals, Farideh thought. How disappointing. She glanced at her sister. Ara had the before-weeping look: compressed lips and luminous eyes.

"It's all right," Farideh whispered. "We won't get a reading. We'll just stand near the door in the waiting room. There's always a waiting room."

Ara nodded and clutched the hand Farideh still had wrapped over her sister's upper arm.

12

"Why ever do your parents not want you to have a fortune telling?" Sylvie called back.

"We don't know, but our mother dislikes occultism," Farideh said.

"Yes, she said so," Ara insisted. "And we're to have nothing to do with the nonsense."

"Hmm. Just as expected. You're suffering from superstition," Sylvie said and minced onward. "Occultism is all the rage. Everyone does it."

Farideh cast an eye-brow-lifted grimace at her back.

"Isn't refusing occultism the opposite of superstition?" Ara said.

"Not if you're afraid of it," Sylvie replied.

"She does have a point," Ara muttered.

"Well, we don't have to agree," Farideh said, "because we're not afraid of superstition or occultism, whichever she meant."

Ara smirked and bit her lip to stop a laugh.

"Have you been to this Madame Vazeem before?" Farideh asked, because Sylvie seemed to know exactly where she wanted to go.

"No. But I know the address. Carlotta gave it to me. With a description. Carlotta is brilliant with descriptions. We've already passed the flower shop, the tavern with the fat man sign and …." She looked distastefully at a black man sweeping the sidewalk near his shoe shine stand. "And this. We're not far off now."

The black man looked up, glanced at Sylvie and then passed his gaze to the twins. They smiled. He smiled and nodded a polite hello. The girls inclined their heads in unison and continued on. They both felt better after. Farideh sensed it from her sister's relaxed fingers. Being nice always made them feel better. Being nice, as their mother said, cost nothing and brought the world to their doorstep. Being nasty always made a person pay. Eventually.

"Ah! La voici!" Sylvie said. "Oh, dear. We must cross the street."

"Did Carlotta forget to mention that?"

"Yes, she did," Sylvie said, a displeased huff coming out of her mouth directly after.

The nanny took charge of the cavalcade. She brushed past the twins and grasped Sylvie's hand. "You will follow me, girls," she said. She chose her moment and began the dangerous expedition across the busy avenue.

The twins didn't feel the least inclined to practice the languid walk. Hands clasped, they scurried across on the nanny's heels, both shrieking when a car tooted at them. Although they lived in Toronto, their mother had impressed upon them the importance of crossing only at guarded cross walks, and they'd paid keen attention to safety after witnessing a gruesome hit-and-run outside their father's office building when they'd been seven. As well, they had a chauffeur who drove them everywhere, straight to the shop door usually. Crossing streets wasn't necessary. Really.

"I don't like this!" Ara said, her voice rising with each word.

"I don't either!" Farideh agreed.

"Why couldn't we have gotten a taxi?" Ara added.

"Nonsense!" Martha said, and her voice reached them despite another blare from a car. A few steps later, she marched her charges onto the opposite sidewalk and to safety. "There we are. A taxi! Girls, what are you thinking? We were just across the street."

Farideh considered mentioning the hit-and-run, but decided against it. The nanny's stern expression suggested repercussions if more 'nonsense' should arise from her or her sister.

"Now, then. Into Madame Vazeem's," Martha said. She strode to the boutique door and gave it a firm shove. Bells tinkled, and a boy yelped.

"Oh, dear. I am sorry," Martha said.

Ara, still with her sister near the edge of the sidewalk, whispered, "I stopped liking her Scottish accent, but perhaps it's not so bad after all. She sounds nicer when she says sorry."

Everyone sounded nicer when they said sorry—usually—but Farideh didn't remind her sister of that. She focused on the boy in the boutique. He looked a little older than them, thirteen or fourteen with the first symptoms of 'the change', a term her friends liked to use when they had a giggle-gossip tea party. His yelp had crackled with high and low notes. His chin had a bright red pimple large enough to be visible despite the distance of the wide sidewalk and his position in the shade, and he was rangy, a bit too much so, though not that tall yet.

Rather than a casual striped jacket and light-coloured suit pants, he wore an immaculate dark suit that was a little too short in the legs. He held a fedora in one hand. His hair was dark. Unruly spikes stuck upward from his forehead, she supposed because of the hat. That or it was curly and the hat had cramped most of it down.

"Would you look at him," Farideh breathed. "He's dressed to the nines."

14

"I'm looking," Ara said, and her breathy tone had Farideh pinning Ara with a sharp glance. Oh, no. Love. Despite the pimple.

"You're only twelve, Ara. Stop it."

"What?" she said faintly.

"Are you going to stand there all day, young man? You're blocking the entrance," the nanny said.

"Sorry," he said and stepped a few paces back. Farideh decided he must be waiting, because he glanced back at something or someone in the building.

"There you are, young lady," Martha said to Sylvie. "In you go."

Sylvie had been standing quietly during all this, the image of purity, her hands folded together in front. She smiled a shy mouth-closed smile at the boy and all but floated inward.

"Those ballet classes do make for a lovely stride," Ara mentioned, and Farideh's sharp gaze pinned on her again, because that comment had borne a less-than-pleased tone. Ara was the dreamy sort. She almost never had a tone other than mildly surprised or contentedly happy.

"Ara!" Farideh complained. "You'll never see him again after today."

"Yes, I will, because that's what I'm asking the fortune teller to tell me."

Farideh's mouth gaped. Her sister had melted her baby spoon. At twelve! "What? But we're forbidden!" Farideh hissed. "We're staying at the door!"

"Why are we forbidden?" Ara demanded. "Haven't you learned anything from Maman's diary?"

Dear Lord! "You knew about my secret operation?"

"Of course, I knew about that," Ara said. "As your handler, I was monitoring the situation."

Handler? "You did nothing, Ara. I worked alone."

"Really? So those three times I distracted the maid, the butler and then mother were nothing?"

Well, darn. "You're a better spy than me, Ara. Why didn't you say?"

"Girls!" the nanny barked.

"Coming, ma'am," Ara said and commenced the languid walk forward with Farideh. "I will not be outdone by ballet lessons," she muttered.

"If you knew I was reading the war diary, why didn't you ask about it?" Farideh whispered.

"I didn't think it proper to pry on Maman's love story with Papa. It's about that, isn't it? You're always red-faced after reading it, especially the next day when you see Maman or Papa."

Farideh breathed a very nasty word that made her sister pause in shock. "Farideh!"

"Sorry. Anyhow, there's nothing about the fortune telling in the war diary."

Ara commenced walking again. "She must have it in an earlier one. You will have to find it."

Farideh gaped at her sister all the way into the boutique and past the beautiful boy, at which point she bumped into something taller that had arrived at his side.

"Oh, dear. Terribly sorry," said a mildly accented voice.

Farideh couldn't quite place it. Somewhere Germanic, maybe? She looked up at an angel and squeaked rather than apologised. She could have died of mortification.

"Are you all right?" the angel said.

He had a definite resemblance to the beautiful boy, excluding the pimple. "Are you his father?" Farideh blurted. Oh, no. She was going to die of mortification and a thunderclap of social doom. All the cultured charm she'd practiced at the tea parties, gone in seconds.

"What? No," the man said, smiling. "His uncle."

"Girls! How rude. Do come along. I'm terribly sorry, sir," the nanny said. "They've been rattled since crossing the avenue, of all things."

"Oh, not to worry." The angel smiled in Martha's direction. "I myself detest crossing streets. I'd rather take a taxi or have some rickshaw carry me over."

"I'm sorry," Farideh said.

"Not at all, my dear. It was a perfectly reasonable question."

"He's as good as my father," the boy said.

"Yes, well, one must make do," the uncle replied, his attractive smile acquiring a wry lopsidedness.

Farideh, with a flaming face, glanced at the boy and lost herself in 'the eternal gaze', as Daniella referred to the 'ew-yuck' love stare— Farideh's description of it. Farideh's baby spoon didn't just melt. It exploded.

From somewhere far away, where her mind still existed under the smothering blanket of puppy love—and her mind very much hoped it was only puppy love—Farideh became aware of a body with fingers that were being squeezed mercilessly. She blinked and realized they were her fingers and Ara squeezed them.

"Sorry," she mumbled and lowered her gaze.

"This is my sister, Farideh," Ara said. "I'm Ara Tremblay. We're from Toronto, Canada. Are you residents of New York?"

"No, Montreal," the boy said.

"Oh, really! These girls! Why are darkies so ungodly forward?" the nanny muttered.

Farideh's gaze lifted. The blanket of puppy love had just incinerated, most of it. She found the boy staring at the nanny. His expression …. Well, it was expressionless, except ….

His attention returned to Farideh, and the remains of her blanket frosted over. He had the coldest soul she'd ever seen; there, in dark eyes with flecks of gold; there, where seconds earlier a spark of interest had roasted her intelligence. Now she saw nothing but icy calculation. Farideh felt twelve years old again and very frightened.

And unwanted and … dark. Next to her, Ara was very still with breath caught, and Farideh knew she felt the same.

"Well, on then," the uncle said a little quickly. He grasped the boy by the upper arm, yanked open the boutique door, which set the bell to jangling in an alarming fashion, and ushered his nephew out into the sunlight. Their dark brown hair fired with a multitude of golden highlights. Several rushed steps later, they passed beyond the shop window and out of view.

Farideh remained motionless for a few seconds longer. Then she and Ara turned to face the nanny. Darkies. They understood now the meaning behind 'girls'. Not 'young ladies', but 'girls.' They didn't count as young ladies, not to this woman. For this woman, they would always be darkies.

The helpless shame that Farideh had been feeling fired into resentment. Always the same, her reaction. First it was shock that someone, anyone, didn't see her and Ara as persons. Then came the shame of not being a person, of being a darkie. Then the resentment arrived, always hot and ferocious, with murderous intention entwined throughout. And after ….

Ara gently squeezed Farideh's fingers. Farideh shut her eyes and tried to regain her calm, because after resentment Farideh tucked the anger away for another day. She had never managed to expunge the fury with tears in privacy like Ara did. All Farideh could do was wait until it exploded out of her.

Last time she'd broken furniture. She didn't remember how she'd broken furniture, but she'd found herself in her shared bedroom with Ara, and the fancy boudoir dresser they used for dress up had been in three places on the parquet floor. Ara had been white-faced and frightened, up against the curtain near the window. The floor had been scratched in a circular pattern, as if the dresser had spun around from the force of a cyclone, and Farideh somehow had been standing yards away rather than near the wreckage.

She remembered arriving in the room. It had been directly after the chauffeur brought them home from school. Sylvie had been whispering 'nigger twins' and other things too quiet to hear all that day. There had been sniggering and nasty looks, even from girls who weren't in Sylvie's entourage. Farideh had endured the classes and the car ride home, but seconds after stepping into her bedroom ….

Well, that was it. That's all she remembered: stepping into her bedroom. After that it was a blink of her eyes, a return of reason, and witnessing Ara's terrorized expression and the results of destruction. The maid had run in to save them from whatever disaster had befallen, only to find the girls standing far apart, not a scratch on either. Farideh hadn't been breathing hard. Her arms didn't hurt from lifting up the dresser, though they should have. Somehow she still held her school bag. Even so, the destruction had been her fault. She'd known it without being told.

Later that evening her mother had visited the bedroom. She'd looked at the scratched floor—the dresser had been removed hours ago—and looked at Ara, who read a book aloud while seated against plumped up cushions next to Farideh. Then their mother had walked over to sit on the bed. Farideh had been running a fever since the episode. Their mother had settled a cool hand on her forehead, tucked her in more comfortably and kissed her on the cheek, never a sign of anger or reproach in her expression. She'd made them hot chocolate to drink before bed and said she loved them both, just like always.

But here they were in a boutique of occultism with a glassed-in counter displaying natural crystals, tarot cards, spirit boards, incense, and globes of glass or polished quartz. If that huge portrait between extravagantly large potted plants didn't lie, they were in a shop where

18

the white owner played dress up, who wore a turban above a fancy flapper dress, who hired a light-skinned black woman to work the counter and costumed her like some kerchiefed slave from dime novels of the American south.

The beginnings of a fever fogged Farideh's thoughts. The clanging door bell as another customer entered seemed a distant tinkle. Everything of Sylvie would die today: her atrocious humour, her nanny, her belief in elite white-skinned occultists who lied about their skills.

A strong hand grabbed Farideh's arm and startled a gasp from her. The fog, the fever, both vanished. Clarity returned and the comprehension that the boy had re-entered the shop. He'd seized her arm with a vice-like grip. He released it as she blinked up at him in dumbfounded surprise.

"I don't think you're forward. Either of you," he said. The icy calculation she'd witnessed earlier had hidden beneath a concerned expression in which little wrinkles scrunched between his eyebrows, and his gold-flecked eyes displayed awareness rather than intellectual distance.

He backed a step, smiled faintly, and bowed. "Ladies," he said. When he straightened, he topped his head with the fedora, grinned outright, though somehow he still looked sad, and opened the door again. "Adieu, Mlles. Tremblay."

A few quick steps after, he vanished from view again.

Chapter Three

Dark clouds and fortunes.

"Well, darn it," Ara said. "We still didn't get his name. Didn't you think his uncle looked like the angel Michael?"

"My first thought was Gabriel," Farideh said numbly. Ara's fingers shivered against Farideh. Her sister was frightened still. Farideh had no doubt she'd sensed the oncoming destructive passion of her twin.

"Welcome to the shop," the counter help interrupted. The twins glanced at her, but found her looking at Sylvie and the nanny. "Are you here for a reading?"

"Yes, we are," the nanny said. Her tone added a clip to the words, and when she finished speaking, her lips firmed together and her gaze darted toward the twins in a disapproving manner.

"Please make yourselves comfortable," the help said. "I'll check if Madame Vazeem is ready to receive." The woman moved briskly toward a lacy red and black curtain at the back of the shop.

Sylvie looked at the plush armchairs near the large potted plants and sat in one. The nanny claimed the second, and that left the row of stiff wooden chairs lined along the shop window.

"Well, if Maman does happen along, those should be far enough away that she won't be angry with us for coming here," Farideh said.

"She won't be angry with us. She'll be angry with the nanny for her rudeness in forcing us to come here, and so will Papa," Ara said, and she didn't lower her voice either.

"How dare you?" Martha spat.

Ara ignored her and chose a seat at the furthest end of the row. Farideh sat beside her. Rather than disregard the nanny, she gazed directly at her without blinking. Martha flushed an angrier hue, but still averted her gaze first. One of the things Farideh had learned long ago about her unusual blue eyes, they could be disconcerting if directed at a person she disliked. She really disliked the nanny.

She glanced at Sylvie. Her nemesis wore an angry pout, the lower lip all but vanished under the upper, and Farideh realized a delightful fact. During both brief encounters, which had seemed like two brushes with forever, the boy had ignored Sylvie entirely. For a second, Farideh wanted to pull a stunt learned from her nemesis, a smug smile of victory to mock the loser and tarnish the memory of the day forever, but she hesitated. Not because of Sylvie, but because of her mother. The most important tenet of the war diary flashed through her mind. In situations of little risk, rather than a firearm, the best weapon was emotional disarmament.

Farideh looked away from Sylvie. Oh, dear, but what a failure she'd made of practicing her mother's methods when she'd stared the nanny down. Ara's unusual anger hadn't helped there, but Farideh had never mentioned their mother's tricks to Ara before. Aside from not wanting to reveal her clandestine peeks into the war diary, Farideh hadn't seen the need to pass the information on. Ara had always possessed their mother's skills of charm and tact. She'd been born with them. Today was the first day ever that Ara had behaved more like Farideh.

"Fairy, you almost blew a cyclone in the boutique," Ara whispered.

Farideh blinked and then looked at her sister. "Fairy?"

"I like that nickname. We're taking it away from Sylvie. Mother already did anyhow. And it suits you."

"What should we nickname you?"

Ara smiled. "Nothing. My name is short enough."

"What did you mean about blowing a cyclone?"

Ara gave her a surprised stare. "Well, that's what you do, you know, when you're … upset."

"A cyclone?"

Ara's stare grew a frown. "Well, yes. But you knew, didn't you?"

"No!"

The counter help returned. "Madame Vazeem will see you now," she said to Sylvie and the nanny. "This way, please."

The pair rose and followed the woman through the curtain. Ara sighed heavily. "They don't read to black people in this store. You can tell by the way even the help ignores us."

The help shoved through the curtain with an expression that indicated she'd overheard, and her response confirmed it, but she moved away from the inner room before saying it.

"You girls don't want that old fake reading for you anyhow," she said with a hushed voice and waved them closer. "Come on, now.

Get over here before someone comes in to interrupt. Oh, wait! Turn the open sigh over to closed and lock that door! Hurry it!"

The twins didn't hurry it, too amazed to move. The woman huffed something naughty and rushed to do it herself. "Here, now. Move your sorry bottoms. We don't have much time. You need this reading. If you want to survive this storm without either of you losing your souls, you come here and listen."

The sign flipped, the key turned in the lock, and the extra bolts clicked home. The woman scurried back to the counter and snatched out a deck of tarot cards from the pocket of her old-fashioned white apron.

Ara lifted up and walked to the counter. Farideh hurried after her. "Why do you say lose our souls?" Ara asked.

"Been seeing a dark cloud looming over you both since you walked in, and it wasn't no cloud of your sister's," the woman said. "Some things are worse than death, child. This cloud is coming for you. I know you feel it."

"I only wanted to ask you about finding that boy," Ara said, her voice faint.

The woman gave her a sharp look. "That boy and his uncle came here to see me, just so you know. But it's too late to call them back. I already saw. They won't be here again, not for many years to come."

"At least tell us his name," Ara begged. Farideh gave her a disbelieving stare. This woman spoke to them of a cloud of doom, and Ara still wanted to know the boy's name?

"Girl, I didn't ask, and you don't need to know."

"But I do. At least tell me when they will return," Ara pleaded.

"Oh, you got it bad," the woman said, smiling briefly. She glanced at Farideh. "She didn't see the pimple at all."

A laugh burst out of Farideh.

"What pimple?" Ara said, frowning.

Farideh put both hands over her mouth to prevent another very ungirlish guffaw from breaking loose.

"Enough of that. Shuffle these cards, girl," the woman said. She pushed them toward Ara, looked at Farideh and added, "You're gonna cut."

Ara reached for the cards, a pack that had seen better days. The edges were worn, the backings, as Ara shuffled them, were faded, all bearing the dark marks of stains where fingers had handled them throughout the years. One even had a minor cigarette burn near a corner. Several had nicked, tattered or bent corners. Ara riffled the cards slowly three times, taking care not to add further damage to any. She passed the deck to Farideh after.

Farideh hesitated, thinking of her mother's certain disappointment for breaking a promise to stay away from occultism.

"It's too late for uncertainty, child," the woman said. "The orbs have held your images for minutes now. You been seen." She pointed at the row of crystal balls in the display case. "You wanna live, you cut those cards."

Ara's arm wound around Farideh's waist. "Cut them, Fairy. Hurry."

Farideh squinted at the nearest crystal, a smallish sphere with a paper tag labelled 'quartz' beneath it. Reflections from the shop played on the surface: their blue dresses, the brown of the wood case, the fast flipping motion of the ceiling fan.

A shadow moved within the sphere, there beneath the reflections of the real world.

The counter help slid open the back of the display case and threw her kerchief over the crystal. She straightened. Her crinkly hair began to fan in a huge lion mane at the back of her head.

"Don't look at it. Hurry with those cards."

Farideh reached for the tarot. The loss of souls had been mentioned, a shadow had moved in the nearest ball, and she had a sister to protect. Her fingertips prickled before she touched the topmost card. She seized the pack and dropped the bottom five.

"Them the ones," the woman said. She snatched all five. "No time for the usual mumbo jumbo. We'll work with the chosen cards."

She flipped them over and spread them out, revealing a man face down, multiple swords stabbed into his back; a woman in a white robe and elaborate headdress seated between pillars of black and white; a tower with two people falling away from it, one of them possibly a woman; a naked man and woman beneath an angel; and Death on a pale horse.

"Oh, that's good. The Tower is reversed," the woman muttered. "Listen up." She pointed at the Ten of Swords. "You got a big change coming, and it gonna be harsh. Things you don't know, things you shoulda been told, they gonna hurt." Her finger moved to the sunlight beyond the murdered man. "But there's always a part of the secret that can save you. You just got to find what it is."

24

Her finger passed to the High Priestess, but settled on the black pillar. "One of you got to make a fatal decision." The finger passed to the white pillar. "One of you got to guard the future. And then …." She shoved The Tower closer. "One of you gonna land on your feet where you can find this man. You got to marry him."

She moved too quickly past The Lovers and on to Death. Every girl wanted details about the man she married—his eyes, his hair, how tall, how many babies together, what he'd do for a living—but the woman didn't care for any detail but career prospects.

"He a cold blooded murderer, and you gonna be darned glad of it."

The boutique door rattled.

"And there are your parents." She snatched up the cards and the deck, shoved them back into her apron and started around the counter. "Make sure you marry the killer," she said as she hurried to the door. The twins' father had just shaken it again. "You want to survive, you got to side with the enemy of your enemy, and Death wants your enemy bad. He darned ready to make use of the weapon she gave him. Umpteen generations going as far back as war over the Holy Land, her own Ten of Swords was bound to catch up with her. Marry the angel of death."

"But who is he?" Farideh asked. "Where do we find him?"

"I don't know! The cloud in here is too big! There are curses twisting with curses in your past, present and future. Oh, and the secret that will save you? I keep seeing a blue crystal. Keep your eye out for a blue crystal."

The key turned. The door opened. The bell tinkled. "Welcome to Madame Vazeem's. Please take your girls outta here before all the crystal balls get cursed with the evil eye. I can't sell no crystals with shadows floating in them. I'll be cleaning out evil spirits for hours as it is. Well, get on with you, ladies."

The twins shook free of the bewildered fog that had enshrouded their minds and moved ensemble to the door, Ara still hugging Farideh's waist. They walked past the black woman and into the waning light of the day. The bell tinkled and the door clicked shut behind them before they thought to ask anything about the reading.

But they wouldn't have been able to in any case. Their mother clutched them both in arm-wide desperation. "Oh, thank God," she breathed. "Thank God. Thank God."

Farideh was closest to the shop window. She glanced within and found the counter help removing the handkerchief from the cursed crystal ball. The ball she tucked within a silk sack and dropped into her apron. The kerchief went back on her head.

Farideh became aware of her mother shaking both herself and Ara. Hands on shoulders, ducked down to fix them with a stern but still frightened gaze, their mother rattled them again. "How could you both go in there? How could you?"

"She made us go in. The nanny did. She called us darkies and said we were ungodly forward," Ara replied. "Farideh almost blasted a cyclone in the boutique, but the nephew of the angel rushed back in and stopped her, and I didn't get to ask anything about him. All I know is that he lives in Montreal." Ara burst into tears and threw both hands over her eyes.

"A boy?" their father said. "There was a boy? And where is this Scottish nanny? This paragon of no nonsense?"

"An angel?" Deena uttered, frowning in mystification. Her gaze shot to the boutique, and the frown strengthened. Farideh worried that she'd march in and argue with the counter help.

"The nanny is in the reading room with Sylvie," Farideh said quickly. "She did make us enter the boutique. When we discovered it wasn't a frippery, we tried to go back to the coffee shop, but she wouldn't let us. She accused us of nonsense, and she made us cross the street. Cars honked. Twice! We screamed."

"I was very frightened," Ara added with a shaky voice and a shakier sniffle.

"We are never hiring a Scottish nanny," their father said. He glanced behind. "Oh, there you are, Muise. You're puffing like a steam engine. Don't you golf?"

"Of course I golf," Mr. Muise said. "You know I golf. You golf with me."

"Oh, that's right. Perhaps you should start carrying your own bag."

"Don't be ridiculous. I have a caddie for that. You should get one."

"And end up puffing like you? I think not."

"What was the meaning of rushing from the coffee shop like that?" Mr. Muise asked. "I had to leave my wife behind to pay the cheque."

"I'm so sorry, Mr. Muise," Deena said, stepping away from the girls. "I have a dreadful fear of occultists. When Marie-Joseph spoke of getting a reading from this Madame Vazeem, I panicked."

"Yes, you hared out of the coffee shop as spry as a girl half your age, my dear. I've never seen you move so fast." Muise gave the twins' father a cynical glance. "Him, now, I've seen run for cover, leap walls and shrubs, and tackle men twice his size, which is what he did when some blustering big Yankee wouldn't get out of his way when he chased after you. You'd have thought the poor man was a German."

Oh, yes. Farideh remembered that Mr. Muise had survived the early days of the war in the trenches with her father, but then David Tremblay had gone off to be their mother's handler, and he hadn't seen Richard Muise again until after the war, when they'd started a stock dealership together. Mr. Muise had been a sergeant major at the end of the war. He'd started as a private. The twins' father had started as a private as well. He'd retired from service as a major, but whenever anyone asked, he claimed to be a sergeant major.

Actually, Farideh wasn't entirely certain he was retired. There were business trips with Deena that seemed suspicious. Investment concerns were a good cover for espionage.

"Oh, dear. Is the Yankee dead?" Deena asked.

"Of course he's not dead," her husband said. "He was with a date. I'm not that rude."

"Oh, yes. Sorry, darling."

Farideh stared warily at Mr. Muise. The question, answer and apology had been uttered with the sort of certainty that only existed in customary circumstances. Mr. Muise frowned with a faintly puzzled air. Then he smiled as if the Tremblays had been joking. "Well, no harm done, I suppose, except the wounded pride of that Yankee. Oh, and my wife's going to be irritated as a nest of bees when we get back."

"Oh, please, Richard. Do give her my apologies, but the shock has been enough to set off a migraine. Will you forgive me?" Deena said. "I must return to the hotel."

"Oh, yes …." Mr. Muise glanced at David.

"I'm afraid we'll have to chat later, Muise. I'll need to see after the girls tonight."

"You really should hire a nanny," Muise said. "I'm sure the hotel staff has one handy for occasional work. Just ask the concierge."

"Yes, I'm sure they do, but I won't leave Deena alone with a migraine. I'll see you Monday, Muise." David offered his arm to his wife.

"Oh, but …?" Muise said, hesitating.

"A discussion won't change my mind, Richard," David said. "It won't change it now, on Sunday or on Monday. I don't agree to the stock purchase. I think we should sell."

"So you're going to do it, just throw it all away on Monday, force me to take another partner."

"Sorry, Richard, but I have a bad feeling. I'm putting my money in something durable, something I can touch." He pulled Deena away and toward the edge of the sidewalk, where he waved at a taxi passing in the other direction. The taxi braked and set off a cacophony of blaring horns and cursing drivers. Then it did a u-turn in the middle of the avenue. More horns tooted and more curses sullied the atmosphere, including an almost muffled one from Mr. Muise.

"David!" Muise began.

"I'm out, Richard. Buy me out of the business if you want, but I suggest you do the same as me and sell everything. Put your money in something real."

"You're insane."

"Hmm."

The taxi rolled up and parked with a screech of brakes. "Yes, sir?" the driver called.

David handed in his wife, his daughters, and shut the door. He glanced at Muise with a pitiless stare that reminded Farideh of the look she'd seen on the beautiful boy earlier—and which gave her a chill down her spine, to finally witness such ruthlessness in her father—and then he opened the front door and climbed in next to the taxi driver. "The Plaza," David said.

"Yes, sir!" the driver said with even more enthusiasm. He shoved the car into gear and roared off to the discordant disapproval of further honking.

Farideh stared back at Mr. Muise. He looked like Sylvie just now, with his lower lip almost hidden beneath the upper.

Ara's hand settled over hers and squeezed. "He's going to regret it, but he's not going to listen," she said. "He really should listen."

"Did that woman's fortune-telling gift rub off on you, Ara?" Farideh asked.

28

"I've always been sighted, Fairy. That's what makes me a better handler."

Farideh turned to frown at her. Really? Ara was sighted? But she'd never said. Why hadn't she said?

"Handler?" their mother repeated. "Girls? Is there something you should tell me?"

"That the Querent card no longer represents you," Ara said, her expression sleepy. She slumped toward Farideh. "The High Priestess is no longer you. I'm sorry, Maman. I read books in Daniella's family library when we had our play visits." She mumbled a few last words into Farideh's neck. "But I didn't understand until I touched the deck and Farideh dropped the five cards. They told me more than the fortune teller said."

Ara fell asleep. Farideh's wide-eyed gaze locked with her mother's.

"What five cards?" Deena asked. Her voice was calm, but her expression tight. She hid either anger or fear. Or both.

"The Ten of Swords, the High Priestess, the Tower upside down, the Lovers, and Death," Farideh said. "She said …. It wasn't Madame Vazeem. It was the counter help who was the real fortune teller. She said we had to listen to her or lose our souls. I'm sorry. I decided to listen."

"Farideh, this is very important," Deena said. "You must tell me everything that woman said. Everything. As close as you remember it."

"Maman, Ara is running a fever," Farideh said anxiously. "I can feel the heat on my neck."

"I know, my darling. It can't be helped. She'll be fine later. Now tell me all of it. Now, before you forget any of it."

Farideh did her best, while her father and the taxi driver listened. Her parents were silent after, but the driver was the type prone to rambling chatter and burst the disturbed silence a mere minute after Farideh finished.

"That Eliza Mayhew is the best in the state, you know. It's a big secret, right. All the rich folk, begging your pardon, seeing as how you're rich, but seeing as how you're tourists, it ain't so bad, right? But anyhow, it's Eliza Mayhew who does the real deal in that boutique. Madam Vazeem is her front. The old woman's too dumb to notice, see? Most rich folk're too dumb to notice either. Unlike

29

you, of course. Most rich folk don't look at black folk long enough to see what's what, most of them. Yep."

The driver made a squealing turn around a corner and continued speaking to his confined audience. "Yep, most of the customers walk right on in to that back room without glancing at Elizah, but the smart ones wait for the old biddy to get out of the way and then they go talk to her. Anyone who gets a reading from Eliza's a lucky fella. Or gal," he added, glancing back at Farideh. "She's known for telling the harsh truth. If she says you got a chance, then you got a chance, because when you don't, you'll run crying from the shop, 'cause she won't cushion the blow. No sir."

Another squealing turn had the car shooting down another busy New York street. "Good thing you came to New York. Yes, indeed. No better fortune teller in the state than Eliza Mayhew. Why, I said the same thing to the pair of Norwegians who hired the taxi earlier. Or was it Scandinavians? Yeah, it was Scandinavian. Anyhow, they wanted to know who was the best, and I said, 'Eliza Mayhew', I did, and I drove them all the way to the shop. They were good tippers, too."

"From where?" Farideh asked quickly.

"Eh?"

"From where did you drive them?" Farideh clarified.

"Oh, the train station. Got off the in-bound from Canada, if I'm not mistaken, given the time. Funny accent, the father. Sounded German. I almost threw him out of the cab until the boy said they were Scandinavian. 'Scandinavian?' I said. 'Isn't that another type of German?' And he said, 'No, sir. That's Viking. The very nasty sort.' And his father said, 'Not the least,' like some British guy, but without sounding British. He was very polite like a British guy too.

"The boy didn't sound Scandinavian to me, though, or British, but he said he was born in Halifax, Nova Scotia, of all places. Never seen a kid with eyes that cold. Got a shiver down my spine fit to shake the bones loose. I figured they wanted to see Eliza to exorcise a demon from that kid. Scary young fella. Never seen eyes like that before on a kid. I said seven Hail Mary's the second he stepped out of the cab. Worse than driving the mafia. Kids born in Halifax must have the North Pole in their bones. Got some sort of Eskimo hoo doo blowing into their houses all year long. Mix that in with Viking and hoo boy!"

"Halifax is not a part of the arctic," Farideh's father said.

"Eh? It's not? But it's in Canada."

"All the same. Much of Canada is about the same as New York State. The most populated areas of my country are very far from the North Pole. Most of the population is very close to the U.S. border. We really are close neighbours."

"You don't say? Well, I'll be darned. Learn something new every day. How does anyone get to and from the pole, then?"

"Most no one bothers."

"You don't say? Why the heck not?"

"It's too cold and inhospitable. It's actually a spot on the arctic ice flows, which means ocean beneath and no land for hundreds of miles in any direction, and no one can survive on a diet of snow and ice."

"Oh. Really?"

"Yes. Really."

"Well, I'll be darned."

Farideh glanced at her mother, but given the distant, worried gaze, she realized her mother wasn't paying the least attention to the driver now that he'd rambled away from talk of fortune tellers. Farideh focused on the conversation, just in case the Halifax-born Scandinavian boy came up again, but for the rest of the ride, Farideh's father kept up a pleasant dialogue with the cabbie while correcting him of his many misconceptions, some of which were as brilliantly funny as Halifax being a part of the North Pole.

Farideh wished Ara were awake to hear it, but the fever still flourished, warming Farideh's body along the side where her sister lay slumped. She held Ara up as best she could during each successive screeching turn, but her attention always returned to the conversation after.

Their mother passed a hand over Ara's forehead once, but other than that remained subdued, and Farideh briefly wondered why she wasn't fussing over Ara more or cradling her instead. But their mother had left Ara in charge of Farideh's recovery back when Farideh had the strange sickness. Farideh supposed it was just as well, because she would have been reluctant to give Ara up to someone else right now.

Eventually, despite the careening driving style of the driver, they arrived at the hotel, and Farideh did have to give her sister up for a short time. Their father carried Ara into the hotel and to the elevator while their mother paid the taxi driver. Farideh hovered nearby even then, hoping for one last tidbit concerning the boy. She was afraid to ask anything in front of her mother, who still bore a distant air, and then it was too late. The driver grinned, saluted with his generous payment plus tip, and roared off, setting several cars to honking, including one limousine, whose driver shouted out the window as well.

"Ti ammazzo! Cretino! Che palle!" *I'll kill you! Idiot! What balls!*

"Oh, there's the mafia," Deena muttered and turned away without much interest. "Come along, Farideh. Your sister needs you."

Farideh backed away from the big black limousine and its cussing driver. That did sound Italian. Many root words were shared between French and Italian, or so their mother said. Learn the roots, learn the language quicker: Deena Tremblay's maxim, straight from the war diary. Farideh wasn't entirely certain, however, that she should apply it to cussing.

A man thrust open the passenger door of the limousine and stepped onto the sidewalk. He said something quickly to the driver and slammed the door shut. He was tall, slender, his complexion and features of Mediterranean descent, and he dressed in a spiffy black suit with a matching Fedora. He turned, and his gaze fell on Farideh. A slow and lazy smile spread on his face.

"Salve, bella bambina." *Hi, beautiful little girl.*

The man's attention drifted toward Farideh's mother, who waited by the door the porter held open. His smile lost the lazy overtones and sharpened to a toothy menace. "Bella bambina, bella madonna," he said. *Beautiful girl, beautiful lady.*

"Farideh, do come," her mother urged.

"Yes, Maman." Farideh hurried into the hotel and entered the elevator with her mother. The Italian followed them as far as the lobby and grinned at them as the elevator door shut.

"Those are the worst sort of men, Farideh," her mother said when their view of him was cut off. "The smile is a dead giveaway."

The elevator operator glanced at them. His skin reddened, and he focused on the panel again.

"He looked like the sort to follow people," Farideh said.

"You have good instincts. He was probably meeting someone, or I think he would have."

"What would you have done?"

"That would depend on the circumstances, but in this case, I would have endured the elevator ride in his company. He can be as much of a boor as he likes, but in front of witnesses, that type will only press the advantage if they think they have one. He's a minion, and therefore has a superior to whom he must answer. Causing a scene will force him to answer, and I doubt he would find the interview with his superior pleasant. Am I right, John?"

She directed this last at the operator. Farideh noted a little late that he had a metal name tag pinned to his uniform.

"Yes, ma'am. That about sums it up," John said, yet more pink but also grinning. He didn't quite meet their gazes. Evidently he was a shy sort around females.

"Thank you, John. I thought so."

When they exited the elevator, Deena gave the operator a smile and a handsome tip, which won a salute and a huger blush that lowered into John's collar. Farideh practiced the serene walk alongside of her mother as they continued to the suite door, very aware of John watching.

"One must be a queen before every potential knight, my darling," Deena breathed to her daughter. "One never knows when one will need a knight, so do endeavour to be an admirable queen at the very least and never forget the power of bribery."

"A tip is bribery?" Farideh whispered back.

"Well, of course it is. Bribery is how most of the world works, but try to refrain from the distasteful sort."

"Yes, maman," Farideh said. She wasn't entirely certain what sort of bribery was distasteful, but she did hope she was on her way to being an admirable queen. Better yet, she'd like to be an inspiring one like her mother. Farideh was darn certain Sir John of the Magical Rising Room would stand and fight for Her Majesty Deena Tremblay without hesitation if the opportunity arose, just for another smile.

Chapter Four

Manhattan, New York. In The Plaza before supper.

A single step back placed him near an ornamental pillar and a tall, leafy potted plant. The girl and the woman hurried through the open door. A side step had him positioned slightly forward of the pillar and facing the door. The woman glanced his way. He pasted on a smile for the next patron entering the hotel, a man in a sharp black suit, but the patron ignored him. The fellow—he looked Italian—had no bags to carry in any case. Instead he had nerve, he had cheek, and he regained the woman's attention and riveted the girl's.

Caspar edged a bit to the side for a better view. The Italian halted in the lobby and leered at the woman and girl. Within the elevator now, they stared back, both faces impassive. No fear, no return of interest, no gain for the shark who trawled for prey in the wrong territory.

The elevator doors shut. The Italian cussed a word, inaudible at this distance. Caspar headed for the dining room. Moving like he had a purpose, he entered and walked through the comfortable dimness toward the kitchen. He shoved the nearest swinging door open a crack and glanced back at his target. He widened his eyes. Then he smiled and nodded politely.

Yes, the target watched, and he smiled back and crooked a finger. Caspar hesitated as if uncertain of his duty. He dropped his hand from the door and approached the middle-aged, burly man seated alone at a table for two. The table was at the side of the room near the rear, a good location for a modicum of privacy.

"Yes, sir?" Caspar said, acting hopeful, earnest.

"You look like an enterprising boy," the man said. His gaze wandered down Caspar's body and up again. "I need an enterprising boy later. Say around nine. That sound good to you?"

"Enterprising?" Caspar repeated. He focused on the target's smile. Another shark smile, but meant to be reassuring, fatherly. It wasn't a complete failure. Actually, it would have been perfect if the man's mark were an innocent ... or someone on the make.

"You like money, don't you?"

Caspar allowed a slow grin to broaden his lips. Innocent wouldn't work for him. Wickedness suited his purpose better. "Yes, sir."

The target's smile broadened as well. He gave Caspar his room number. "I have a meeting. I don't mind if it's interrupted. Actually, I'd like it to be interrupted, but only if you do it. You know what I'm saying? You make it a good interruption, you get more money. But keep it quiet. You understand?"

The target slid a dollar bill toward the table edge. Caspar plucked it from the surface and shoved it into his vest pocket. The tinkling of cutlery, the murmured conversation of other patrons, none of it altered during the exchange. He was just another unimportant bellhop taking a commission from a customer.

"Yes, sir. At nine, sir." Caspar performed a short bow and retreated to the kitchen. He navigated the hot, busy confines and slipped out the alley door before someone stopped him and demanded he work for real.

He met his uncle near a trash bin. "This stinks."

"And there are rats," his uncle said. "Rats as big as poodles."

"I hate Grandma's dog."

"Kill it."

"She'll hate me."

His uncle threw his cigarette butt on the dirty asphalt and tromped it flat. "Here, Caspar. Get your outfit straightened up. I'm surprised no one booted you from the hotel. That's as sloppy as I've ever seen an outfit, but never before on you."

"I only had minutes to get it on. The boy left? With my clothes?"

"Yes. He's assured me he'll keep his nose out of the hotel until tomorrow."

"I want my suit back."

"It didn't fit you any longer, Caspar. We'll get you another later."

"Hmm. Why didn't you say kill Grandma?"

"Not funny."

"I think she'd like to go with the dog."

"Stop it, Caspar." His uncle commenced to tuck in the shirt Caspar seemed disinclined to tidy.

"Do you think she'd noticed if we replaced the poodle with a rat?"

"Caspar!" his uncle complained. He finished tucking, patted down the vest, tugged the bellhop jacket straight at Caspar's shoulders and yanked the little bow tie out of its slightly crooked position. "There." He stepped back. "The target?"

"Nine."

"What? Nine? What about nine?"

"I've a rendezvous with him at nine. He offered money."

"So it was true."

"Yes, everything she predicted. He likes skinny, pimply boys."

"She did not say pimply."

"Well, he's getting pimply."

"I don't know that one pimple counts as pimply."

"That girl, it's all she looked at."

"Girl? The girl at the fortune teller's? You're still on about her?"

"If I'd had two heads, she still would have stared at the pimple."

A smile flittered across his uncle's face and vanished. He tried to resist, but it returned in seconds. "Damn, Caspar. I had no idea you were vain."

"Vain? In this monkey suit?"

A laugh burst from his uncle. "Dear Lord. You are!"

"I've definitely decided to kill the dog."

"Caspar! I was joking!"

"I'm not."

His uncle swore a vile thing in his native tongue and endeavoured to change Caspar's mind. He apologized for calling him vain, swore he'd never tease about pimples again, promised a visit to the most reputable tailor in Montreal for a well-fitted new suit. Caspar drew out his pocket watch, noted the time, spotted a rat scurrying through rubbish only feet away, heard the back door of the hotel kitchen swing open. He pulled his uncle further off into the shelter of another back entrance.

A scullery boy shoved out of the hotel with a pail of messy vegetables parings. He walked closer, bored, oblivious, and paused at the open trash bin. He slung the mess inward. His aim was sloppy, and half the contents dropped down the front, where alert rats watched and scampered into view as he lumbered back to the kitchen.

"Please don't kill the dog! Or my mother!" Caspar's uncle begged in an urgent whisper. "Please!"

The alley door swung shut.

"Fine. Give me a cigarette," Caspar said.

"No!"

"I'm killing the dog."

"Caspar!"

Caspar ignored him.

"Fine! Here!"

His uncle hauled out his silver case, withdrew two cigarettes and lit them. He handed one over. A single inhalation and a bout of hoarse coughing convinced Caspar to drop the burning stick and smash it dead with a heel.

"Damn! That's not the least elegant," Caspar said, grimacing at the messy remains of his attempt at suave classiness. His uncle laughed at him. Caspar looked up sharply. His uncle's gaze veered away. An exhaled drag obscured his face.

"Hacking up yellow spit each morning isn't very elegant either, Caspar. Don't take up the vice. It's not worth it."

"Uncle?"

"Hmm."

"You should quit."

The air cleared. His uncles face reappeared wearing a sceptical expression. "I can't just quit."

"Why not?"

"Well …! I don't know! I can't just quit. There. Just be glad you haven't taken up the vice."

"Should I stuff the dog after?"

"Caspar!" his uncle protested. "I'm not quitting!"

"Not even for Grandma? Oh, I suppose we can stuff her too."

"Onda brorson från helvetet!" his uncle said. *Evil nephew from hell!* Scowling, he dropped the cigarette and rubbed the smoking end dead with the toe of his shoe. "I don't believe you."

"Then why did you put out the cigarette?"

"I don't feel like smoking now."

"Then I suppose we shall discuss this again when you light another cigarette. Say in … fifteen minutes?" Caspar said, glancing at his watch. He pocketed it while listening to his uncle demonstrate the less dignified elements of the Scandinavian language.

Chapter Five

July 27, 1929. Early evening before escaping New York.

Despite Ara's fever, a fierce and quiet argument ensued in the hotel suite. The twins' mother packed their bags with the intention of catching an overnight train to Canada. Deena refused to remain in the hotel. She would be at the train station within the next hour, early or not, and she would leave New York with their daughters whether her husband accompanied them or not.

But of course their father would never let them travel without escort, and of course their mother knew it. David Tremblay accused his wife of being all sorts of a superstitious woman, but she wouldn't give in. At last he did. "I damned well had stocks to sell! A business to sell!"

"Sell next week and keep your voice down. If it's so urgent, why don't you just have Muise sell for you?"

"That cheat? Like hell. He's decent cover for our other interests and nothing more. Damn it, Deena!"

"Do your daughters mean nothing to you?" she demanded.

"You know they mean everything." His shadow appeared near the bedroom entrance. Farideh commenced reading the novel again, choosing a random spot half a page down from earlier.

"'That proves you are unusual,' returned the Scarecrow, 'and I am convinced that the only people worthy of consideration in this world are the unusual ones. For the common folks are like the leaves of a tree, and live and die unnoticed.'"

Farideh's father paused at the door. A scowl marred his usually smooth brow. Farideh looked up. He attempted a reassuring smile, but it failed to be more than an aggrieved grimace. He moved out of view again. Farideh started the next sentence, but Ara's hand settled on her forearm and stopped her.

"Maman will be in next. You don't have to pretend. They know we're listening."

"I haven't seen a blue crystal anywhere," Farideh whispered.

"We'll just have to ask outright," Ara said.

Farideh sat up and placed a palm on her sister's forehead. "Your skin is still hot."

"I'm still asking," Ara said. "Doesn't matter how hot my skin gets, I'm asking."

"All this unnerving business isn't good for you."

"Stop sounding like Maman. Did you like that passage, by the way?"

"What passage?"

"The one you just read, silly," Ara replied.

"I don't remember it. I was acting."

Ara giggled. "Good actresses remember their lines."

"This one doesn't," Farideh said a little snippily. "I work best at impromptu."

"That only makes you a half-way decent spy. Read the passage again."

"Which one?"

Before Ara answered, their mother entered. She moved to the bed and placed a hand where Farideh's had just been. "You seem a little cooler," she said to Ara.

"She's not," Farideh contradicted. "But since you want to feel better about forcing us to end our holiday early, I suppose she feels cooler."

"Fairy!" Ara said.

"I'm sorry," their mother replied. "We can't stay. We'll go on holiday elsewhere." She turned toward their lightweight summer sweaters, which were draped on a nearby chair. She lifted one. "Let's get you bundled and ready for the taxi, Ara."

"Do you have a blue crystal, Maman?" Ara asked.

Their mother froze. "No," she said without looking back.

"Did she just lie to us?" Farideh asked.

"I'm not sure," Ara said.

Farideh decided their mother had. "Why would you lie to us?" she cried. "I told you what the fortune teller said! I told you everything! She said there were things we should have been told! Tell us what we should have been told!"

Their mother whirled to face them. "There is nothing you should have been told!" She thrust the sweater toward Farideh. "Get your sister ready."

40

Farideh grabbed the sweater with a mulish glower. Their mother marched out of the room. They listened to her thump into her own. The door slammed shut. A muffled sob filtered back to them.

"Fairy!" Ara scolded.

"Why won't she tell us?"

"I don't know."

"Here!" Farideh shoved the cashmere sweater at her sister and hopped off the bed, blue dress rippling down over her knees. She started for the door.

"Fairy!" Ara protested.

"I'm not listening!" Farideh said. Someone had to protect her sister since their mother wasn't doing it right.

Their father appeared in the doorway, and Farideh stalled. "Girls, have you unsettled your mother?" he said with an uncompromising stare.

"Do you have a blue crystal, Papa?" Ara asked.

For a few seconds, the uncompromising stare remained in place, but then it crumbled. Sort of. Farideh thought his reaction was a mix of melt and crumble. Papa never could resist Ara's well-practiced innocent-little-girl gaze.

"Uh …."

"Oh, how wonderful," Ara cried. "May I see it?"

He glanced nervously at the other bedroom and entered theirs. He approached the bed while reaching down into his shirt and undershirt. Of course, they'd seen the golden chain before, and of course they'd seen the tiny caged crystal before. It was Papa's good luck trinket from somewhere in the Middle East. But it was also a dusky mix of grey and black.

"Papa!" Farideh complained. "It's black!"

He halted a few feet from the bed. His shoulders hunched a little as if her lack of faith had deflated him. His expression wry, he switched the bed light on. He pulled the lamp shade off and dangled the golden cage before the incandescent bulb. "Your mother is going to bust my head," he muttered.

With the lamp light shining from behind, the heart of the crystal was blue.

Quietly, their father gave his awed daughters some of their mother's secret. "Your mother thinks her family is cursed, and the key to ending the curse is this crystal. She wouldn't marry me until I agreed to wear it. She performed a little ceremony before she placed it around my neck. She spoke of an ancient prophecy. She held the crystal before a candle and showed me the blue heart and made me swear to protect our children with my life. I would have sworn that in any case without this marvellous family heirloom as a bribe."

"What is this curse?" Ara asked.

"David!"

He and Farideh faced the entrance. Deena had returned.

"David! Put it back on!"

He lowered it away from the bulb, but rather than place it back over his head, he handed it to Ara. Deena burst out with protests in Persian and perhaps German. He answered in kind. Farideh looked down at the crystal on Ara's lap. It was dusky black and grey again.

"It doesn't glow!" David snapped. "It has never glowed! Light shining from behind the crystal is not a glow! If I were the man in this prophecy, it would be glowing all the time, wouldn't it? Deena! This is …. This is madness! It's the twentieth century, for God's sake!"

"The century makes no difference!" Deena said.

"It's just a little fever, Deena. The girls are perfectly healthy. The doctors have given both a clean bill of health time and again. Ara will be fine."

"It's not Ara!" Deena cried. "It's always the strong one!" Deena gasped, looked at Farideh and clapped both hands over her mouth. Farideh at last understood the odd expression of having one's stomach drop out, because hers had. It had plummeted below the earth's surface. She felt empty, not a girl any longer, but a hollowed container filled with shock and disbelief.

"It's always the strong one," Ara repeated. "Of course it is."

Deena's breath quivered inward. She regained her composure and attempted to undo the disastrous blow to her children's belief in a happy future together. "It's just a silly family legend," she said. "I've only carried it on because of tradition. Ara, give the talisman back to your father. We have a train to catch."

Ara, the sweet and obedient daughter, refused. "He's not the right murderer. You are no longer the Querent."

Deena's composure shattered again. "Oh, God! Oh, God!"

"Now that's just enough, young lady," David said.

"You are a murderer, Papa. Don't deny it. Even if you do it for your country, you do it very well, or Maman wouldn't have chosen you. But you're still not the right murderer. She is not the High

42

Priestess, not any longer. I am." Ara's feverish gaze settled on her mother. "Papa has good instincts, Maman. He may not believe, but he put the crystal where it belongs. Whether you tell me the truth now or later, I'm not giving it back." She raised the necklace and lowered it over her head. "Fairy," she called.

Still feeling numb and hollow, Farideh returned to her sister's side. Ara plucked at the sweater. Farideh lifted it and helped her sister put it on, listening to their mother's desolate sobs, her father's apologetic reassurances, and wishing she didn't have to hear either or comprehend the reason for their distress.

"She kept the secret so I wouldn't feel this way," Farideh muttered.

"The apple was eaten," Ara whispered back. "Even if you vomit it back up, a taste remains."

"I don't like vomit," Farideh said.

"Then don't vomit. Eat the flesh of every apple life gives you before it all rots."

"Ew! Ara! You sound like a fortune teller, a gloomy one."

"I am one. I'm sorry for being gloomy. My head is all fuzzy with images and places. I understand now why that woman said the cloud was too big. Everything is tumbling about, and I can hardly pin a single thing down. All I know is you better hang on to your apples, Fairy."

"Her name was Elizah Mayhew, the woman in the shop."

"Oh. I'm glad you remember it. I don't recall that she said her name."

"She didn't. Our taxi driver did."

"Odd."

"He drove the beautiful boy to the fortune teller's before he picked us up. He said so."

"Do you think it's only a coincidence?" Ara asked.

"Aren't you the fortune teller?"

"The cloud is very bad right now. Try to see for me. Here. Hold the end of this." Ara lifted the talisman. A little hesitantly, Farideh cupped it in her palm.

"What do I do?"

"No idea. I wondered if it would turn blue if we both touched it."

Farideh dropped the golden cage. "Ara! Just say so! I don't need to be more nervous!"

Ara sniggered. Farideh huffed and glanced at their parents. Their mother still sobbed against their father's shoulder, but he was watching them with a mystified frown.

"Fairy?" Ara called. "Try again, but think of that boy. Please?"

"Oh, fine." This time Farideh sat at the bedside and clasped the cage without faltering. She thought of the boy. Of all things, his pimple bloomed in her mind.

"Ew!" Ara exclaimed.

"Did you see that?" Farideh whispered, suffering a prickle of awe up her spine.

"I did now! Can't you remember something else besides that?"

"Mmm, no. His uncle was much nicer looking."

"Well, of course he was. No pimples at all," Ara said. "You're supposed to be concentrating on the boy."

"Sorry, but his uncle felt comfortable and the boy didn't."

"Yes, I did notice that. Do you think the pimple was evil?"

Farideh snorted a laugh up her nose and covered her lower face with one hand. "Oh, no. I did the pig laugh again."

"Papa thinks we're being perfectly childish," Ara whispered, "and now he feels relieved. He really doesn't believe any of this."

"Well, I'm glad he's relieved. He has the stare, you know, the cold stare the boy showed us."

"Well, of course. He's a murderer."

"Ara!" Farideh lowered her voice. "I don't think warfare counts."

"So it is in the war diary? He really did."

"Yes, he really did, but it was duty. Duty to country doesn't count. Oh, and neither does smashing a man's head in with a pipe wrench for touching Maman."

"It counts in the bible," Ara argued, but quickly added, "except the pipe wrench."

"Are you saying our Papa is going to hell?"

"No. He'll get absolution first."

"Absolutely."

This time Ara set loose a tiny pig snigger.

"Can I let go of this thing now?" Farideh asked.

"Yes, but ...."

"But what?"

"Can you get me a flashlight?"

"Papa always has one somewhere. Maman said so in the diary. He adores flashlights."

44

"Well, get it. I feel badly in need of a flashlight."

"Fine." Farideh decided to wait until their father settled their mother a little better.

"Go on, then," David said after a little more comforting. "Freshen up. Get your make-up fixed. I'll get the trunks to the door."

When Deena walked out of the room, still with a few shaky sniffles, Farideh attempted her sister's innocent girl gaze and hurried after her distracted father. "Papa?"

"Yes, Farideh?" He didn't quite look at her, so the gaze was a waste.

"Can Ara and I use your flashlight?" Farideh asked.

His focus left the main bedroom doorway and sharpened on her, after she'd already let the gaze lapse. "Why would you need my flashlight?" he asked.

Farideh opted to answer in her usual forthright manner. "We're conducting experiments on the crystal of course."

"Oh. Fine. Put it under as much scientific scrutiny as you want, but don't break it. It's worth something to some collector of ancient artefacts somewhere."

"Would you really sell it?"

"Shh! No."

He was such a liar. He'd sell it in a flat second if he needed cash for an escape. Good thing the need had never arisen. She loved her father, but he was definitely not the right murderer. Farideh was certain the right murderer would have felt some sort of attachment to the talisman.

She followed him as far as the master bedroom door and then hovered just to the side of the frame, not wanting to attract her mother's attention. Deena moved listlessly about the room. Farideh had never seen her like this before, hopeless and looking abandoned.

It was always the strong one.

Farideh blinked. The strong one. Did that mean …?

Oh, no. Her mother had a sister, and the sister was ….

Deena looked up and saw her staring. "Farideh," she breathed and said words in Persian.

"What does it mean?" Farideh asked.

"May evil pass over you," her father said, arriving with the flashlight. He'd just dug it out of the top drawer of his steamer trunk. "And don't worry. It will pass over you. There you are. Off to Ara.

Wait by the suite door. We'll go down to the taxi soon. If they let us on the train early, we can settle you for a good night's sleep."

"And if they don't?"

"Then we play cards in the train station for a few hours."

"All right." Farideh backed off with the flashlight in hand, feeling hollow again, certain that evil had not passed over her mother's sister. If the secret were as old as the talisman, then evil had not passed over many generations of sisters.

Chapter Six

Jimmy Russo, with a wry grin, smashed his cigarette into an ashtray and lifted up from the stool at the hotel bar. He'd begged a quarter hour break from Judge Brown, who detested tobacco smoke of any sort. The judge had agreed, adding that he would put the fifteen minutes to good use in the bathtub before heading out on the town.

"Take your time. Take a half hour," he'd said. "Have a drink. I intend to get good and spiffy."

Jimmy's wry smiled widened. Of course the old boy would hit the town. It was all on the boss's tab, so why the hell not? Booze, gambling and girls, and plenty of all of it. Jimmy would have taken more than half an hour bathing and sprucing up in his best suit. But still, he wished the judge hadn't been so eager to delay the outcome of their meeting. Maybe the judge shouldn't be so concerned with how he looked. Money and power didn't need looks. Man was ugly anyhow. And old.

Well, the half hour was up. Time to get back to Old Judge Brown and wrap up the deal.

He and the judge had started the negotiations in the dining room. Most of the conversation had been pleasantries and hints—the better lawyers were good at pleasantries and hints—but Jimmy was fairly certain the deal was done except for the handshake. His brother Eddie would be out of Sing Sing on a technicality before autumn.

He sauntered out of the barroom and into the lobby, where he remembered the woman and girl with the captivating blue eyes. Their skin had been a little dark, like coffee with a lot of cream. He'd pegged them for old world immigrants, somewhere Mediterranean maybe, but the woman's accent hadn't sounded old world. She'd had a cultured voice with a trace of a French lilt. So maybe southern France, though the woman's features had seemed more like those he'd find further east and south. She looked like an Arabian houri, and he damned well wanted her in his harem, wearing nothing but a veil and some jewels. Wait a few years, and he'd have the girl in the harem too.

The same operator manned the elevator as earlier, a fellow with a tag naming him John. He was a careful sort who kept his eyes focused on the cage door or the panel most of the time. "Where to, sir?" he asked.

"Same as before. The top," Jimmy said.

"Yes, sir." The operator got the box in motion and remained at attention, eyes front.

"There was a lady in here earlier, around supper time. Beautiful blue eyes. Had a girl with her. Same beautiful blue eyes. Know anything about them?"

"No, sir. I don't rightly recall anything about a woman and girl. A lot of people go up and down at supper time."

"They were hard to miss." Jimmy pulled out his wallet and played with the bill fold, riffling the wad of ones and twos. "Really beautiful. Woman had a light beige dress and sweater and wore a short-brimmed straw hat. She looked old world. Olive skin, face that belongs on a painting of a harem girl, body to match. The girl had a dusky blue-coloured dress. She had a Coney Island pin stuck to the bodice."

"Sorry, sir. I don't rightly recall."

Jimmy squinted hard at the operator, who faced front same as before. The man hadn't even looked when Jimmy started the dance with the dollars, and most everyone looked when the paper started whispering. People liked the whisper of green paper.

"You know a lot about her," Jimmy said.

"No, sir. Sorry."

"At least tell me what floor she's on."

"No, sir."

"She must be a hell of a tipper," Jimmy said.

"I don't rightly recall, sir."

Jimmy shoved his wallet back into his inner jacket pocket, stumped. Bribery had failed, and he couldn't resort to the usual methods when his favourite non-violent means had been unsuccessful, not here in The Plaza and definitely not now. He couldn't afford to alienate Judge Brown.

Jimmy settled against the elevator wall, scowling, which did nothing to unnerve the operator, because the stubborn cretino continued staring at the panel. What the hell was wrong with the

48

man? He didn't like money? Jimmy would have gladly doubled whatever the woman had given him, but for some reason, elevator operator John had gotten all cocky for some woman.

"Top floor, sir," John said and hauled the cage open. "Have a good evening, sir." Jimmy stepped out and turned to face the operator, but John pulled the cage shut and disappeared from view as the inner doors closed, without once looking at him.

"Damn it," Jimmy said. No weak points, no advantage. The man had been as effective as a brick wall. Shaking his head in disgust, Jimmy headed for the judge's suite.

Up ahead, a skinny bellhop wrestled a heavy trunk on a trolley toward the service elevator further down. Jimmy had missed which room the boy had issued from.

"They should have sent someone with more muscle to get that done," Jimmy commented as he stopped at the judge's door. He gave the wood a sharp rap.

"No, sir. I can manage," the boy said.

"Yeah, you got no choice," Jimmy replied.

"Right you are, sir." The boy narrowly avoided ramming the trolley into a decorative desk along the hall. "Bad wheel on the left," he said.

Jimmy watched him manage the heavy load to the elevator. Did he have wet jacket sleeves?

The boy jammed his finger on the call button, faced away and fussed with the trolley, setting it up for a push when the elevator arrived. The jacket sleeves hid from Jimmy's view.

Jimmy frowned at the suite door, realizing his knock hadn't been answered. He rapped again, this time more loudly. After a few more seconds without a response, he tried the door handle. It was locked. He pressed his ear to the panels. He thought he heard water running.

"Judge?" he called through. He knocked again.

The service elevator door opened. Jimmy paused to glance in that direction. The boy heaved the trolley into motion and shoved out of sight. Jimmy's distracted gaze returned to the door.

"Judge?" He banged the wood.

The elevator door shut.

Jimmy banged the wood again.

Some ten minutes later and now very hesitant even to knock quietly, because rich folk had come out into the hall to glare at him, Jimmy stepped away from the door and returned to the lobby. He checked the dining room. He checked the smoky bar and the billiard area. He stepped outside to see if the judge's chunky body stood out amongst the casual strollers on the sidewalk, but the judge wasn't in any of these places.

At the concierge's desk, he asked the clerk on duty to telephone the judge's suite. When the judge didn't pick up, the clerk suggested the guest in that room may have checked out of the hotel; but after the clerk ran his fingers through the book and confirmed that Old Judge Brown had not, Jimmy made the green paper in his wallet whisper and convinced the concierge on night duty to accompany him to the top floor, where they unlocked the suite door.

Inside the bedroom, they found a large pile of clothes dumped on the floor and one small overnight suitcase lying open on the bed with the clothes still packed inside. There was no sign of the judge.

Jimmy moved with trepidation to the bathroom. Water trickled from an open faucet. The door was ajar. He shoved it. He and the concierge stared inward.

The concierge sagged with relief and entered to shut off the tap at the sink. "He must have stepped out for a bit," he suggested. "Perhaps you should check the dining room again."

"Yeah, sure," Jimmy said, gazing at the trail of water that led from the filled bath to the bathroom door. He followed it with his eyes, a successively lighter pattern of drip marks that stopped near the bed. He started back to that location.

"Sir?" the concierge said. "Sir, I really must lock up now."

"Yeah, be right with you." Jimmy stared at the discarded pile of clothes. Most were still nicely folded. He at last noted a triangular bit sticking out at one edge. He prodded this with a toe and realized it was the wooden tray of a trunk. "Son of a bitch," he breathed.

"Sir?"

"Yeah, I'm on my way," Jimmy said, backing off a few steps. He turned and marched out of the suite, not waiting for the concierge to lock up. He had to get out of this hotel, out of view and hopefully out of everyone's memory, because that little bastard bellhop had just screwed him over big time. If the judge showed up dead later, Jimmy didn't want to take the blame.

He almost didn't wait for the elevator, but then figured he'd look too suspicious if he used the stairs. In the end, he travelled down with the concierge and elevator man John, who kept his stolid gaze to the front as usual.

50

"If the Judge returns, shall I give him a message?" the concierge asked.

"Yeah, tell him Danny Major stopped in to see him," Jimmy said. "He knows how to reach me."

"Very good, sir."

Jimmy waited with false patience for the elevator to descend, and he sounded normal as he thanked the concierge for his help. He moved at an unhurried pace to the door and out into the warm New York summer evening air. He didn't see the boss's limo anywhere. Good thing. The boss wouldn't want to be involved in this mess. No use taking a taxi either, not this close to The Plaza. Jimmy set off down the street with long strides. He'd get a few blocks between him and the hotel before flagging down a ride.

"Figlio di puttana bastardo!" he said. "Io lo ucciderà!" *Son of a bitch bastard! I will kill him.*

Unless this was a kidnapping for ransom, old Judge Brown was either dead or would be soon. Either way, that skinny little bastard had put an end to Eddie, because without the judge's influence, he had no hope of getting Eddie out. His brother would die in prison now, electrocuted or hanged, whatever means Eddie finally decided on.

"Bastardo! Bastardo!" Jimmy spat.

"Mister! Watch your mouth!" someone said.

"Vaffanculo." *Go fuck yourself.*

"How dare you!"

Jimmy quieted down and hurried onward. He couldn't afford to attract more attention, but someday he'd find out who that little bastard was, hunt him down and kill him.

Chapter Seven

July 28, 1929. New York State. In a milk delivery truck just after midnight.

A muffled shout sounded from the trunk. Startled, Godefroy glanced back through the narrow aperture leading to the rear of the truck. The truck swerved. Godefroy jerked his attention to front and narrowly avoided tilting the clumsy vehicle into a ditch. He wrestled with the steering for a few more seconds, breathing hard and trying not to panic.

"Focus on driving, Uncle," Caspar said.

"Ja," Godefroy croaked. He swallowed an uncomfortable knot and peeked at his nephew. The eyes gave him the situation. This had never been intended as a quick kill and disposal.

"Caspar—"

"Nothing you say will change this," Caspar interrupted.

"How did you get a man that fat in the trunk? And without a struggle?"

"He's curled up like a drowned tomcat, only not quite drowned. It only took a little petting for him to let his guard down. The hardest thing was lifting him, really."

All the necessary hints in one answer. Godefroy swallowed another knot, reached into his vest pocket and pulled out a flask. He handed it to Caspar. "Open it for me."

Caspar undid the cap and passed the flask back. Godefroy drank, lowered the flask, waited for the burn to subside and drank again. "It's hell. Newfoundland Screech is hell in a bottle," he said after, wheezing just a little. He gave the flask to Caspar, who capped it for him.

"Why do you put it in your flask, then?" his nephew asked, though he didn't sound very interested.

"Half way through, I water it down. Then it's about as strong as regular rum," Godefroy said. "I get twice as much use out of the flask, so to speak."

"You've already drunk more than half without watering it down."

"I forgot. Caspar—"

"You don't have to watch," Caspar interrupted again. "As soon as we get to where we need to go, just leave with the truck for a while." He pressed the flask toward his uncle, who grasped it clumsily and almost dropped it.

"I have to stay," Godefroy said, hurrying to place the flask between his legs until the narrow road wasn't a dying snake's tangle of unpredictable curves.

"Yes, I read that in one of the family tomes. 'One who witnesses, one who perpetrates.' If that's the case, shouldn't the curse have kept my twin alive?"

Godefroy wished the flask were still uncapped.

"Uncle?" Caspar prodded. "How did my brother die? You've yet to add that history to the volumes."

"I don't have to add anything. I just have to witness."

"Doesn't matter. I found your diary and read that part."

"Jesus!" Godefroy spat. "Even where I hid it?"

"That was a stupid place to hide it. Wedged behind the flush toilet? Really? Even oil cloth might not protect it from a spill. You're always on the toilet, Uncle."

"The spills happen from the bowl. Helvete! How much did you read?" *Damn it!*

"Just the part about how you found Helge smothered next to my strangled mother when we were two. My father was about to smother me, and then you banged on the water closet door because you were suffering another of your emergencies and I had to hide the book."

"Jesus, Jesus," Godefroy breathed.

"Was my father mad already?"

"No. Yes. He was trying to end the curse. He intended to murder me after you, and then himself."

"Well, your usual after supper bout with the runs interrupted the story, and when I returned, you'd already moved the diary, I presume to write in it. It's been a great game trying to find it again, which I haven't yet. So? Why aren't you and I dead?"

"He passed out. He had the pillow over you. I rushed to stop him, but he collapsed on the floor. I couldn't wake him up for a week."

"That must have been messy."

"Damn it, Caspar," Godefroy said. "Yes, it was messy. You try to clean a bed day after day when it's been pissed in once too often."

"No, thank you. You must have been tired. All that work. Two bodies to bury, a child to feed and diaper, and an insensate man to clean. I suppose you were very glad when Grandma moved in to save you the trouble."

"Caspar, stop it."

"So why didn't my father try again later?"

With an effort, Godefroy loosened his tight grip on the steering wheel. "He did, and he passed out again. You would know this if you really did read the family tomes. One must witness, one must perpetrate. Your father killed your witness, and I was all that remained, and the heir cannot be killed until he has sired an heir himself."

"I did read the tomes actually, the pages that didn't crumble at my touch. I just wanted you to admit it. You never did well with secrecy. The runs, Uncle. All the runs the last few days. Even Grandma has complained."

"Oh, shut up."

A shout from the trunk sounded again. This time Godefroy thought he understood words.

"Help me! Dear God! Help me!"

Godefroy's grip tightened again. Soon, very soon, he'd be forced to witness something appalling. Death was never clean, but some sorts were messier than others.

"Please! Help me!"

"How is he even still breathing?" Godefroy asked.

"I knifed off some wood near the hinges."

"Oh."

One of Caspar's hands settled on Godefroy's sleeve. "Uncle. Relax your arms. You'll be too tired to drive if you continue like that."

"Can't you just knife him quickly," Godefroy begged.

"I'll try not to be too untidy, but that's all I can promise. You know why."

"Yes. Yes, I know why."

"You should have realized he wasn't dead. You are the witness, after all."

"I don't need to see the actual kill, not if you show me the body. It was easy enough to know it happened just by how your father behaved."

"Seriously? You thought I already killed him? Based on my behaviour? Do I look satisfied?"

"Oh, dear God!" a muffled voice cried.

"No, you don't look satisfied!" Godefroy said. "You don't look anything usually. And your father never looked satisfied. Before or after."

"Oh. Then how did he look?"

"Relieved." Godefroy eased his anxious grip on the steering wheel yet again. "I just mistook your calm for the same thing."

"Sorry."

"What's the use of being sorry for that?" Godefroy demanded.

"No use. I'll try to look relieved after."

"Don't you dare. And stop teasing."

"Sorry," Caspar repeated. "So you don't need to see the actual killing?"

"Not if the body is claimed for the curse."

"How can you possibly know it's my work?"

Godefroy hesitated, but then said, "I can feel the kill."

His nephew's stare was like a rasp scraping his skin. "You can feel it?"

"Ja. Sometimes."

"Sometimes? Why sometimes?"

"I don't like it. The drink helps it go away."

"If it's true that you can feel a kill, why do you even need to see it happen?" Caspar asked.

"The witness pays his debt with sorrow, Caspar! The curse doesn't give us as much if I don't see the body."

"Fine. I'm sorry. Don't get in a lather." They said nothing for a bit. Then Caspar asked, "So what does a kill feel like to you?"

"Caspar! Give it a rest!"

"All right! Fine!"

They were silent again for a short time, until a grief-stricken, terrified howl bled through the wood of the trunk. Godefroy spoke the first thing that popped into his mind to drown out the sobs that followed. "The first time I've seen you brighten up in months was in front of those girls. Beautiful names, Farideh and Ara. Persian, I believe."

"Persian like some of our distant ancestors," Caspar added. "Perhaps we should go back and murder them."

"For God's sake, Caspar! Not because they're Persian. You don't murder little girls just for being Persian."

"I suppose not. They were half Canadian from the looks of it, and that would be bad form, seeing as how I'm Canadian by birth. But they can't be far removed from the Persian family tree, don't you think? They still had coffee candy skin. The type made with cream, I mean."

"Please! Please, don't kill me!"

"Yes, I know what you mean." Godefroy tried to hand the flask back to his nephew, but Caspar refused to grasp it.

"Drive, uncle. You can have more Screech later."

Godefroy's jangled nerves knotted into an unmanageable panic. "Go back and shut him up! Just shut him up! Why should I put up with your messy kill? Tell me? When did I agree to a messy kill? You were supposed to murder him and then sneak me up to see the body! That was all! But now we have complications! Ja! Complications!"

"Sorry. I'll see after it." Caspar started moving from his seat.

"Just stab him and be done with it!"

"I can't do that." The boy grabbed his uncle's flask, uncapped it, handed the flask over and tossed the cap on Godefroy's lap. Then he squeezed through the narrow gap in the back wall of the driver's cabin and moved into the dimness at the rear of the truck. Godefroy glanced back, caught sight of his nephew withdrawing the switchblade from his coat pocket, and jerked his gaze to front.

"Not messy. Not messy," he breathed. He lifted the flask, drank and drove, resting the flask against the wheel after one more swallow. A thumping bang occurred in back, and he knew the trunk lid had slammed open.

"Please! Please, don't kill me! I'll do anything you ask! I've got money! I've got contacts! Name it! Name it! Don't kill me!"

"I'm not the least bit familiar to you, am I?" Caspar said. He sounded as calm and distant as before.

"No! I'm sorry! No!" A shaky breath ensued and then louder shouts of negation. "No! No! Don't kill me!"

"I'm just getting closer so you can see. Here. I'll turn on this flashlight." A ray of light swung crazily and settled into a mild glow directed to one side of the truck. "There. Do you recognise me at all?"

"You're the bellhop from The Plaza. You almost tore my balls off and then drowned me."

"Yes, well, drowning you was easier while you were distracted. Testicles are rather delicate nuggets. Yours are particularly ugly, by the way. I washed my hands five times after stuffing you in the trunk. I still feel disgusted. Oh, and I vomited in the sink too. Your breath stinks and your mouth tastes foul."

After a brief hesitation, the victim said, "What do you want? Why did you kidnap me?"

"What about the name Grace? Do you remember anyone by the name of Grace?"

"No! Why …." A small inhalation suggested shock.

"Yes?"

"Grace? Edward …?"

"Edvard. Edvard Grace, a Canadian landed immigrant."

"Oh, dear Lord."

"So I do remind you of him," Caspar said.

"You're his son? He had family?"

"Are you an idiot? Who do you think paid for his lawyer?"

"But no one ever came to the trial! We couldn't find any relations."

"My father didn't want my uncle arrested too. Grace is a translation. You really are an idiot, you and your investigators."

"Your father was a murderer! He strangled and beat to death five men in prison! He broke the arms of a guard and ripped the ear off another! You've no right to kidnap me for—!" A short pause, then: "Stop! Stop! I'm sorry! Please don't!"

"I need to know some names," Caspar said.

"Anything! Anything!"

"My father had a good lawyer. He had a good argument that should have dismissed his case: he was running from a gunfight in the dark and shot at people he thought were trying to murder him. No one found bullets in any bodies that matched his pistol. But the argument didn't work. Things went bad with the jury and with you."

"No, no. He didn't have a good argu—! Stop! Stop! Oh, God! Jesus! I'm bleeding!"

"Prisoners in Sing Sing tried to make good on a contract for his life. So did some guards. Are you listening?"

"Aaaa! Jesus! Jesus!"

"Pay attention."

"Yes, I'm sorry! Please don't stick me again!"

"A trial that turns sour and a series of prison assassination contracts isn't the sort of thing that happens to a man who was in the wrong place at the wrong time. One of the men who died at Beau Lake was important to someone," Caspar said. "Who did my father kill that was important?"

"Frankie Russo! He killed Frankie Russo! Please don't hurt me again. Please don't!"

"And who was Frankie important to?"

"Don Antonio Russo. Frankie was his nephew."

"Don Antonio Russo bribed the jury?"

"Yes! Yes!"

"And you? Did he bribe you?"

"Please! Please! No! Aaaah, God, have mercy! Have mercy!"

"Did he bribe you?"

"Yes! I'm sorry! I'm sorry! Please, I'm sorry!"

"We'll be done soon. You just have to give me another name. You can do that, right?"

"Yes! Yes, anything! I'll do anything!"

"The man you were with tonight? Who was he?"

"What? Jimmy Russo. Why should he matter?"

"He's related to Don Russo?"

"He's another nephew, but he had nothing to do with your father. Look. You let me go, right? And Don Russo will owe you. Jimmy's brother is in Sing Sing on death row. He's innocent. I can get him out, but only if you let me go. All right? You let me go, and the Russo family will owe you."

"How would you know if Jimmy's brother is innocent?"

"Because he says he is. No! I'll talk! I'll talk! Jimmy said he did it! But Eddie took the fall for him!"

"Eddie? His brother's name is Edward?" Caspar asked.

"Eduardo. It's Eduardo. Jesus, God!"

"An Eduardo for an Edvard," Caspar said.

"What? No! He's innocent, I said."

"How innocent? Has he committed other crimes?"

"He's in the mafia! Of course he's committed—! Grrggkh!"

Disgusting noises burbled in the back, sounds Godefroy had heard too many times before, of blood in breath, of a struggle for continued life, of helpless, wordless protest. The hairs on Godefroy's body prickled.

The trunk lid thumped shut and cut off the worst of the ordeal. Caspar squeezed back into the front and sat down on the passenger seat. He pulled out a handkerchief and wiped clean his switchblade.

"The mess is still in the trunk, Uncle."

"This Jimmy Rus ...." Godefroy's voice was breathy. He cleared his throat. "This Jimmy Russo?

"Pull over, Uncle. Teach me to drive."

"You're too young."

"I'm not. Pull over. You're going to be too drunk soon in any case."

"This Jimmy Russo?"

"He was there at the hotel."

"I heard that. But why?"

"She was there at the hotel. Farideh. She didn't see me. As a bellhop, I was virtually invisible."

"And how does it relate to this Jimmy?"

"He looked at her wrong. He looked at her mother wrong. Pull over, Uncle."

"We're not staying. We're going back to Canada. We still have time to make the Niagara train at least. We're not far from the next station."

"I know. Later, Uncle, perhaps when we come back for the prosecution lawyer or a member of the jury. I'll do Jimmy later. But for now, pull over. Teach me to drive. You can look at the body before we dump it."

"Ja. Ja." Godefroy slowed the vehicle and parked it at the side of the road. He turned the key, and the engine halted. They didn't move. The headlights played over asphalt and weeds. Night insects whirred through the air. The sounds in the back had stopped. The silence of the country reigned until crickets found their courage and sung love ballads to each other again.

"I'm so sorry, Caspar," Godefroy whispered.

"Ja, Uncle. I know."

Neither looked at each other. Caspar pushed open the delivery door and stepped out. After a few seconds delay, Godefroy retrieved the cap of his flask and exchanged seats with his nephew.

Chapter Eight

July 28, 1929. On the train to Niagara Falls.

Farideh lifted the curtain and peeked out. On the platform, a station worker rolled out a flat trolley topped with cargo headed for some destination elsewhere down the track. He looked up as he passed. Farideh dropped the curtain lower and spied with one eye. He smiled and continued on. Behind her, the flashlight clicked on again.

"Ara," she complained. "The batteries are running out." She lowered the curtain entirely and slumped with her back to the car wall. "You can't charge the crystal with a flashlight. It's just not going to stay blue."

"Don't talk so loud," Ara whispered. "You'll have Maman in here. You know she only just managed to fall asleep."

Their parents were in the neighbouring sleeping compartment. The walls were thin enough their father could punch his way in with an ear, let alone listen to an unguarded conversation. He'd warned them to hush up and keep the flashlight off, but Farideh was feeling grumpy, enervated and useless, and Ara, despite the unabated fever, was frantic to uncover the secrets of the crystal.

Ara's efforts had been interrupted for hours. Either their father or their mother had sat in the compartment with them up until a half hour ago. They hadn't been able to conduct a conversation or do much but annoy their father by incessantly turning on the flashlight under the blankets. But their father had left to check on their mother and hadn't returned. They'd heard him moving about in the other compartment, but then silence had fallen. Farideh suspected he'd gone to sleep.

Their door was locked. They were in easy scream-for-help distance. Even they could punch a hole through the separating wall, though they'd use the armchair or some other moveable object and not their ears, but sleep was out of the question for both of them. Their parents might think they were safe now that the train had moved from New York to this outlying town, but the twins weren't prepared to believe it.

"Ara," Farideh whispered.

Ara shook the flashlight and focused the dying beam on the little cage.

"Ara!"

"Hmm?"

"Do you realize what it means?" Farideh asked. "That stuff about the strong one?"

"Yes. Maman had a sister."

"Who died," Farideh added. "She had a sister who died. I'm going to be next."

"Who says you're the strong one?" Ara asked absently.

Farideh hunched a little further down the wall, bunching up her night dress all the more. She hated night dresses, but her mother hadn't packed any of the soft harem-style trousers she liked to use at home. "Maman looked at me."

Ara slammed the flashlight vigorously in the air, but the beam remained a feeble plea for power compared to the strident attention-demanding ray of before.

"Oh, shut that off," Farideh said.

"I don't want to be in the dark."

"Then turn on the bed lamp."

"I don't want Papa to notice a warm light bulb if he comes back in. He was very stern about us sleeping. He only let us keep this flashlight because the batteries are all but dead."

"I'll open the curtain."

"I don't want to be seen."

Farideh didn't want to be seen either, but she couldn't resist peeking out from beneath a raised edge of curtain again. "I think we can turn on the lamp. I'm pretty sure he knew we wouldn't sleep. He's left us on guard duty."

"Oh? Really? I hadn't thought of that."

"It's in the war diary. Papa will put a soldier to work if the soldier has energy to spare. We're on night watch, and he'll have all the more energy to stand duty later."

"Maman is still going to be annoyed with him," Ara said, "even if he is only a scream and a cardboard wall away."

"He doesn't believe any of it."

Ara leaned off the bed and switched on the lamp. She rolled and came up against her sister's back. They shared a narrow bed in a luxury cabin for unmarried folk, as they thought of these sorts of

62

compartments. Farideh had shoved the second bunk out of the way and locked it in place. Although the twins had always been given the option of their own beds, neither liked sleeping alone.

"I wish I could put the lamp in bed with us," Ara said, "but its wall mounted."

"Can you imagine how many lamps would go missing from the railroad if they weren't wall mounted?" Farideh said.

"Who would steal a lamp from a luxury cabin?"

"Someone in need of a lamp."

"Farideh!"

"I think the porters are almost done loading the parcels on the train."

"Why do you suppose Papa doesn't believe any of it?" Ara asked. Farideh almost sat on her sister lowering away from the window. "Ow! Fairy!"

"Shh!"

"Don't put your bum on my nose, then."

Farideh giggled and wormed around to the other end of the bed. "Let's sleep foot to face."

"No kicking."

"I don't kick."

"You did last time. Well? What about Papa not believing?"

"I don't think he's seen anything to make him believe."

"So there's nothing in the war diary," Ara stated. "I was hoping Maman had written about strange goings on and mystical occurrences that had saved their lives during ferocious battles and escapes."

"It wasn't the Arabian Nights," Farideh said dryly. "Most of it is about her feelings for Papa."

Ara tossed the talisman at her. "Go and hold this up to the light. My legs are too rubbery."

Sighing dismally, Farideh plucked the chain from her lap and hopped off the bed. She dangled the cage in front of the wall lamp and watched the little crystal glow in the centre. She and her sister said nothing for a little bit. The train whistle blew a short note, and a few second later, the car jerked. Farideh hit the wall.

"And we're off," she said. After another second, she added, "At the pace of a snail."

"It takes so long for trains to get going," Ara agreed.

"And stop."

"They're so long."

"Like a tower of rectangles shooting down a track."

Ara's sleepy expression sharpened. "A tower?" she repeated.

"Yes, that was a stupid image," Farideh said. "I'll do better." She staggered a little. The train had shuddered again.

"Fairy ...? Fairy, what if Maman's sister didn't die of a fever?"

"What?"

"What if the danger isn't an illness or fever?"

"But—?"

"Why else would we need a murderer but to murder something worse than a fever?" Ara continued, almost frantic. "We're on the tower! Fairy! We're on the tower. The danger is already here!"

"Oh, no! But you have to get off!" Farideh said.

"No! Not me! You! Stop trying to protect me!"

"But ...!"

Ara shoved free of the sheets and blankets and rose on her knees. She thrust the curtain wide. "It's not going that fast yet. You can still jump off."

"But ...! Wait. Shouldn't we just shout for Papa?"

"I don't believe he left us on guard duty," Ara said, a hand plastered to glass, the curtain clutched in one fist. "I just don't. This is the tower. Fairy, if you don't listen to me, the tower won't reverse."

"I'm not leaving you here!" Ara protested.

"Oh, no!" Ara cried. She looked back at Farideh. "I've been the wrong one all along! It isn't the Querent! It's never the Querent! It isn't me who needs to pass the crystal to the murderer! It's you!"

"Ara!"

"I can't run! Fairy! I can't run! Look out the window!"

Farideh lunged onto the bed and plastered her hands to the glass as well. Their car was traversing a quiet town road. Beyond the lowered crossing gate, a milk delivery truck idled, and in the driver's seat sat the beautiful boy. He and his uncle stared at them as they passed.

"It's not coincidence! It's not coincidence!" Ara shoved Farideh in the flank. "Fairy! Run! Get off this train and get the crystal to the boy! Now! Now! Go!"

"Ara!" Farideh wailed.

Ara seized her wrist, and a shock of mind-focusing terror ripped through Farideh. "She never eats the witness," Ara spat. "She only eats the rightful heir. Break the chain of destruction and break her!"

64

The next word that issued from Ara's mouth sounded as if a thousand voices bellowed it. "Survive!"

Farideh scrambled off the bed. She banged into the door, tried to yank it open, found it locked, regained enough sense to shove the lock open and slam the door aside. She charged from the compartment and collided with someone only a few yards away, someone wrapped in perfume and a fur coat, someone with lacquered nails, a black hat and veil, and a faint tobacco smell. Farideh saw that much before they both fell. She landed face first against a bosom with sharp metal buttons over the bodice. They scratched her cheek.

"Run!" the thousand voices howled from inside the compartment. Farideh clambered over her collision victim, stepped on something soft, ignored the yelp and curse, and barrelled down the corridor to the end of the car. She barged through to the little platform between cars.

"Chienne!" she heard a woman say. *Bitch!*

"Sorry!" she called back. She leaned her head out to view the crossroad. It was already far behind, and the train picked up speed as she hesitated. The truck …? Was it …?

Oh, no! It was backing from the intersection! They were leaving!

"Little girl?" a woman said at the car door. "Here, little girl. You seem confused. Let me help—!"

With arms and feet braced, Farideh lunged her torso backward. Her head brushed past red-painted fingernails on a hand reaching toward her, a hand whose fingers, she vaguely realized, had a clawed arrangement. Then she whipped forward with all her strength and launched her body off the train. The fingers snatched hair near her temple and ripped them from her scalp. She shrieked, sailed through air and staggered onto broken rock at the side of the track. Agony spiked the soles of her bare feet. She managed several clumsy, excruciating steps to retain her balance, but tumbled onto the grassy ditch further off and rolled down it.

"Ara!" she wailed and burst into huge sobs of grief, terror and pain. Alone. Alone for the first time in her life.

Then the milk truck rattled up, screeched to a stop at the roadside and brought with it, of all things, a smell of skunk instead of milk.

Chapter Nine

July 28, 1929. New York State. In the milk truck while missing the train.

"Oh, dear Lord," his uncle said. Again. Feet planted far apart, Godefroy clutched the dash and the driver's backrest to remain on the passenger seat.

"It was a perfectly executed turn," Caspar responded.

"The truck tilted halfway to the ditch!" his uncle cried. "Caspar! Slow down!"

"Exaggeration. And I can't slow down. We'll miss the train."

"We can catch the next! The last thing we need is attention drawn to this truck!"

"No bad luck today, Uncle," Caspar said. "You're the only witness. I'm the only heir. A murder has just been committed, and I can drive like a madman if I want."

"Stop wanting to!"

"Stop worrying. We'll have the luck of the devil tonight," Caspar said, and then he hit the skunk. He barely had time to notice it before it made its last sound.

Thud.

And then the stink arrived.

"Dear Lord!" his uncle howled. "Caspar!"

"That wasn't my fault at all," he said. "How was I to expect a skunk in the middle of a sleepy town?"

"Because it's the middle of a sleepy town! You call that luck?" his uncle snarled. "Slow down now!"

Very much deflated, Caspar eased his foot off the gas peddle. "I want a race car, Uncle."

"Anything. Just stop racing the truck. Gud i himlen, jag ska kräkas. Stop the truck." *God in heaven, I'm going to vomit.*

"We're going to miss the train."

"Fine! We'll miss it! Stop the truck!"

Caspar stopped the truck. His uncle lumbered out of the vehicle and puked at the roadside in front of an old building that looked to have been a farmhouse at one time. Now it was one of many houses along a narrow street facing more buildings on the other side, most of them built in the last thirty years. Caspar glanced at the windows of the nearby residences. Despite his uncle's awful noise, none of the curtains lifted and no lights turned on.

"And how is it good luck to hit a skunk?" he muttered. If the rules of the curse were immutable, and apparently they were, then the murder should have brought his family extraordinary good luck in the first few hours alone, and since he had yet to father an heir, that luck included him. Grandma, in whichever casino she currently lurked, should have recouped the family fortune already. Perhaps she even had gangsters kissing her feet and painting her toenails. So why the skunk wandering under his wheel now, in the middle of this sleepy town just before catching a train?

"Gud! Helvetet!" *God! Hell!* Godefroy lurched upright. He wiped his mouth, turned and blinked at the fender. "Is that ...? Is that a skunk's tail?"

"What? Where?" Caspar asked.

"In the fender of all places. How did it get up there?"

"No, idea. It bounced off the wheel perhaps. If you're done being disgusting, get in."

"No! Get out here, and get rid of it."

"I'm not touching it."

"Well, neither am I!"

"Then get in."

"The smell, Caspar!"

"What smell?"

"Caspar!"

Caspar put the truck in gear and forced his uncle to race for the passenger door.

"Damn it, Caspar!" His uncle scooted onto his seat, and the door slammed shut.

Caspar ignored him and jarred the truck out of first, but he was clumsy with the clutch. The gears protested. "Whoops. I thought I'd learned not to do that."

"Practice lower speeds for a bit, why don't you?" his uncle said dryly, digging into his coat pocket. He started to raise his flask and then realized it was empty. "Damn." He lowered the container and slumped with an arm on the open window. "Damn the stink."

"We must be close to the station by now," Caspar said.

"Yes, I think so," his uncle agreed. A train whistle confirmed their speculation. "Oh, dear."

"Uncle, vomiting is a nuisance, time-wasting vice, and I should like you to stop."

"As if a person can just stop vomiting!" his uncle said. "Don't be childish!"

Caspar grabbed the flask from lax fingers and tossed it out the window past his uncle's nose. Godefroy let out a string of rapid curses that even Caspar couldn't easily follow. Caspar pulled to a stop at an intersection.

"It looks like a ... left turn?" he guessed. "The train sounded left, didn't it?"

"Yes, go left," Godefroy said, pinching the bridge of his nose with one hand. He had the other palm splayed over his forehead. "Varför, Gud? Varför denna pojke?" *Why, God? Why this boy?*

"My twin would have liked me," Caspar said, turning left.

"I like you, Caspar."

"No, you don't."

"Caspar! Damn it! I like you!"

"Aren't you supposed to love me? I'm your precious nephew, after all. You're going to make me feel unwanted."

"Grandma loves you," Godefroy said.

"She tolerates me, and you avoided saying you love me, Uncle. You should say you love me, your pitiable nephew who must live with a lifetime burden of guilt for your benefit."

"Yes, and let's see what threat you have to make for that to happen," Godefroy retorted. "Why don't you swear to butcher every poodle you ever come across? Then I'll say I love you."

"I knew you didn't like that breed of dog. There's the train. It's going to cross in front of us."

"Ja, ja. Let it cross. I'm so tired." Godefroy stopped pinching the bridge of his nose. The other palm swiped down his face and lowered to rest on his thigh. "This," he muttered. "It has to be this mood. Not relief. Playfulness, of all things."

"You're tired because of the alcohol. You won't feel so old after the liquor fades from your blood," Caspar said. "And it's the driving that's made me happy, not the murder. I like driving."

"Be quiet. Damn I want a cigarette."

"Grandma's dog or ...?"

"Shut up, Caspar!"

Caspar rolled the truck to a stop and put it in park before the gate blocking the track. He and his uncle watched the flashing light of the wigwag overhead.

"The bell isn't sounding," Caspar mentioned.

"Half of those things are always broken," Godefroy said.

"If the gates hadn't come down, I might have been able to cross before the train."

"Caspar, if you ever mention such stupidity again, you shall never have any car, let alone a race car."

"Then I shall keep the truck."

Apparently his uncle was too weary to argue now, because he said nothing. He stared glumly forward. Caspar looked down the length of the train and spotted muted lights shining from a few windows in the cars rolling closer. The engine passed the crossroad.

"Those cars must have private compartments," Caspar said.

"Hmm."

"I could have crossed. You can't die and neither can I, not until our heirs are born."

"Ja, ja," Godefroy said wearily. "It's very easy to murder from a wheelchair. There are guns now, after all. Guns make it all simpler. We'll hire menservants to push us both into range."

"Oh," Caspar said. "I didn't think of that."

"You like being able to walk, ja?"

"Ja," Caspar admitted. A light in an oncoming train car suddenly brightened. Someone had just pulled a curtain back. He focused on the window. His uncle leaned forward.

"Is that …?"

"Ja," Caspar said. "The sister."

Farideh suddenly plastered herself to the window as well and gaped at them. Caspar and his uncle stared at the twins until the train car trundled them from view. Then Caspar jammed the truck into reverse. The engine roared, and he drove the cumbersome vehicle backward until he'd crossed an earlier intersection a few hundred yards back, narrowly avoiding the ditches to either side thrice.

His uncle clung to the dash again. "Caspar, we can't race the train to the next station. Slow down. Caspar!"

"Not slowing down!" Caspar said. He changed gears, pressed the gas pedal to the floor and followed the road parallel to the track.

"Yes, you are! Now! Slow down now!"

"No!"

70

But yes, he slowed, because up ahead, something white launched from the gap where two cars joined together. The figure staggered several paces down the rocky border of the track and tumbled out of view into the weed-choked ditch. Caspar slammed his foot on the brake pedal. The truck screeched, his uncle banged into the dash, and Caspar craned to see. They'd passed the figure, and the headlights provided no illumination into the ditch.

"Gud i helvetet! My nose!" *God in hell!*

Caspar shoved the gears into park and slammed out of the vehicle. He scrabbled down the bank. "Farideh?"

She sobbed a desolate, wordless cry. He yanked weeds away from her face.

"Farideh?" his uncle said. He scrambled into the ditch at her other side. Up on the track, car after train car passed.

"Farideh? Did you jump from the train?" Godefroy tugged weeds away from her face on his side. "Farideh? Why did you jump?"

One hand lifted to the dark sky. She had a chain in her grip. Something dangled from the end. Caspar and his uncle reached for it together. Their fingers tangled with metal, and a tiny star caught life inside a little cage. They both jerked their hands back, except Caspar clung to the chain. He pulled the luminous object out of Farideh's grasp.

"What is this?" Godefroy said, while Caspar raised the tiny miracle higher and stared.

"It's some sort of blue stone," he said. "It has its own fire inside."

The last passenger car trundled by. Farideh wailed again. Caspar startled, realized they needed answers—now!—and pinched her nose.

"Ow!"

"Why did you jump from the train?" he asked.

"She's on the train!" Farideh bleated, both hands over her nose. "She's on the train with my sister! She's going to hurt her!"

Without further information, Caspar clambered up the ditch, chased the caboose and grabbed the rail, the tiny blue star trailing from one hand.

Chapter Ten

Chasing the train.

"Up you get, min flicka," the uncle said. He worked his hands beneath Farideh's back and knees, lifted her and staggered up the slope toward the truck. Once he was on level ground, he had no difficulty carrying her. He rounded the truck and set her on the passenger seat. Farideh huddled on it, shivering with cold and shock.

"Aj, aj, that looks bad," he said, inspecting her feet. He stretched out of his coat and handed it up to her. "Put it on, min flicka."

"What does that mean?"

"Min flicka? My girl. It's just … one of those things we say."

"Yes, to reassure useless, screaming girls who leap from trains," Farideh said. Instead of wrapping the coat around her shoulders, she lifted it and sobbed against sturdy material that smelled of cigarettes. The train moved faster and faster, taking away her sister, her mother, her father, the boy with the shining talisman.

"Aj, aj, not to worry about screaming. I'd have screamed too," the uncle said. "Jumping from trains is not fun, especially unprepared and without shoes."

She blinked back tears. He'd said that like he really understood, as if jumping out from between passenger cars was not an unbelievably stupid thing, but perhaps an activity that sometimes had to be done.

"Here, now. I'm going to give you my shirt too," he said. "We'll have to wrap your feet in it, ja? Your little feet, they're not in a good way."

She lowered the coat enough to speak. "Yes, all right."

He unbuttoned and shrugged out of his white shirt, and with only an undershirt remaining on his torso, wound the garment around both her feet. It felt warm from his body heat. He had nice shoulders. She caught a whiff of alcohol as he lifted straight.

"What will happen?" she asked. "Will he kill the woman who wants to hurt us?"

His concerned gaze hardened, and he didn't look nearly as gentle. "Caspar? No. Of course not."

"But he is a murderer, isn't he? I'm supposed to give the crystal to the right murderer." She gasped. "Oh, no! Was it you? You both touched it! But he took it! Please! You have to catch the train and kill that woman!"

"We'll catch the train," he said, his expression stern, "but there will be no talk of killing, ja? You want to get Caspar in trouble?"

"No. No, of course not, but ...! But she wants to kill us."

"Who is this woman?" he asked.

"I don't know, but she wants to kill us."

He squinted at her for a second and then stepped back a pace. "Watch your hands and feet."

Farideh huddled smaller behind the coat. She felt stupid and desperate, but she really didn't know anything. She wished she did. How awful to disappoint her rescuer by being a stupid girl who sounded like she'd panicked for no good reason and jumped from the train like an idiot.

He shut the passenger door and rounded to the driver's side. Just before entering the truck, he stared into the distance, and once again Farideh thought he looked like an angel. But ...?

"Why are you in a milk truck?" she asked as he settled on the driver's seat.

"Oh! Uh ...."

"Did you steal it? Why does it smell like a skunk?" Her teeth began to chatter.

"You have an alarming way of viewing things, min flicka. As if anyone would steal a milk truck."

"So it's yours? You bought a milk truck?"

He didn't answer. Instead, he said, "Put the coat on, child. You're in shock. Stay warm."

"Oh, yes. My mother wrote about that in the war diary. Stay warm; stay calm."

He gave her another sharp look, put the truck in gear and drove down the road after the train. "Hang on."

She shoved her arms into the coat sleeves and gripped the door frame with white-knuckled hands. The truck sped up rapidly. She peered ahead, caught sight of the train's dark shape between distant farmhouses, and looked at him again. She wondered how old he was. He didn't seem that old. He didn't have lines or crinkles. He was perhaps younger than her father. Her father was thirty-nine.

"Why are you both here now?" she asked.

74

"We were trying to catch that train, actually, and here we are, still trying to catch that train. But ja, bit of a mess regarding who is accompanying who."

"What's your name?"

"Godefroy. Godefroy Grace."

She thought a slight hesitation occurred between first and last name. "It's a beautiful name, but is Grace Scandinavian?"

"Now how would you know I'm Scandinavian?" he asked, flicking a frown her way.

"The taxi driver," she said. "Back at Coney Island."

"The garrulous fellow with the freckles mostly on one cheek?"

"I didn't notice about the freckles, that they were mostly on one side, I mean. He had crooked teeth, though. He had you as a fare before us."

"Ja, a girl would remember crooked teeth."

"Why would she?"

"Why …? Ha! Uh … never mind. Strange coincidence, yes? Having the same taxi driver."

"Yes, I thought so too. So are you the angel of death? Because I'm supposed to marry the angel of death."

This time he jerked the steering wheel when he looked at her. The truck swerved a little. He faced front again, blinking and obviously struggling to find words. He definitely didn't look that old. She wondered if he'd participated in the war. He didn't seem the type who'd like being a soldier, but he did have those nice muscles. He was tall and lean and just how Farideh thought a handsome man should look while improperly dressed and driving a milk truck.

"I thought it might be your nephew, the angel of death," Farideh ran on, knowing she was running on but entirely unable to stop, "because I melted my baby spoon when I looked into his eyes, but now that I think on it, I may have melted it late after bumping into you. Because you would have looked that way when you were that young, wouldn't you have? Like him, I mean. Except maybe not with the pimple. Did he pop it?"

"Min flicka … uh, Farideh, you're in shock."

"Yes, but she said so. Elizah Mayhew. She said I had to marry my cold-blooded murderer, the one I find after falling off the tower, and that I'll be glad he is one. I'm already glad, really, if you or … Caspar?"

"Ja, Caspar."

"Yes, if you or Caspar can save Ara."

"How old are you?" he asked.

"Twelve. How old are you?"

He didn't tell her. "Farideh, you're a little young to be worrying over marriage, ja?"

"No. That's all girls do. What else do we have to do? What else do you men let us do?"

"Aj, aj, a twelve year old suffragist. He'd deserve this, ja."

The vehicle went over a bump and jarred Farideh enough to jam her soles on the truck floor and send pain shooting up her legs from her injuries. Panic built in her chest again. "Oh! Do you think he'll arrive on time?" she cried. "Will he save Ara?"

"Ja," the uncle said. "Ja, and we'll catch the train, because it's stopping. He's pulled the emergency brake, I think. And there goes the train whistle."

Yes, she heard it, a distant wail in the early morning gloom. "Oh, thank God, thank God," Farideh breathed.

Absently she set her fingers against her temple. When her hand lowered, she found blood. She didn't remember much of the truck ride after that. Godefroy Grace pulled her from the passenger seat and carried her to the train, where travellers and train employees milled on the broken rocks bordering the track. She was aware of his arms holding her securely against his warm chest, of faces staring and voices uttering concerned sounds, of entering a narrow corridor and her mother shrieking her name. After that, the world dimmed entirely.

Chapter Eleven

Stopping the train.

Caspar hauled himself onto the little platform at the back of the caboose. He tried the door and discovered it locked. A startled man looked up from a bunk, saw him and heaved up from the mattress. A blue light swung near Caspar's torso. He remembered the luminous stone and shoved it into his coat pocket. The door opened.

"What the hell, boy? Are you stupid? You're stuck on this train until the next stop, now aren't you? I hope you like your little stay in the joint after, because that's where you'll be until your parents fetch you."

A burly hand reached for him. Caspar knocked it high and charged into the caboose.

"Hey! Get back here!"

He sped past another sleepy man in a second bunk, and reached the opposite entrance. He hauled it wide and escaped. The first train employee shouted an obscenity, and the chase commenced.

"Get back here, you little bastard!"

Caspar fled through a kitchen car manned by a couple of staff who looked up but didn't move from their counters.

"Hey! Why'd you let him by?"

"Not our job," someone said. "Have fun."

"Yeah, thanks a lot."

In the next car, lethargic passengers in the dining car looked up as Caspar raced by. "Why's he running?" someone said.

A thump and a curse and the noise of dancing crockery sounded to his rear.

"Watch it!"

"Sorry, sir! The boy got on without a ticket."

"Doesn't mean you can crash into me."

"Sorry."

Caspar exited the car, thumped across adjoining platforms and rushed into the next. The man in pursuit didn't shout, but Caspar heard the heavy tread of his larger body as he entered seconds later.

Caspar sped past bored and sleepy passengers in a third class car and shot into the night air again.

The next car was third class again, filled with yet more sleepy and bored passengers. After that he entered a sleeper car, and this time he brushed by an attendant seated on a folding chair and reading a newspaper in the glow of soft lamplight.

"Hey!"

Caspar snatched a loose belt hanging beneath a privacy curtain and fled onward. In the fourth car, he had two men chasing him, but he slowed them down at the fifth after latching a door shut with the belt. The buckle wouldn't hold for long. He backed away from a pair of angry faces. Ignoring thumping yanks at the door and demands to open it, he turned and faced forward. He'd arrived in a first class car with seats. Some passengers stared at him. Others were rousing from a light slumber.

"What are you doing, boy?" an elderly woman asked as he moved onward.

"Rescue mission, ma'am."

"You're a stowaway," she said. "Shame on you."

"No, ma'am. That would be someone who hides his presence." Caspar hurried through to the next car and found cabins at last. One door in the middle stood open. A light played out on the corridor floor. He slowed to a walk and approached the opening. The atmosphere here felt odd, sort of heavy and thick. The air became less satisfying, and each inhalation more difficult. He crept to a halt near the door. The scent of cigarette smoke drifted into his nostrils, and the demand on his lungs became a harsh need for good air.

"I've decided," a woman said. "Would you like to know your punishment before I deal it out?"

"You don't think murdering my sister is enough?" a weepy voice replied.

A short pause, then the woman continued speaking. "Not the least. I am tired of dealing with naughty girls, and these last few generations, I have seen one too many naughty girls. Your mother's mother hid herself and her daughters from me. It was fun for a bit, that game of hide and seek, but then your mother hid despite the lesson I gave her. And you? You frightened your sister from this cabin and off the train. It's a small nuisance. I will find her again, but you have been disobedient and obstructive. Little, unimportant girls should learn never to be disobedient or obstructive."

A chair creaked from within the cabin. Dizzy, unable to breathe, Caspar sagged against the wall, his head slumping down toward his chin. Something blue glowed within his pocket.

"You were raised by a naughty bitch. You're just as likely to be a naughty bitch, so I'll get rid of your mother, your father, and raise you in chains."

"No! Please don't hurt my Maman!" the girl wailed. "Papa! Papa!"

Caspar stuck his hand in the pocket. The atmosphere ceased being too thick, too heavy, and air entered his lungs again. He inhaled hoarsely. The pleas in the cabin hid the desperate sound.

"Please! Please! Don't hurt them!"

"She's no longer the witness! You are! I no longer need her. The world no longer needs her. Your little womb is sufficient, hmm? I'll choose a nice looking man to fill your belly, yes? You'll like that part. Don't worry; I'll pad the chains on your wrists and ankles. You'll be very comfortable while he ploughs you senseless every night, until you give me an obedient little witness, and yes, another sacrifice, because after your mother and her mother made me wait so long, I'll still be very hungry once I'm done with your sister."

"Stop! Stop!"

Caspar stepped into view. A veiled woman in a black fur coat froze in the middle of stubbing out a cigarette on the tiny bedside table. The girl in the rumpled bed stared at him with huge, tear-filled eyes. Caspar smiled and retreated from sight. Quick footsteps followed him out into the corridor.

"Boy! Boy! Come here!"

He ignored the demand, ignored the tug on his sleeve, but not the words spoken in a language he'd heard in echoes from pages of crumbling books, a language his uncle whispered during nightmares.

Bleed. Bleed from lungs. Bleed from nose and ears, eyes and throat. Bleed out your life.

His grip on the caged stone tightened. He yanked free of her clutching hand and backed away from another that rose with a hat pin in the fingers. The metal looked old. It was too long, too thick. Perhaps not a hat pin. Perhaps an ornamented awl.

His spine met the end of the car. He lifted his free arm chest high. She paused. The red-painted lips firmed into a wary line. Then her hand darted toward him, and the awl bit. She withdrew the weapon, a smile now on her face.

"You're pretty, but you won't die pretty."

"No, ma'am." He glanced at the blood dripping from the awl, at the line of red winding down his hand from the hole in his wrist. He looked at her again. Her smile had begun to curl down into a displeased grimace. He smiled instead. "You should brace yourself."

"Who are you?"

He reached up, knocked the emergency box open and pulled the brake cord. Within seconds the train braked, and the wheels screamed on the track. The woman fell backward. Caspar landed on his knees and both hands before a set of shapely legs exposed past the knees. She wore sheer silk stockings, and yes, a lacy garter, there, just barely visible on one inner thigh.

For a brief instant the air was again too heavy, too thick, but then alarmed cries issued from the cabins. Doors yanked wide. People thrust into view. The spell shattered, and Caspar inhaled with a gasp.

"What is it? Are we crashing?"

"She pushed a girl off the train!" Caspar shouted, lurching away from legs and perfume and secrets he knew of but wasn't supposed to view yet. "She pushed a little girl off!"

The woman rolled and lurched to her knees. From inside the girl's cabin, a high-pitched shriek joined the tumult of screaming metal and alarmed questions. "Papa!" the girl wailed. "Papa! Papa!"

"What is it? What's happening?" someone demanded.

"She threw a girl off the train!" Caspar repeated, pointing at the woman. "I saw her do it!"

The woman staggered upright, bloody pin in her grasp, hat askew, veil tilted, one eye visible. The colour of the iris matched Farideh's startling blue ones. Her black fur coat gaped open, revealing a curvaceous body and low cut dress. An array of tiny diamonds draped the top of her bosom.

"Dear Lord! That woman is injured!" a man said. "She's been stuck with her hat pin!"

Caspar almost despaired. High society males could be so annoyingly stupid in the presence of an attractive woman. "She stuck me with the pin!" he snapped, showing his bloody wrist. "She's insane! She threw a little girl from the train and threatened another!"

"Good God, boy? Are you mad?"

"Gud i helvet," Caspar said. *God in hell.*

"He's a German!" an outraged female passenger spat.

Caspar's shoulders slumped. "Maudite marde." *Damn shit.*

"But that's French," the man said.

80

"No, it is not."

"Are we crashing or not?" someone else demanded. "Why should we be woken up if we're not crashing?"

"Papa!"

Apparently the papa was just not going to wake up. Caspar hesitated, but then pressed on with the rescue. "That's the girl's sister! This woman has drugged her rich parents! Stop looking at me! It's the woman! She's a kidnapper!"

"Boy? Are you wearing a bellhop uniform under that coat?"

"J'm'en câlice!" Caspar howled. *I don't give a damn!*

"That is so French. This boy is from Quebec."

"I don't care where overseas he is from!" the snippy female passenger said. "He should be tossed from this train!"

The veiled woman stepped toward Caspar. He pressed back against the wall.

"You! Boy! Who are you?"

"An obstruction, ma'am," he said, staring into one blue eye. "A disobedient little obstruction."

"You little bastard! Tell me who you are!"

"How vulgar! Is that woman black?" the snippy woman said. "What is a nigger doing in this car? Where is the conductor? I demand to see the conductor!"

"This little girl is black too," another person said.

"Maman!" the girl howled.

"Farideh!" a woman shrieked from inside a cabin. "Farideh!"

"Maman!"

The cabin door crashed wide. "Ara!" A man darted into view and staggered to a stop at the girl's doorway. "Ara! Where is Farideh?"

"She fell off the train! A bad woman is here! Maman!"

The father turned in Caspar's direction. His arm lifted. In his hand he carried a Browning pistol. Caspar suffered an instant attack of murderous envy. He wanted one.

The veiled woman glanced back. The father's eyes widened and then hardened into ferocious promises of murder. Caspar squeezed into the corner, and the pistol fired. Women screamed and retreated into cabins. Men shouted and did likewise. The veiled woman grunted and staggered into Caspar's flank. One arm wound around his waist. Her perfume filled his nostrils. She looked up at him. The pistol fired again. She winced.

"Two bullets in the heart," Caspar said, "and yet you don't die, or … are you already dead?"

"Who are you?" she hissed. A tiny spot of blood flecked her lip, almost invisible against the red lipstick.

"You smell unfortunately lovely for a woman who commits murder," he replied.

Another shot blasted into her, this time from a closer range. The atmosphere shifted, grew dense, and swirled toward the attacking father. The cyclone slammed him spiralling along the corridor. He didn't release his grasp on the pistol throughout. One of his feet narrowly missed the head of a woman who watched from just within her cabin. Farideh's mother. "David!" she screamed.

"Maman!" the girl wailed.

"Damn, I've forgotten her name again already," Caspar muttered. "And someone just said it. Aj!" *Ouch!*

The veiled woman had just jammed the awl into his flank. It had sunk inches deep. "You!" she spat. "Why didn't my curse kill you?"

"Sorry, no idea," he croaked.

"Liar! Haa!" She almost pulled away, but he wrapped his free arm around her and clutched the soft fur of her coat.

"I very badly want a Browning right now," he said, "but all I have is this switchblade between your ribs. It must hurt worse than an awl." The air was getting thick again. He lowered his nose near her veiled ear and gasped words. "You're the first woman I've ever held. I like this feeling. Perhaps …." He wheezed inward. "Perhaps it's better than driving."

A weapon fired. This time the bullet damaged the back of her head. Blood splattered out from beneath the veil. She wrenched free, of Caspar, the knife, but not the coat. He wouldn't release it. While he sank into a seated position in the corner, she spun out of her coat and staggered through the exit, blood staining the back of her neck and her dress. Wind blasted into the train car. A man outside yelped. The girl's father lunged toward the open door, pistol up. Caspar struggled a breath inward.

"Don't shoot! Don't shoot!" a man begged.

"Move!" the father said. He too suffered breathlessness. The command issued throaty and not very loud.

The air lightened, and Caspar's next inhalation eased into his body like a blessing.

82

The father stepped out of the car. "Where is she? Did you see which way she ran?"

"No! There was a tornado or something! She blew away!"

"She blew away?"

"David! Farideh is gone! She's gone!"

The father re-entered the car, weapon hanging near his thigh. He looked down at Caspar, who slowly drew the last inch of the awl from his flank.

"You don't have to worry about, Farideh," Caspar gritted out. "We saw her jump from the train. My uncle has her. He's driving her here even now."

"Why are you wearing a bellhop uniform from The Plaza?" the father asked.

Caspar sagged in defeat. "How is this good luck?" he asked himself. Heroism ignored. Inelegant monkey suit a flaming signal of social ineptitude. That and the pimple.

"Not lucky at all," the father replied. "You look like an unhappy bleeding monkey who's missing his little hat."

"David!" his wife cried.

"There's no need to worry, darling. Farideh is on her way apparently."

She answered with a sob. David moved toward her. Caspar laid his head against the wall and shut his eyes to rest, but not before he hauled the fur over his gaping coat to hide the bellhop outfit. A heavy tread thudded the car floor near him.

"If you try to throw me off this train now, I will bleed you like a pig," Caspar said. He twitched both the awl and his large, bloody switchblade.

The owner of the heavy tread retreated back out the exit.

Chapter Twelve

July 28, 1929. Early morning. Bribes, revelations and dislikes.

Godefroy craned to the side of his seat. Farideh's father still spoke with the local authorities in the gap between two train cars. A police officer glanced into the first class coach. Godefroy sank back into his chair.

"Uncle, relax," Caspar whispered.

"Too many cops. Too much attention," Godefroy breathed. "We should have left."

"The cops were already parking their cars around the milk truck by the time you laid that girl in her bed."

Godefroy grimaced. Yes, he'd heard the sirens even as he carried the girl on board. He'd intended to hand the girl to her parents, snatch Caspar off the floor and flee, but the girl's mother had been in too much shock to walk. The husband had held her, and Godefroy had been forced to bring Farideh to the cabin himself under her father's direction.

He'd placed the girl on her bed next to the pallid twin, only to have Farideh's fingers remained gnarled in his undershirt. When he'd tried to pull away, she'd whimpered and curled around his pelvis. He didn't think his skin had ever been redder in his life.

In the end, he'd given up his undershirt. He'd wormed out from beneath it while the girl's mother and sister held her steady. He'd accepted a replacement from the father and had a borrowed shirt as well, but Farideh huddled in bed with his sweaty undershirt even now. The cops had arrived in the doorway and that had been that. They'd been pinned like moths and remained in full view even now.

"Caspar, didn't I see you with a fur coat when I boarded?" Godefroy whispered.

"Yes."

"What happened to it?"

"I hung it in the closet of Farideh's cabin. Don't worry. I took everything from the pockets first."

"Did you find cigarettes?"

Caspar sighed heavily and shifted away from him.

From the gap between trains, Godefroy overheard the words 'milk truck' spoken loudly. He almost hung his head in chagrin. "Aj! Why did it have to be a milk truck?"

"The pickup was in worse shape," Caspar replied. "Like you said, it probably wouldn't have started again after the first stop. It's not your fault, Uncle. The milk truck was the only other truck in that alley. They're not going to arrest us. How can they arrest us? No heirs, right? No heirs, no doom."

"Ja." But thank God the body had already been dumped along with the incriminating steamer trunk with the fancy gold lettering on the top. Caspar had joked when they'd dragged it down a wooded slope and shoved it off a small rise into a fern-smothered gully.

"There. All settled in, though I doubt he expected to be in such a cramped coffin. Nice lettering though. There'll be no doubt who resides within should it be found."

All the same, Godefroy had insisted on tossing a small fallen tree into the gully to make the trunk less visible. The criss-crossing branches had done a fair job of camouflaging the varnished wood in the dim location.

He glanced at his nephew. Caspar sagged with his head against the train window, an exhausted boy with a bloody spot on the side of his coat and a bit more sprayed across his right shoulder. The coat was firmly buttoned, hiding the telltale upper clothes of the bellhop uniform. Farideh's father had reminded Caspar to do up his buttons and hide 'the monkey suit' mere seconds before the police barged in.

"He's very astute, this father of Farideh, yes?" Godefroy whispered, looking forward again. "He knew without us saying that the bellhop uniform should not be seen."

Caspar grunted a noise that could have been interest or disinterest.

"He passed on some of his features to the twins, I think. The narrow nose, the little dimple in the chin. These are surprisingly delicate on the girls."

"He doesn't like you."

"Aj! That's not what I am talking about!" Godefroy hissed.

"I don't like you. Why did you make the girl fall in love with you? I'm the one who rescued her sister."

Godefroy slapped a hand over his face. "Ja, I am the type to want a little girl in love with me. Since when, Caspar?"

After a short delay, his nephew said, "Sorry."

86

Godefroy lowered his hand.

Caspar shifted restlessly again, his head straightening, his body slouching further down the seat. "What's her name, by the way? The other girl."

"Ara."

"Right. Farideh is in love with you. Since the fortune teller's, I think."

"Don't be so sure of this."

"She was perfectly stupid after looking in your eyes."

"Because I jarred her when I bumped into her."

"She bumped into you. She chose you without even looking."

"She's not in love with me." Godefroy glanced again at the gap between cars. He witnessed a hurried movement, a hand shoving something deep into a pocket. "I think this man is taking care of our little problem with the milk truck."

"His name is David. I heard the mother say it."

"David Tremblay, ja." Godefroy tucked the name away for later.

"And how would you know he's taking care of the milk truck problem?" Caspar asked.

"The cops were loud. This is usual for cops when they sniff something out of place. But now they are quiet. Something nice pads their pockets. This truck will find a remote parking place, I think, and be forgotten for a while."

"Good. Fine. I don't care."

Godefroy sighed inaudibly and endeavoured to remain patient. At the end of the car, David Tremblay glanced in at them and away again. His sharp stare reminded Godefroy of Caspar's less moodier ones.

"That woman …," Caspar said.

"Hmm?"

"That woman who tried to kill Farideh. She had the same blue eyes."

"Ja? Perhaps this is some sort of family squabble."

"She spoke Persian. She cursed me in Persian."

Godefroy's gaze riveted to his nephew.

"The curse failed, but her voice matched the one in my nightmares, in the echoes of the nightmares of every man who scrawled his pain in the family tomes."

"Har du prova?" Godefroy asked. *Did you try?*

"Att döda henne?" *To kill her?* "Ja, but you weren't there."

"Yes. Right."

"Even with a witness, it hasn't worked for anyone else. You know that."

"Ja, I know. Did she recognise you?"

"Would I still be here if she did? You'd be desperate to father the heirs right now if she'd recognised me."

Godefroy said nothing, and his nephew continued speaking after a few seconds.

"Farideh's father tried. Four shots, one in the head. She lived. He has a Browning. I want a Browning."

"Ja, ja," Godefroy said, still dealing with his nephew's unexpected disclosure. Movement at the end of the car attracted Godefroy's attention. He tapped Caspar on the arm. "They're leaving at last. This train might actually start moving."

"About time. I'm so tired."

"The father signals to us."

"Ignore him."

Godefroy considered it, but then sighed heavily and rose from his seat. "Come."

Caspar heaved out an aggrieved breath and lifted up to follow. They met Tremblay on the platform between cars. Tremblay waited until Caspar shut the coach door before speaking.

"Do you have it?" he asked.

"Have what?" Godefroy replied.

"The crystal. Do either of you have it?"

Godefroy glanced at Caspar. "Yes, I have it," Caspar said.

"Let me see it."

"Why?"

"Boy, do not test me."

"Again why?"

Godefroy forestalled a nasty confrontation with a shove of his hand into Caspar's coat pocket. He stuck himself with something sharp. "Aj! Damn it!"

He pulled out both a thick needle and the chain. The needle was stuck in the side of his forefinger, riding up the side under his skin. "Here." He shoved the chain at Tremblay and seized the wrist of his injured hand. "Aj, that hurts!"

"Hurts worse two inches deep in the flank." Caspar grabbed the ornamental head and yanked the pointed end out.

"Aj!" Godefroy hissed and flapped his hand about after. "Why does this sting so much?"

"It's an evil awl. What else?" Caspar said. He dropped it back into his pocket.

"An evil awl?"

Caspar shrugged. "Don't worry. I think it missed my spleen."

Godefroy gobbled without making a sound until, "Spleen?" finally spat out. "Caspar?"

"I'm fine. It's sore but not unbearable."

Godefroy's gaze shot down to the bloody spot on the flank of the coat. He'd mistaken it for the blood of Caspar's earlier victim, but realized now it was the stain of life surfacing from beneath the coat. "Are you still bleeding?"

"Not sure."

"Aj!" Godefroy hissed, touching his nephews side. "I will need to look at this."

"Later."

Caspar glanced at the man with them. Godefroy noticed Tremblay's quiet at last. He faced the girl's father. Tremblay stared from nephew to uncle, the chain clutched in one hand, the tiny cage swinging loose beneath. The crystal within was dark and all but invisible in the early morning gloom.

"Ja? What?" Godefroy said. "You have it back. Can we go sit now? I have an injured boy to see after. Uh … wait? Did you pay for our tickets by any chance?"

Instead of answering, Tremblay held the chain toward Godefroy. "Take this for a second," he said.

Godefroy hesitated. Then he pinched the chain with forefinger and thumb. He tugged lightly. Tremblay released it. Godefroy stared at him while beneath his hand the little crystal fired a happy, fluttery blue. "Ja? It did this before. I drink too much perhaps. Alcohol fumes. Ha, ha."

Caspar snorted derisively. Down at the side of the train, footsteps clattered over rock. Farideh's father snatched the chain and shoved the crystal into his jacket pocket.

"Sirs?" a train employee said. "The train will be starting soon. I have to ask you to step inside your cars."

"Yes, of course," Tremblay replied. "This way, gentlemen, and yes, I will take care of your tickets if the conductor asks for them, but I doubt he will. You're both heroes."

He opened the door of the Pullman and stepped in. Godefroy followed with Caspar. Passengers peeked from their doors or stepped aside as they navigated the narrow corridor to Tremblay's set of cabins. Godefroy frowned at a snobbish woman who harrumphed in disapproval. He bumped into Tremblay, who'd halted abruptly.

"You have something you want to say to me, Madam?" Tremblay said sharply.

The middle-aged gentleman in her company rushed forward. "I'm so terribly sorry. She's very tired." The panel door slapped shut, and Tremblay headed onward.

"Trångsynt tik," Caspar uttered, his face close to the door. *Bigoted bitch.*

"They're Germans!" the woman's voice said stridently from within.

Caspar laughed. Godefroy hauled him after Tremblay, who wore a faint smile when he looked back.

"My wife is with my daughters," Tremblay said. "We can continue our discussion inside this cabin." He waved them in. Godefroy entered and waited in the centre of the luxuriant sleeping cabin while Tremblay slid the door shut. "Have a seat," Tremblay invited.

Godefroy chose the single upholstered armchair. Caspar leaned on the wall near him, his level gaze fixed on Tremblay. Tremblay gave the boy a wry glance and sat on the end of the rumpled bed.

"We should keep our voices down until the train starts and perhaps after as well," Tremblay said. "The walls are little more than paper. Cheapest Pullman I've ever slept in."

"Ja. I've seen better."

Tremblay squinted at Godefroy. Then he reached into his pocket and fetched out the crystal. "Here, Caspar, isn't it? That's what I heard your father say."

"Uncle. He's my uncle," Caspar said.

"Is he? I did wonder." Tremblay looked at Godefroy. "You did seem young to be the father of a boy this old."

Caspar spoke before Godefroy did. "He's my father's twin. My father's dead."

"Sorry to hear that. So how old are you, Caspar's uncle?"

"Godefroy. Godefroy Grace," Godefroy said.

"Yes, and? How old are you?"

"Twenty-nine."

90

"Twenty-nine? And the boy is?"

"Fourteen."

"Your brother started his family young, didn't he?"

"It happens this way sometimes, ja?"

"He was the same age as me. My mother was five years older than him," Caspar said. "She's dead too."

Godefroy watched Tremblay almost say something, change his mind and say something else. "Grace isn't a Scandinavian name."

"Yes, we already know," Caspar interrupted.

"Boy! Exactly why do you have it in for me?" Tremblay snapped. Caspar stared without responding.

"He's upset," Godefroy explained. "This business with teasing him over the monkey suit."

Tremblay's stern expression switched to wry again. "You don't joke when you're nervous, Caspar?"

"Ja, he does," Godefroy said. "And he grows huge pimples, as you can see."

"Uncle!" Caspar complained. He lifted away from the wall.

Godefroy fixed an irritated glower on him. "Yes, and you'll tease me later about my little episodes in the water closet. Ja?"

"No," Caspar said, hunching a little. "I'm sorry for that." He leaned on the wall again, but without the earlier stiffness, and his gaze lowered in submission.

"Caspar? Do you mind holding this?" Tremblay said. He held out the crystal.

Caspar reached forward without hesitation, nabbed it and put it back in his pocket. "I'm keeping it."

"Aj, aj!" Godefroy breathed, shaking his head in dismal resignation. "No sleep, no patience, no wisdom."

"Yes, well, hold it up for a second before you do that," Tremblay said.

Caspar mulishly didn't until Godefroy lifted off the chair to glower down at him.

"Fine," the boy said peevishly and pulled the chain back out. They contemplated the shining crystal within.

"It's odd, ja? It's not a happy blue when you hold it. It's more a …."

"A what?" Caspar demanded.

"A light to cut a heart out," Tremblay offered.

"Now that would be something," Caspar said, lifting it before his face. The rays played devil fire on his skin and in his pupils. "A light that can cut a heart out." He lowered and pocketed the trinket. "So? Is it magic?" he asked.

"Yes, it's magic," Tremblay said after a short pause. His expression was neutral, but Godefroy sensed tension. Godefroy decided to relieve some of it by seating himself again.

"And why did you want both of us to hold it?" Caspar asked.

The train car creaked and jerked a few inches. Caspar staggered a little. Godefroy reached up to steady him. Caspar set a hand on the chair back, and Godefroy refocused on Tremblay.

"It's a family tradition of my wife's," Tremblay said, "that a daughter of her line must pass the crystal to the man who will make it glow, the man she must marry."

Godefroy stared at Tremblay and then glanced at Caspar. Caspar stared at Tremblay and then glanced at Godefroy.

"As you have already concluded, gentlemen. I have a problem with Farideh marrying two men."

"Well, of course it will be Caspar," Godefroy said.

"I'm not sure I like Caspar."

"That doesn't matter to me," Caspar said.

"And I'm not sure I like you," Tremblay said to Godefroy. "We have a long train ride ahead of us, gentlemen, and you're not leaving this compartment until I decide what to do with you. Maybe you should start thinking of why I should like either of you."

"Do you mean aside from the fact that you, your wife, and both your daughter's are still alive because of us?" Caspar said.

"Yes."

"Oh, you're hard," Godefroy said. "What will the other eleven Labours be?"

Tremblay's mouth twitched upward slightly. "All right. You I might like with only a little more convincing, but the boy …?"

"I'm sorry that he's rude. Will you let him sleep for a while? His day was hard. So was his night. He's injured. A little rest for this weary soldier, ja?"

Tremblay considered it, relented, and said, "Ja."

92

Chapter Thirteen

Bringing the bloodlines together. Badly.

Tremblay gave up the luxury cabin to the Grace's and retired into the neighbouring one with his wife and daughters, but he returned a few hours later. "Farideh woke up, and she's asked to see you both," he said, pocketing the cabin key. "Look, she's all set to panic if you don't show up. Could you take a minute to prove you're both here? If she gets off the bed, she'll open the cuts on her feet."

Godefroy moved groggily to the end of the bed. Caspar waited until his body was out of the way and crept down to sit with him. They slouched in their socks and underwear, yawned and each scratched a shoulder at the same time. Caspar looked up and witnessed a quizzical frown on Tremblay's face.

"What?" Caspar said.

"It's like watching a pair of twins born fifteen years apart."

"Yes, but he's the ugly one."

Tremblay smiled faintly. "Are you feeling better?" he asked.

"Yes. Thank you."

Godefroy's hands splayed over his face. "Gud i himlen! Let me have a cigarette!" *God in heaven!*

"No," Caspar said. "You're quitting. You agreed."

"I changed my mind. Kill the dog." Godefroy charged off the bed and leapt on Caspar's coat. Caspar launched after him. They struggled, hands clenched in gabardine. Objects fell: a comb, the switchblade, the crystal in the cage, the awl, small change, a beaded clip purse, a match box, and a gilded cigarette case.

"Ha!" Godefroy exclaimed and lunged downward. Caspar grabbed the thick brown curls on his uncle's head. "Ow! Caspar!"

"No smoking."

"I said kill the dog!"

"I'll kill more than the dog."

A blistering round of obscenities fouled the air, but his uncle capitulated. His muscles lost their tension, and Caspar released him. Still cursing, Godefroy moved away to snatch his suit pants from the armchair, passing Tremblay who had both eyebrows raised.

"Whose dog are you killing?" Tremblay asked.

"My grandmother's. It's a poodle," Caspar said.

"I highly recommend you sneak one more cigarette, Grace," Tremblay said to Caspar's uncle. Godefroy angrily shoved a leg into his pants.

"No drinking either, Uncle," Caspar reminded. Godefroy stopped moving, only one pant leg on, his head sagging in despair.

"You're harder than me," Tremblay said. "Take one or the other, but not both at once."

"He smokes when he drinks. It's both at once or it will never work." Caspar moved to the pile of clothes near the end of the bed. He picked up the bellboy jacket, bow tie and vest, walked to the window, opened it and threw them out. They fluttered out of view with satisfying rapidity. He returned for the white shirt and pants and pulled these on. "Damn the stripes," he said about the pants.

Tremblay ignored the complaint. "You think a lot of your uncle, don't you?" he said instead.

"He's as good as my father. Actually, he's better. He's always been better."

"Aj, Caspar," his uncle said wearily.

"Are you affiliated with the mafia?" Tremblay asked.

"The mafia?" Godefroy repeated. "No. Why?"

"Just wondering. Ties to a clingy family might be a little problematic right now."

"Clingy? The mafia?" Caspar repeated, grinning.

"There aren't many of us left," Godefroy said, at last buttoning his pants. "The family fortune hasn't been good these last few decades. There's myself, Caspar and my mother."

"You must have family in the old world," Tremblay prodded.

"No. The war wasn't good for us."

"The war wasn't good for a lot of people," Tremblay said. "Scandinavia wasn't really involved. Neutral, wasn't it?"

"Yes, Scandinavia was neutral, but my family was involved."

"How?"

"My father and his brother enlisted in the German army."

"And they died," Caspar added. "In the first month, no less. They were blown apart by their own Minenwerfer, or so the official letter of condolence said."

Godefroy almost snapped a suspender button off. "Damn it, Caspar! Stay out of my diary!"

94

"Sorry."

"Why would two men of a neutral country enlist in a foreign army?" Tremblay asked.

"Their reasons were complicated," Godefroy said, pulling his cuffs straight and pressing the silk knots in. "These are very nice. Is this shirt a Charvet? I wondered last night, but I put it on again without looking at the label."

"I have them tailored without labels. I despise labels. You know of Charvet?"

"Doesn't everyone?"

"I don't believe so," Tremblay said. "You realize how patrician you sounded just now?"

"Patrician? Not the least." Godefroy laughed the remark off and reached for his suit vest, which had seen better days.

"Uncle, I want a set of suits from Anderson and Sheppard," Caspar inserted.

"Yes, of course. Myself as well. We'll go on a voyage and take a long tour around Britain in your new car after, yes?"

"Without Grandma? Or the dog?"

"Yes."

"Then yes. Very yes."

Tremblay hesitated visibly and then forged onward with the interrogation. He focused on Caspar's uncle. "So what were these complicated reasons for your father and uncle enlisting in the German army? In a nutshell perhaps, hmm?"

"If you don't mind, I'd rather not discuss it. It's sad. And embarrassing."

"Yes, they chose the losing side," Caspar said.

Godefroy shook his head and muttered another profanity. Caspar shoved into his shoes, impenitent, pitiless. They'd known, Godefroy's father and uncle. Caspar was certain they'd read the tomes of the inglorious dead just like every other victim of the curse. Warfare kills: at best they'd give the family a week or two of grace, if that. And trying to dodge the curse with honourable or rightful kills? That could bring on a disaster if you already had an heir. For Godefroy's father and uncle, the defective Minenwerfer had been the disaster.

Caspar's father and uncle, along with their mother, had suffered poverty, scorn and starvation after the loss of Godefroy's father, until Edvard, just turned fourteen, pushed a little girl out a third floor apartment window. Godefroy lied to the authorities and said she'd fallen while reaching to feed a pigeon. Godefroy had witnessed the murder from across the street, where he'd been chatting with a shop owner whose back had been turned from the crime. Godefroy had such a disarming, angelic disposition, of course the authorities had believed him.

The girl had been the daughter of the building owner, the man who'd been using their mother for sexual relief, but still beating her after for not paying the rent. Edvard murdered him with rat poison a few days later, and Godefroy lied again. He told the police the landlord had concocted himself a drink of the powder because he was unhappy over his daughter's death. Again the authorities believed him, especially after he added that the victim had touched him in a certain place and then felt very bad about it.

Of the two deaths, the innocent girl's should have given the family the longest run of good luck, and it did monetarily. The family recouped its fortune enough to immigrate and start fresh in another country, a necessary action every two generations or so. Rumours and suspicions were a force nearly as strong as the curse and usually led to the quick death of a perpetrator and his witness if they already had heirs.

In a new land, without a history to drag at their steps, Edvard shouldn't have needed to murder again for another seven years, but their mother had a breakdown and abandoned them only days after their ship docked in Halifax Harbour. Edvard suffered remorse and tried to end the family line three years later, beginning with the strangulation of Caspar's mother, a prostitute he'd impregnated and married back in the old country.

Godefroy easily blamed the tragedy on Edvard's youthful lack of wisdom and his wife's sordid past; he told neighbours she ran off with another man, taking her favourite twin son. Everyone had commiserated with Edvard, who'd collapsed and succumbed to a deep apathy afterward. Broken hearts were more nobly romantic than bloody attempts to end an evil curse. Helpful matrons and hopeful young women had arrived with home-cooked food. They'd stayed to dust furniture, or have tea and chat with Godefroy. Some had helped him plant rose bushes in the new flower bed where he'd laid Caspar's mother and twin brother to rest.

The details were all there in Godefroy's diary, if one could find it and hole up long enough to read the thing. Some day, when Godefroy was dead, it would be another grim tome in the family collection, a testament to an adroit understanding and misuse of human nature. In his own subdued way, Caspar's uncle was as monstrous as any of the family perpetrators, and yes, Caspar thought a lot of him.

Caspar shrugged his coat on and squatted to pick up the items that had fallen from his pocket, and as he gathered and sorted them, he listened to his uncle play Farideh's father. Just enough truth to be credible while sidestepping the details; truly his uncle was a genius. Tremblay liked him already, perhaps halfway trusted him, though it was doubtful Tremblay would ever trust anyone entirely. But he certainly found Godefroy interesting and curious and therefore would keep him close for the time being. Caspar's return home was a guaranteed all-expense paid trip, and it had nothing to do with devil's luck, unless Godefroy was the devil in disguise.

"All set, Caspar?" Godefroy asked.

"Yes. All set."

"Oh, wait. My hair. Damn! Where is my hat?"

"Likely you left it in the milk truck."

"Of all things." Godefroy moved to a mirror and slicked his hair into a semblance of order with water poured from a pitcher. Caspar's uncle despised hair creams and waxes, 'the most noxious grease to have on one's head after several days of soapless, unwashed discomfort while on the run.' Caspar had for once listened to him and not used any for this trip. He was glad of it now while following his uncle's example and slicking down his own hair. It had risen up in five places after only a few hours of bed pressing, as his uncle called the effects of sleep on hair, but that was preferable to the filthy, dust-laden, lifeless, greasy mess it would have been, had he used hair cream.

"Is it possible to bathe on a train?" Caspar asked. Godefroy passed him the damp face towel he'd just used to sponge the after-sleep shine from his face. "That's not what I meant."

"Warm water can be brought in for a sponge bath," Tremblay said. "I'll arrange it for you if you like."

Caspar finished with the towel and tossed it down. "Yes, I'd like that, thank you."

"Shall we?" Tremblay said. He let them out and locked the door again. Ignoring other passengers who lurked in the corridor, Tremblay gave a warning knock and entered the other cabin. He waved the Grace's in and shut the door after them.

The girls' mother lifted up from the armchair and approached with hands open in welcome. "Thank you," she said, reaching for Caspar.

She held his face near the jaw and kissed both cheeks. He wasn't much taller than her. She had the vivid blue eyes, but the skin was lighter than the woman of last night. Small differences in features set her off as an individual, but the similarities placed her in the same family.

"Thank you so much for saving my daughters." She turned to Godefroy, set a hand lightly on his chest, and stretched on tiptoes to kiss one cheek. "Thank you. Thank you both." She retreated a few paces.

Caspar contemplated her choice of perfume, a rose-petal musk, while Godefroy smiled and did his thing: charm. "You're welcome, Madame Tremblay." He placed a palm over his heart and gave a light bow.

"Please, come and sit near the girls for a few minutes. They're both anxious to thank you as well." She indicated the second bunk.

The twins were together on the window-side bed. Ara was properly dressed and sat at the foot of the mattress in a well-mannered pose with hands folded, but Farideh still wore her nightdress. Pillows bolstered her back. The blankets covered her to her waist, and she'd put on a sweater, which was buttoned to the collar. As for which stimuli caused the bright red flush over her entire face, given how she peeked at his uncle and looked away, peeked and looked away again, Caspar was certain the heavy blankets and sweater had nothing to do with it.

Godefroy hesitated and glanced at Caspar, but when Caspar didn't make the first move, did so himself. He walked to the second bunk and seated himself near the pillows, giving room for Caspar, who delayed briefly before moving to sit with him. Farideh, with the screamingly silent redness of a lobster dying in boiling water, lifted arms that shook and offered a folded white bundle to Godefroy.

"Oh! Yes," Godefroy said. He gently removed the undershirt from her hands. "Thank you." He tried tucking the garment beneath his suit jacket, but it created too big a lump. He set it down on his knee instead, a weak grin on his face, and now his skin was flushed too. Caspar wanted to kick him until his shins were black and blue. No one could be more disarmingly clumsy than his uncle.

"The, um, shirt is ruined," Farideh said shyly.

98

"No need to worry about that," Godefroy said. "Your father loaned me another."

"Thank you for saving us," the twin sister said, looking at Caspar.

Again Godefroy glanced at his nephew, and again he stepped into the breach when Caspar offered no reaction other than to continue staring at Farideh. "You're very welcome. I should hope you shall never have to endure such a thing again."

"Yes, but we will," Ara said with an air of absolute certainty.

"Oh, uh …." Obviously disconcerted, Godefroy faltered and glanced at her parents.

"May I see it? The crystal?" Ara asked.

Caspar, still without looking, dug into the upper pocket inside his coat and pulled it out. He tossed it at Ara's lap and at last gained Farideh's attention. The flush on her cheeks ebbed.

"Oh, but …! But that was too quick," Ara said. "I'd like to see you hold it."

"Give it to my uncle," Caspar said. Farideh's gaze narrowed into a leery squint.

"Oh, but …!" Ara faltered and looked imploringly at him. He ignored her.

"Here, now, Caspar," Godefroy said. "Be a little nicer, ja?"

"Saving her from sexual slavery for the purpose of birthing replacement sacrifices wasn't nice enough?"

Ara's hands fluttered up to cover her mouth. "Don't make my sister cry!" Farideh said.

Caspar grinned his most evil. "Or what? Are you going to blast me with a cyclone? Go on. Show me how strong you are compared to your great great aunt or whatever relation she is."

"Caspar!" Godefroy barked. "You're being absolutely detestable!"

"I don't …! I wouldn't …!" Farideh stuttered.

"The lack of air in your vicinity, it has the same feel as the stifling atmosphere of your aunt, though not as strong," Caspar continued. "It was there in the fortune teller's shop when you wanted to murder a stupid, spoiled girl and her nanny."

Farideh's hands fluttered up to cover her mouth as well. "I didn't! I didn't!" she said behind her fingers.

"You did. You wanted to commit murder, but I interrupted."

"Oh!" Ara gasped. "But we'd never—!"

"I know you'd never. You're boring," Caspar said. "If you could have stopped her, you would have, but you're too boring even for that."

"Don't be mean to my sister! And that's not what happened!" Farideh cried. "That's not at all what happened!"

"Go ahead and lie to yourself, but none of us believe you."

"I'm not lying!"

"I chased after the train for you," Caspar said. "I upset train employees for you. I saved your boring sister for you. I suffered the attack of a witch for you. I was stuck in the flank with a four inch awl! Shots were fired! Bullets came within inches of my body!"

"Don't complain about that," Tremblay interjected. "My aim was perfect."

"I put up with your arrogant father for you," Caspar continued. "And there you are, making eyes at my uncle. Do you really think you can string me along while flirting with him? Fight your maternal aunt yourself next time."

"Aj, aj, aj," Godefroy muttered. "The jealousy of a half-grown puppy. The bite is harsh."

Caspar launched to a stand. Godefroy launched with him.

"Go ahead! Ja? See if you can hurt me."

Caspar stared up at him, because he couldn't. He couldn't hurt his witness. But his witness could hurt him … up to an extent. The ears were particularly vulnerable. Godefroy grabbed him by one. "Ow!"

"Apologies. Now!" his uncle said.

"I'm terribly sorry."

"Not to me!"

"Ha, ha, ah! Ow! Esti de tarbarnak! Ça fait crissement mal!" *God damn it! That hurts like hell!*

"Caspar!"

"Isn't that a Persian name?" Madame Tremblay said, the epitome of cultured self-control despite Caspar's rudeness.

"What? Oh, yes," Godefroy replied.

"Please, let go of my ear."

"Now why would your brave nephew have a Persian name?" Madame Tremblay asked.

"Oh, it's a family tradition from long ago. There was an ancestor who went on a Crusade. He returned from war with a Persian wife and a pair of children. Twins."

100

"Twins?"

"Uncle!"

"Yes, twins. A girl and a boy. The girl and her mother, they disappeared one day. The crusader was devastated, but the boy remained, and when this boy eventually had children of his own, he had twins. Always and forever since, there have been twins, but since the loss of that girl, these twins have always been boys. This is very interesting, ja?"

"Yes, very."

"Uncle, ayez pitié!" *Have mercy!*

"Apologies," his uncle said, no pity whatsoever in his tone. "Make them to the girls."

"I'm sorry, Farideh, Ara, for my rude behaviour," Caspar said. His uncle released him, and Caspar clutched his ear, grimacing still.

"Seems he didn't sleep enough," Tremblay mentioned.

"I think perhaps a lack of breakfast," Godefroy said.

"Yes. Right. Getting missed by a dead shot does give a man a hell of an appetite."

"The pimple needs feeding," Farideh said.

Caspar's gaze sped away from Tremblay's smug face and froze on her irate one. Before he could respond, Godefroy spun him around and marched him to the door.

"Ja! I shall feed him right now."

"Farideh," Madame Tremblay said disapprovingly.

"He started it."

"A lady never continues it."

"Oh, wait!" Ara cried. "The crystal! You have to take the crystal! Please!"

Godefroy seat-boosted Caspar out the door, which slammed him into the further wall. Caspar twisted toward the cabin while yanking the centre seam of his trousers into a more comfortable lower position.

"Please, don't cry," he heard his uncle say. Godefroy had already moved out of view and back into the cabin. "He'll be nicer later, ja? I'll speak with him. Here, I'll give the little charm to him."

Scowling, Caspar thumped toward the end of the car, brushing past interested bystanders, some who were smirking. He shoved out into the adjoining platforms and stalled the progress of two passengers trying to go in the other direction. They were the snippy bigot and her husband.

"Young man! How rude! Step aside!"

"Sorry," Caspar said. He did a slow turn that set him facing the gap between cars and which forced them to navigate around him. "Are you coming back from breakfast? How is the service?"

The man paused to answer, which brought his irritated wife to a standstill since he held her elbow. "Oh, it was superlative. Breakfast was very good. I recommend the bacon. Canadian, I believe."

"Canadian? That's the best sort." Caspar glanced through the door window at the Tremblay's cabin. His uncle stood outside whilst finishing the conversation with whichever Tremblay spoke from within. He was the centre of attention in the narrow corridor, the tall, handsome angel brightening everyone's dull morning.

"Yes, I very much agree. It really is the bes—!"

Simultaneous hard pushes to both chests. That was it. Husband and snippy wife plummeted over the guard rail, hit the corner of the rearward car and vanished from view. Other than the first harsh thump, and a small yelp beforehand from Caspar when a sharp-toed shoe hit his chin, the murders occurred in relative quiet.

Somehow the husband's Fedora had toppled forward onto the metal grid. It looked a lot like Godefroy's Borsalino, only newer and with a nicer black silk band. Caspar fetched it up and lifted his gaze to the forward car. His uncle stared at him with a blank expression.

Godefroy blinked and responded to someone in the cabin. Then he moved toward the exit. He stepped out to meet Caspar.

"Uncle, someone found your hat and brought it to the train," Caspar said. "An employee just handed it to me now." He shoved the Fedora at his uncle's chest.

Godefroy snatched it before it blew away. He glanced inside at the label, read it with a grim compression of lips and then plucked the pin off the hat band and tossed it off the train. "Shall we have breakfast, Caspar?"

"Yes, I'd like that."

Godefroy opened the door of the next car. The hat went on his head. He handed a handkerchief back to Caspar. "For your chin. Small cut. Wipe the blood off your neck."

"Oh, yes." They entered the first class coach car, where bored passengers read newspapers, knitted or snoozed. Despite his throbbing chin, Caspar felt a lot less irritated. "You know, I think I figured this good fortune thing out. It's best to work the necessary events while under the influence of the previous results."

"Aj, Caspar. In front of a coach full of forward-facing passengers," his uncle muttered, pulling him closer to hear.

"Well, it worked, didn't it? No one was looking."

"No heir, no doom, Caspar."

"Oh … yes. Forgot."

"Ja, I know. Stop forgetting. The curse is pushing you to father the heirs, and once you father the heirs, that's the end of it for us."

They stepped out onto the next platform. "Is it pushing you, Uncle? Despite your interests, you've been ready to father heirs a lot longer than me."

Caspar's uncle didn't respond, just opened the next door.

Chapter Fourteen

July 31, 1929. Encounters at The Plaza.

Old Judge Brown was missing. Rumours were already circulating. They began when he didn't arrive on time for his cruise south. Family members made inquiries. His clothes were found in The Plaza, but only one overnight suitcase with them, not enough to hold the large pile he left behind. The Plaza hushed the incident up as much as they could, but the police breathed life into the salacious gossip with every person they questioned.

No warrants were issued, but the name of a man, a certain Danny Major, cropped up in the whispers of high society families and in furtive discussions amongst certain sordid folk. A boy vanished as well, a bell hop who took a day off work without permission. The police sought to question him, but the day after he was fired, his parents reported him missing.

More boys were mentioned, but not in context with the disappearance. These rumours were most often discussed between men, most of whom showed evidence of disgust when the topic came up. Old Judge Brown's family quietly removed themselves from New York City and retreated to their country house to wait for the results of the police investigation, and Jimmy Russo, despite the risk, lurked near The Plaza searching for more clues.

He'd grown a straight, no-nonsense moustache. He wore a suit of a more business cut, a suit he hated. His hat he hated more. Everything was boring and white-collar plebeian, which made him practically invisible. He looked more like a private detective than a private detective did.

His brother Eddie was as good as dead. Eddie had made the means official; he'd opted for the electric chair. He'd decided to fry instead of hang.

And that son of a bitch boy in the bell hop disguise, the boy with the German father who looked a lot like him, he was nowhere to be found. The bell hop, the real one, he'd been useless except for giving Jimmy a matching description of the imposter inside the hotel along with information about the father. Jimmy liked to put useless people in the bottom of dumpsters after cutting their faces off. In the case of the dim-witted bell hop who liked skipping his job, Jimmy had put him in the dumpster naked. When the kid's body was found at last, what was left of him would be hard to identify.

Jimmy threw his cigarette stub down and squished it with the toe of his shoe. He really didn't know why he hung out here in front of The Plaza any longer. What was there to find? Who was there to question? He was at the end of the same figurative alley as the police. The only person who had anything to lose from pushing the investigation now was him. If he kept coming here, if an employee pegged him as Danny Major, he was as good as fried for Judge Brown's disappearance.

"Brutto bastardo," he muttered. *Ugly bastard.* "Nessuno me lo ficca in culo." *No one sticks me up the ass.*

After hearing the latest rumours about Judge Brown, Jimmy was thoroughly disgusted. Going up to the judge's room like that, all chummy like; he wanted to vomit. His cousins, they looked at him funny now. If he were to get blamed for that sick son of a bitch's disappearance, he'd have liked to slit him a grin in his fat gut first.

A woman walked out of The Plaza. Jimmy had seen her go in fifteen minutes earlier. She wore dove grey, a smart dress and sweater along with a hat and veil. The veil combined with the chic casual style could be expected from a woman widowed almost a year ago, a woman who might be on the lookout for a replacement husband. Jimmy had ignored her when she'd gone in, but he didn't now. She exited the hotel in the company of elevator man John. Jimmy straightened from his slouch against the street lamp.

The lower half of the woman's face was visible. She smiled beneath the veil. John smiled back, blushing and nervous. She said something and held out a hand. He shook it and nodded. With a last smile and a wave, she walked away. John re-entered the hotel, still grinning and blushing. Jimmy followed the woman. The body, the dark-complexioned skin, the smile, they reminded him of the woman with the beautiful girl.

She walked as far as the corner before pausing to dig a silver cigarette case from a beaded purse. "Oh, hell," she muttered, still digging.

"Need a light?" Jimmy asked. She looked up, and he watched her dismiss him because of the suit, the damned plebeian suit. "Here. Don't waste a light because of the boring outfit."

106

He approached with his lighter out. She looked at it. Her mouth opened a tiny fraction. He stared in fascination, hoping for more, a better view of white teeth, a rounder pout, the tip of her tongue.

"That's a lovely lighter," she said.

Her cultured accent provoked a delighted tingle up his spine. He wanted her weeping naked in his bed, her shapely legs and arms squeezing him close, her mouth breathing ragged gasps on his neck and shoulder. "Yeah, I had it custom made."

"You're Italian American."

"Yeah, that's right."

"An Italian American with a custom-made, gold-embossed silver lighter," she said. "In a boring middle-class accountant suit."

A slow smile spread his lips. "Yeah. I guess it doesn't fit. I shoulda brought a less fancy lighter with me. I'm an investigator."

"Who are you investigating?" she asked.

"Right now? A beautiful woman I saw a few days ago. I was hoping to see her again, and here she is."

She stared from beneath her veil for a few seconds. Then she released the catch on her case and drew out two cigarettes. She handed him both and dropped the case back in her purse. Jimmy lit the lighter and sucked the flame into the ends of the cigarettes. He passed her one. She lifted the veil and inhaled a drag. Jimmy stared with a surprised frown, his mouth opening in a mild gape.

She released the drag slowly while looking him over with the sort of lazy, territorial appreciation only a very experienced woman displayed. "I'm related to her," she said. "I've been looking for her. We keep missing each other."

"Is that right? Did you find out much from John, the elevator man?"

"Oh, he just wanted me to pass on a hello to my cousin. He's a very sweet man, and therefore boring. But you don't strike me as sweet. What's your name?"

"Jimmy."

"Jimmy? Are you sweet, Jimmy?"

"No. What's your name, beautiful?"

"Taleyah."

"Talya. It suits you."

"Close enough. Well, Jimmy. Would you like to show me what you have under that boring tax collector's suit?"

He stared without answering, the smile frozen, his burning cigarette forgotten, images of their entwined bodies destroying his ability to respond.

"You don't like women who are direct, Jimmy?" she asked, releasing another cloud of smoke into the air. "What if I told you I'd like to put my mouth where you were imagining it earlier?"

He blinked and came to his senses. If he screwed up this opportunity, the failure would haunt him the rest of his life. "Yeah, I like direct women. You have a place? Or do you want me to take you to a place I know?"

"No, I don't have a place, and no I am not a prostitute. If you take me to a place for one, I'll tear your nuts off."

For the first time in years, his skin fired red like a virgin's. "I didn't think you were a prostitute."

She laughed. The chill in her eyes warmed to an inviting half-lidded stare. "Then take me to your place, Jimmy. I need to relax. You can help me relax, right?"

"Yeah." Jimmy flagged a taxi down and took her to his place.

Chapter Fifteen

July 31, 1929. The Tremblay Residence, Toronto, Ontario.

"Mamma …. No, Mamma …. Mamma! Would you just …! Aj! Mamm—! Ja, ja."

Godefroy's voice lowered, and Farideh stretched further out from the door of the salon. Ara flapped both hands in a frantic shooing motion. She sat on an armchair in the library, the room across the hall.

Farideh ignored Ara's worried attempts to stop her from taking further risk. Godefroy couldn't see her. Farideh's side of the hallway had perfect cover. A decorative table—layered with this morning's mail, a newspaper, and a big vase of flowers—hid her while she crouched on her knees.

"Jag är ledsen." *I'm sorry.* "No, I'm sorry. I should have called sooner. I didn't think you would be back so quickly. Just come, ja? Bring everything. No, we have to live here now. I'll explain later. Caspar? Ja, he's fine. What? Uh … not from the one we expected. Yes, it's better. You noticed, ja? Aj! Mamma! What does it matter why it is better?"

Godefroy listened to his mother speak, and Farideh hung even further out the door, leaning as far on her fingertips as she could get. She caught a one-eyed glimpse of him in front of the telephone table near the kitchen entrance. He'd come down to use the phone without a vest or jacket on. Farideh wished she had a better view of him, of his beautiful, strong shoulders without that white dress shirt and suspenders interfering with her memory of them.

Despite his annoyed tone, he stood in a relaxed position, with one hand in his trousers pocket, but the other hand held the phone away from his ear. His mother's tinny shriek carried to Farideh, though the words weren't very intelligible, a mix of rapidly uttered Swedish, French and English.

"Mamma," he said. "I'm sorry. Listen, I'm sorry. What?" He put the receiver back against his head. "Sorry, what? Seven years, maybe nine …. Ja, there were two incidental events …. What do I mean incidental? They weren't planned, Mamma. What else could I mean?

Oh. Right. Sorry. No, it wasn't that sort of incidental. It was sudden and random and completely unrelated to the planned business. No! He's under control. It's fine. It's all fine."

The noise of conversation in the kitchen intruded into the hall. Godefroy turned in that direction. Farideh won a partially hampered view of not only his shoulders, but his elegant back, waist and hips, and she despaired that she had to see it all while he wore trousers. She'd caught a glimpse of him through the keyhole yesterday morning, while he was in his socks and boxer shorts, but then Caspar had opened the door of his own room, and she'd popped upright and pretended to be coming down from the attic, where she and Ara sometimes played at haunted tea party.

Since then, the keyhole of Godefroy's room had been covered from the inside with the little metal flap that prevented intrusive peeks within. Despite her effort to pretend otherwise, Caspar hadn't believed her cover story, and yet the protective flap on his door remained upright, according to Ara, who'd risked a glance just this morning and seen something to make her skin blush red for nearly an hour after. She'd refused to say what, and Farideh had decided not to press. Her relationship with her twin had been tense and prickly since meeting the Graces.

Ara flapped her hands again, but Farideh wanted a clearer view of Godefroy's tall, masculine body. She should have heeded her twin, because she leaned a little too far, lost her balance and hit her face on the floor. A pained bleat escaped her throat. Godefroy glanced back and spied her.

"Mamma, jag måste gå nu." *I must go now.* "Ja, I love you. I'll pick you up at the station. Phone before you leave. Ja, take care."

He hung up and hurried toward Farideh, who had rolled to face the hall ceiling, both hands over her face. Ara sniggered inside the library.

"Farideh, min flicka?" Godefroy said. "Are you bleeding?" He knelt at her side.

"I think I cracked a tooth," she gave a muffled reply.

"Aj! I hope not. Here, let me look."

He pulled her hands away and squinted at her open mouth. "No, they don't look cracked, but you're going to have a bruised lip."

A grin started at the corners of his mouth. She stared, wishing it would grow. She loved his smile. He had the warmest smile in existence, just as Caspar had the coldest. When they were together,

110

Godefroy and Caspar brought the equator and the North Pole into the same room. Farideh preferred the equator, but somehow, always, stupidly, she did something like this: an act of utter idiocy that made her look like a silly girl.

"But my teeth hurt," she said.

"I'm sure they do. Just look at this dent in the floor."

Ara howled with laughter. Farideh rolled to her hands and knees to see the mark Godefroy pointed at. "That's not from my teeth!"

"No?"

"I did that dropping a lead weight from off a chair."

Godefroy grinned, rose and helped her stand, and Farideh had a moment's satisfaction that her silliness could lift his mood so readily. She just wished she could find a more elegant way to bring that happy expression to his face.

"Careful," he said, holding her steady a bit longer. "Do your feet hurt?"

"Not so much. Maman's poultice is very effective." She wished she'd lied, because he released her directly.

"Ja. Amazingly so. I'd like to have some in my emergency medical kit." Godefroy glanced down at the mark on the floor. "A lead weight? Now why would you drop a lead weight from a chair?"

"To see if it fell at the same speed as the ceramic duck."

"And did it?"

"Yes. And the duck broke, just like I hoped. Gravity was very obedient for me."

Godefroy laughed and stepped away, back toward the phone near the kitchen. "You're a delightful girl, min flicka. Now stop spying on me."

Farideh shot a glare at Ara, who had chortled yet again. "I wasn't spying," she said to Godefroy.

"Hmm."

He dialled a number and waited for an answer. Caspar opened the kitchen door and leaned on the frame, his gaze fixed on Farideh. Godefroy glanced at him. Then someone answered the call and distracted him.

"Hello? Ja. It's Godefroy Bordsbön." He laughed. "Yes, of course you know it's me. Sorry." He spoke rapidly in Swedish at some length, while Farideh and Caspar fought their silent war from the distance. "Ja, start the process. I want it transferred to the Toronto branch as soon as she makes the deposit. Ja, and can you see about a name change?" Again Swedish took over the conversation, until: "Grace. Ja, Grace. G, R, A, C, E. Ja, thank you. Come and see me with any necessary papers, on my bill of course." The unseen contact spoke. Godefroy laughed. "Yes, of course. We'll make a night of it. What? A weekend? That might be problematic. We'll see, ja? All right. Until then."

Godefroy hung up and turned to view the stalemate of his nephew and Farideh. "Ja? And what is happening here?"

"She's lurking around you again," Caspar said.

Farideh reddened with chagrin and anger and shot yet another warning glare at her sniggering sister.

"Come in the kitchen, Uncle. I made tea for myself and Adler. Have a cup with us."

Caspar backed away with a hand on the door to keep it open. Godefroy followed him through to the kitchen, where warm smells permeated the atmosphere. The scents billowed out of the kitchen and washed over Farideh. As the odours of herbs and meat and soup stock skirmished against baked fruit, bread and spices with sugary overtones, Caspar swung the door shut, his gaze mocking. Farideh fisted her hands and stomped toward the kitchen. Ara hurried off the library chair and chased after her. They entered and stood in the doorway together.

Godefroy seated himself in a chair without too many items on the table in front of it. Caspar brought the tea tray over from the counter. The cook stood at the end of the table, chopping vegetables on a huge block. The girls hesitated, their gazes on him. Adler, a heavily muscled man of medium height and very little hair, had certain boundaries as a member of the household staff. The girls skirted one of them simply by opening the kitchen door.

"You know the rules," he said without looking up.

"Rules?" Godefroy repeated. "Did I break one?"

"No, you didn't." The cook pointed his chopping knife at Farideh. "She's not allowed in here."

"Yes, because things happen," Caspar added for his uncle's edification while leering in triumph at Farideh.

"Ja? This is not a girl who should be in a kitchen in any case."

The cook laughed and nodded. "And that's saying something." He went back to chopping. Farideh crossed her arms and stubbornly remained just inside Adler's forbidden realm.

"Aj, aj, I didn't mean it like that," Godefroy said. "Ladies shouldn't have to dirty their hands."

"Yeah, as if that would stop her," Caspar muttered. Farideh squinted a threat at him. He coolly looked away.

"It was only peanut brittle, Adler. Please let me in," Farideh said.

"It was not peanut brittle. It was a burned mess that caught fire in the frying pan and somehow flew in the air to land on a stack of antique china plates." The chopping knife pointed again, this time at the centre of his work space. "I still see that black circle in the table. It's hasn't disappeared, but you better."

"May I come in?" Ara asked.

"How would that be fair to your sister?" Caspar said.

"Farideh won't mind if I sit next to you. Will you, Fairy?"

Farideh did mind, but Caspar spoke before she did.

"I mind," he said. "You lurk too much, like some sort of—I don't know—desperate and boring girl perhaps."

Ara's hands flew up to clutch each other over her heart. She began a hurt protest, only to have Caspar shoot it down. "I don't—!"

"Yes, you do. Your sister is at least amusing enough to fall on her face scampering closer like an industrious little mouse, but you hide in a crack and let her take all the risks. Go do something that boring mice girls do. Go read. Go play with your frilly little dolls. Just go."

Ara's lips shivered into a pout that rapidly transformed into a sob. She ran down the hallway and up the stairs. They listened to her footsteps thump all the way to her room. Caspar watched Farideh's reaction. When she didn't move to follow, a faint, cynical smile formed on his lips.

"Aj, Caspar," Godefroy said wearily.

Caspar's attention diverted to him. "Shall I pour your tea, Uncle?" Godefroy said nothing, just stared flatly at him. Caspar lifted the pot and poured the tea.

Farideh found it odd how he catered to Godefroy. He could be as mocking and nasty with his uncle as he was with anyone else, but always, inevitably, whatever he might say, his actions revolved towards thoughtfulness and concern. She didn't think Caspar was afraid of getting his ear yanked halfway to the heavens again. He wasn't the type to fear punishment. In any other boy, his behaviour would be endearing, but he wasn't any other boy.

"So your name's not actually Grace," the cook said.

"It will be in a few days," Godefroy replied.

"Why change it?"

"We usually do whenever the family migrates to a new home."

The cook shoved together several cloves of garlic, smashed them with the flat of the knife and a thump of his fist, and started mincing them. "Your family migrates? What are you, geese?"

Godefroy laughed. "We only migrate every generation or so. There is no comparison. The geese have us beat."

The cook grinned and dumped the garlic into a stock pot. "And your family name changes everywhere you go?"

"Ja, family tradition. It's a little delayed this time, but the name will be changed again. It was Grace several centuries ago too. We were in England."

"So this Bordsbön? It means Grace?"

"More or less." Godefroy sipped his tea. Since the Graces had arrived, Caspar had been plying his uncle with tea. Farideh had yet to discover the reason for the special treatment.

"They made fun of him back in Scandinavia," Caspar said.

"Aj, Caspar!" Godefroy complained.

"Did they? Why?" the cook asked.

"Because Bordsbön translates as table prayer," Caspar said. "Our forefather didn't pick the best translation."

The cook chuckled. Godefroy grimaced wryly and sipped again.

"So it's grace?" Farideh asked. "The family name, whatever it sounds like, it always means grace?"

"Yes, pretty much," Caspar said. They stopped talking as the cook heaved up the large pot and thump-walked to the stove. "How did you lose the leg?" Caspar asked after Adler shoved the mix onto a burner.

"A goose ate it."

Godefroy laughed. "The geese have us beat."

The cook glanced back, grinning. "It was eaten, but by a grain drill," he said. "I was a boy at the time. Farm accident. Wrong place, wrong time. My father backed the damned thing into the barn over me." He kicked his wooden foot into the stove bottom and made the metal clang. "At least I kept my knee."

"Yes, those are useful," Godefroy said.

The cook laughed and fired up the stove. "Lovely things, gas stoves," he said.

"I wonder how well they blow up," Caspar said.

114

"I think very well," the cook replied. "But I'm not trying it here. Tremblay will chop off my last leg and feed it to the racoons living in the garbage pails."

Caspar chortled, and Farideh understood he liked the cook, therefore Adler was a murderer or a potential one.

Her gaze drifted to Godefroy again. And so was he, or the crystal wouldn't have lit in his hand. She remembered Ara's stunned expression back on the train when he'd lifted it from her palm and tucked it into his vest pocket. The crystal had been beautiful in Godefroy's grasp, a warm, inviting sapphire. Godefroy, the witness on his side of the family tree, was a killer too.

Ara wondered who he'd murdered and why. She suspected he'd done it to protect his family. Farideh didn't care. She was determined to make Godefroy the protector of her own family as well. And Caspar could just …! Well, he could just go suck an egg out of a goose!

The worst thing, the absolutely most horrifically awful thing about having the Graces in the same household was Caspar's presence. His coldness tortured Ara. His sharp attention tormented Farideh, and Farideh still fell under the spell of his brown and gold eyes if she let her guard down, despite that she didn't the least bit like him.

"Your nephew was telling me that your side of the family is distantly related to the missus," the cook said, returning to the table with a rag to wipe the block clean.

"Ja, this is true," Godefroy said.

"The Persian side of your heritage seems to have disappeared from your looks."

"Our side of the family most often lived in Christian countries in Europe," Godefroy replied.

"Nowhere but Christian countries? Here. Pour me a cup." The cook pulled his chair closer and sat.

"There was a great, great, great and great to the umpteenth grandfather who lived in India," Caspar said, teapot lifted and spout tilted. "He was a favourite court guest of some Rajput ruler for a short span."

"Is that so? You have your family tree written that far back?" the cook asked.

"Hmm," Godefroy said over his teacup.

"There was another who lived in South Africa at the time of the Zulu uprising," Caspar added, passing the filled cup to the cook.

"And apparently he survived it," the cook said, smirking.

"No, but his children did."

"Well, that was lucky for you and your uncle," the cook replied.

"Yes, lucky as hell. Did you serve in the war in some capacity?" Caspar asked.

"What? Me?" The cook tapped his prosthesis against a table leg. "No. Missing limb. They wouldn't let me serve."

"Not in any capacity? At all?" Caspar pressed.

"You can't see this fake leg? You want me to take it off and knock you in the head with it?"

"No, I want to know if you have any skills other than cooking and blowing up gas stoves."

"Why should I have skills other than cooking?"

Godefroy inserted a comment before his nephew answered. "You called your employer Tremblay," he said. "Not Mr. Tremblay, but just Tremblay, like a man who's known his employer as someone other than an employer."

"So maybe I knew him before I was a cook," Adler said.

"Being a cook would be a good cover for a body guard," Caspar mentioned. "Someone comfortable with knives would make a decent protector inside a household."

"I'm a cook, just a cook."

"Yeah, all right. How's the tea?" Caspar asked.

"Great. It's just great. Thanks."

"You're welcome. What did the girls' chauffeur do before he was a chauffeur?"

"He was a chauffeur," the cook said stiffly.

"Does he wrestle? He looks like a man who wrestles. Without rules."

"Aj, Caspar, leave Mr. Adler alone. He'd like to enjoy his tea."

"I was just wondering what the girls needed protection from before we arrived," Caspar said.

"There was a hit and run outside Papa's office building," Farideh said and gained the riveted attention of all three males. "I saw it. When the driver looked back, he looked right at us—Maman, Ara and me—and then he kept on driving. He didn't look surprised or sorry or scared. Papa hired the chauffeur directly after, and Adler

116

replaced our old cook. She was a woman, and her meals tasted better."

"Thanks, kid," Alder said with a sour grimace.

"I meant to say that your cooking has improved since."

This addendum didn't improve Alder's disgruntled and censorious expression, and Farideh lowered her gaze. Well, really. Why shouldn't everyone know what Adler did before he was a cook? There was this situation with a witch happening. Papa's small army of family retainers should be cooperating with the Graces.

"Who was hit by the car?" Godefroy asked.

Farideh looked up again. "Papa's secretary," she replied. "He was a nice man, but he was looking at Maman instead of the traffic. She felt very bad about it."

"I'm sure she did, min flicka. Perhaps we should change the sub—"

"So the secretary was killed as a message to your father," Caspar concluded. Adler scowled. Caspar grinned. "And there you are, the cook with the beef for tossing logs on top of buildings."

"Did you just call me beefy?"

Caspar chuckled.

"Caspar, change the subject," Godefroy said. "If you want to know about Adler and the chauffeur, just ask Tremblay. Don't put his employees on the spot."

"I did ask him. He thinks being vague will put me off. I'm not stupid. It's easy enough to see that these are hired guns."

"No, you're not stupid," Adler agreed. "Exactly why did Tremblay bring you in?"

"Bring us in?" Godefroy repeated.

"You're here for the girls, right? Extra protection?"

"Yes, that's right," Caspar agreed.

"From what?"

"Another distant relative of the missus," Caspar said. "A maternal aunt. She has it in for the twins."

"Strange family," Adler muttered.

"I heard that!" Farideh said. "I'm right here!"

They ignored her.

"Our situation has nothing to do with your boss's usual racket, whatever that is," Caspar added, "but he should have mentioned it all the same to you and the driver."

"Yeah, I agree." Adler set his teacup down and frowned at the dregs. "I'll have a chat with him tonight."

"Good." Caspar lifted from his seat and exited the kitchen, pressing past Farideh, who squeezed into the door frame to avoid touching him. She could do without the tingly after effects. They always lasted for minutes on end, and she always became very agitated, enough to break dolls in half. Ara would hate her if she broke another doll in half.

"Did he chat me up just for that?" Adler said, sounding a little miffed.

"Hmm," Godefroy murmured. "I was going to do it if Caspar didn't. I'm surprised Tremblay didn't speak with you."

"He told me to keep an eye on you two, especially the boy."

Godefroy laughed. "Yes, do that too by all means, but watch out for a woman who may share a resemblance to Mrs. Tremblay. If you see such a person, get the girls to safety and keep well back. Distance weapons are more likely to keep you and the girls alive. Shoot bullets or throw knives, but don't let her get close." Godefroy set his half-full cup down, and he too brushed past Farideh and left the kitchen. She didn't squeeze against the frame like she'd done with Caspar, but darn it, Godefroy twisted slightly to avoid contact all the same.

Adler stared after him. Then frowned at Farideh until she edged away from the door and let it swing shut.

"What the hell? Since when is a woman that dangerous?" she heard him mutter. Farideh pivoted in time to see Godefroy stepping into the library. She started toward him.

"Go to your sister," Caspar called down.

She looked up. He stood on the staircase directly above. "No," she said.

"I said go. Let my uncle have some peace. If you want male company, you'll have mine or none. So go to your sister, or put up with me."

"I just want to sit in the library to read," Farideh said.

"He's an adult. Let him alone to have some quiet."

"I'm not a child! I can be quiet!"

His eyes squinted in a warning stare. The fingers clasping the rail briefly tightened, and he started down the stairs.

Farideh's lower lip bunched beneath her upper. "Fine! I'll go to my sister! I'm coming up there, so get out of my way!" She thumped down the hall toward the bottommost step. He stalled in the middle of the staircase and pressed to the wall side as she passed.

"You're detestable!" she spat, nose in the air, face turned away.

"Only toward boring, silly and annoying girls," he replied.

She stalled and opened her mouth to injure him with a more caustic putdown, but he didn't give her the chance. He dove on her like a falcon on a dove. A hand seized her by the back of the head. Another held her chin, and he grasped her bottom lip inside his teeth. She squeaked in surprise. The threatened bite transformed into a slow movement of his lips over her mouth. His tongue stroked the tip of hers, a feathery tickle of presence and nothing more intrusive, and then his teeth gave a gentle squeeze on her upper lips and departed.

It hadn't been a kiss for a child. It had been a kiss a man gives a woman, a man of passion and few boundaries, who threatened while he invited. It had been a kiss far exceeding the imagined ones her mother's war diary had provoked.

"You are twelve," he whispered near her ear, and she shivered from the sensation of warm air blowing past skin that had never been sensitive before now. She didn't entirely grasp his words until his next sentence. "The thing I just did to you?" he breathed, tickling her skin again. "At your age, it's for naughty girls. Stay away from my uncle. You're embarrassing him. If you really want what I gave you just now, you take it from me, not him."

She realized the import of his words. Embarrassment scorched away the fuzzy warmth of seconds ago. She shoved him with all her strength and staggered backward in reaction. She hit the rail and started to topple over it. Caspar grabbed her and pulled her flush against his wiry body. She froze, very aware of the thighs to either side of her own, of the hard bump travelling along his pelvis and squeezing against her lower abdomen.

"You're twelve, Farideh, yes?" he said. "Do you remember what that means?" The hand at her spine pressed her in and slacked off. "Do you?"

She suffered a tormenting ache somewhere lower than her stomach. It radiated into the secret place that wasn't to be discussed. Tears began to track down her cheeks. He confused her. He made her feel this thing, this incredible thing, and forced her to confront her wickedness at the same time, because she was twelve and had chosen to chase this. No veils. No lies. No cloud of girlish notions.

This was what she invited, a hard length that would thrust into her body, there down between her legs. She wasn't ready, not for what all this meant. She wasn't an adult yet. She didn't want to be an adult yet, not with Caspar, who refused to let her hide behind anything, especially romantic lies.

"I want to go to Ara," she said. "Please let me go to Ara."

"That's right. Go to Ara. You're a little girl. Now be a good one and stop pestering my uncle, or you'll answer to me."

He freed her. She stumbled again, but in the direction of the second floor. She climbed the last few steps using hands and feet like a child and fled into the haven of her room of frilly dolls and lacy doilies, play tea sets and childish dress-up boudoirs. But it remained, the memory of Caspar's grip, his pressure, the tingly skin, the ache between her legs, the knowledge that she'd invited Godefroy to cause these feelings when all along he'd known her for a naughty child playing at games she didn't fully understand.

Chapter Sixteen

Family plans in the library.

Caspar rounded the library door and leaned on the frame. His expression bleak, Godefroy turned away from the unlit fireplace and faced him.

"Well," his uncle said, not a question, more a statement of resigned understanding. Godefroy pulled his hands from his trouser pockets, lowered his head and cast his gaze elsewhere.

"I couldn't do it gently, Uncle. You know that. You've already tried the gentler methods."

He sighed heavily. "I despise being so blunt with women."

"And that's why I did it for you. Did you hear what you just said?"

Godefroy looked up. "Ja. I despise being blunt with women."

"She's not a woman, Uncle."

His uncle flushed. "You know what I meant."

"Yes, I know what you meant."

Godefroy reddened further. "Damn it," he muttered and averted his gaze again.

"Your usual interests don't seem to be helping you much, Uncle."

"My usual interests? Do you see any here?"

Caspar smiled. "Adler …."

"No!" Godefroy gave him a disgusted glance and walked to the window.

"Fine. Beefy isn't your thing. The chauffeur?"

"Caspar!"

"Oh, yes, he's rather beefy too. Then … Mr. Tremblay?"

Godefroy spun to face him again, brighter than a lobster. "Not nice, Caspar."

"Yes, you're right. Not an option despite that he fits your usual tastes. Well, your lawyer is coming soon, isn't he?"

"Ja. Just …! Leave it go, Caspar."

"Why do you prefer men who are tall and slender, or at least slender? Your lawyer isn't that tall, is he?"

His uncle's hands fisted. "I said leave it go!"

"Fine, fine. It's better than fat and old, in any case. If you were after fat and old, I'd have to shoot all your interests, because after seeing what Judge Brown wanted to offer, I'd puke if you went near anything like it."

"Caspar! Helvete!" *Damn it!* "Don't make me puke as well, and stop punishing me for how you had to catch Judge Brown. If I'd been the better lure, you know I would have done it."

Caspar rolled his head away, nodding a little as he did. "Yes, I know. I'm sorry." He refocused on Godefroy. "But don't you think it's odd, Uncle, that the curse is finally pushing you this hard? I'm ready. Why is it pushing you when I'm ready?"

"Aj! Caspar, why should I know?"

"Maybe I'm sterile."

Godefroy froze with the stupidest expression Caspar had ever seen on his face: a twisted mix of surprise, disbelief and confusion. "Sterile? You joke. You can't …. None of us are ever sterile!"

"I know. But saying it was worth seeing your reaction." Grinning, Caspar abandoned the door frame and chose a red upholstered chair to lounge on, one leg tossed lazily over the armrest. "Perhaps the curse is tired of having so few of us to torture, and the witness is to do his share of siring the potential victims."

Godefroy chose to lean against a perpendicular surface, the window frame, where he could watch well-to-do pedestrians passing on the sidewalk of the high-society Toronto street the Tremblay's lived on. His hands went back into his pockets. "Ja, all those uncles and aunts, cousins and second cousins. The curse must miss them badly."

"Funny how it wiped them out until only we three remained. You, me, Grandmother, though she did try to separate from our inevitable misfortune."

"It was too late the moment she received my father," Godefroy said.

"Uncle! And you say you don't like to be blunt with women."

"She's not here, and you've heard her say it, Caspar."

"Yes, she drinks more than you."

"Now she does. I've been dry since the night of the train."

Caspar smiled. "True. I suppose I meant to say you've never been as maudlin. You're looking healthier since you gave up smoking and drinking."

"What was the point? Seriously, Caspar? What was the damned point of making me stop?"

"To survive. To survive as long as possible and to hell with this curse," Caspar said. "I'm fighting it, Uncle, and you're going to help me. If you really do love me as a father, then you'll stay sober and stay alert. I'd like a longer run than a few miserable decades. Can you do that for me, Uncle?"

Godefroy raised his eyes to Caspar, and the apology was plain without him speaking, but he gave the promise Caspar wanted to hear in any case. "Ja. I can do that."

"I've scared Farideh away from you. Ara's miserable. If we can hold off on heirs, we might be fine for a bit."

"I give you one month before you go after Farideh again," Godefroy said. He smiled at Caspar's instant glower. "Ja, I know. She's a child. But you still want her. We should make plans to help us keep our suspenders up and our pants on."

"Like what? Chaperones?"

"That might be appropriate."

"I don't need a chaperone. I refuse to father children on a twelve year old. It's disgusting."

"Ja. That's going to get harder to say the more she blossoms."

"You're not getting Farideh."

"Caspar! She's not my usual thing."

"Your usual thing can't have children, and the curse knows it. I suppose it's lucky, your disinterest in females, or you'd have fathered another witness and perhaps my heir, and that might have ended my run before I was ten."

Godefroy stared without responding. After a few seconds, he turned his haunted features toward the window again. Caspar contemplated his uncle's tormented expression and continued speaking.

"It was spectacular, the madness of that child perpetrator, the one who had an heir via his uncle when he was still only nine. What was his name? Oh, yes, Caspar like me. An entire village razed to the ground in the middle of the night. Brilliant strategy for a child of little musculature or means. Fire can be very efficient ..., except when it also burns you alive while you laugh maniacally as your remaining family watch helplessly outside the inferno."

"Caspar, stop."

"I suppose I should thank you for being impervious to women before now, or perhaps I'd have set a new family record as the youngest butcher in the lineage. Odd how his circumstances and mine are almost the same. Why do you think that happens? These occasional bottlenecks in the family population?"

"That one …. It occurred when they hunted her."

Caspar straightened out of his sloppy position and sat upright. "Hunted the witch? Why isn't that in the family histories?"

"It was on one of the crumbling records. That account fell apart as I read it."

"Damn it, Uncle! Why didn't you write a transcription before your memory of it faded?"

"Yes, I should do that," he said faintly, still gazing out the window.

"Uncle … the other bottlenecks? Were they for the same reason? Uncle?" Caspar shot off the armchair and forced his uncle to face him. "The accounts didn't fall apart, did they? You destroyed them. Why did you destroy those records?"

"So we'd keep trying," Godefroy admitted.

Caspar released his arms. "Why do the bottlenecks happen?"

"The curse is alive, Caspar!" Godefroy said impatiently.

"Yes, I know. Answer me."

"It doesn't want to end. If the family is strong and well-connected, the witch has too many enemies to fight. No one's been able to kill her so far, but that doesn't mean she can't be chained and tortured."

"Chained and tortured?"

"This is what it is, Caspar."

"I'm not complaining. Which of my forefathers hunted her recently?"

"My father. My uncle."

"Your father …?" Caspar's forehead lowered to rest on Godefroy's chest. He felt defeated and betrayed, helpless and yet all the more dependent on his witness. "Damn it, Uncle. Is the Minenwerfer account even true?"

"Yes, it's true."

His uncle's respirations gently lifted and lowered Caspar's head, and despite his upset, a spreading calm soothed the turmoil in his heart. He could die like this. If his uncle were with him, he could die at peace.

124

"They tried for years," Godefroy continued, "but they never found her, and the cousins and uncles and aunts dwindled until they were gone in a few short years. I watched them disappear, Caspar. I watched them all disappear. Disease, death, accident. One by one, I lost them all."

"And yet you destroyed the records that warned us not to try," Caspar said. The feeling of betrayal faded. The other emotion, the deep and abiding devotion for his uncle rose up to swamp everything else as usual. He lifted his head. "Never mind about making a transcription. We're down to three, yes? I've seen her, and we're here with the objects of her search. This isn't the time to quit trying. If there's anything we should murder, it's her and this curse."

"Ja," Godefroy said. His tense body sagged against the window frame. "Thank you, Caspar."

"Did you tell Grandmother?"

"No, but I will. She has a right to decide her fate, as much as she can within the confines of the curse's snare."

"The girls? Their salvation prophecy? Did you get the details?"

"Not yet. I think his wife is willing to talk, but Tremblay is being stubborn."

"What the heck for?"

"He's a damned war spy," Godefroy said. "It's to be expected. It's their habit to get without giving."

"A war spy? How do you know?"

Godefroy shrugged. "He just …. I don't know. Farideh mentioned a war diary, he speaks German, and he feels like a soldier and a spy. I'll get the details later, Caspar. Besides, the girls aren't old enough to marry. For now we practice no heir, no doom, ja?"

"Ja." A nasty smile spread over Caspar's face. "Immunity," he said. "Immunity from her power so long as we don't have heirs. That's why she couldn't kill me on the train. Her older curse hampered the simple murder of a witness who got in her way."

"Ja, but apparently she can still make us pass out if the talisman isn't touching skin."

"We should cut the crystal in half, split the necklace, one part for you, one for me."

"I worry this will break the magic of the talisman," Godefroy said.

Frustrated, Caspar retreated a step and stared out the window. Pedestrians glanced at him, curious neighbours who had passed more than once the last few days, all of them intent on learning more of the house guests in the Tremblay residence. "I don't like it, having one of us with a weakness."

"We should take turns with it. When you're guarding the girls, you'll have it."

"No. The one who is hunting the witch should have it."

"Oh. Ja. I can see that, but only if the girls are in a secured location, because you can't work alone."

"Yes, fine. I need a witness, but you don't. Do you uncle? The curse doesn't care if you murder or not. You can hunt without me."

Godefroy's mouth opened a fraction. The eyes widened in confused surprise. He was brilliant, just brilliant, a superlative actor, but Caspar wasn't falling for it. Godefroy had no doubt worked through all the ramifications of their current situation the night they were on the train, but that veneer of guiltlessness: that was Godefroy's shield, and he'd drop it for no one. All the same, Caspar wanted it down. He needed it down. He'd chop off a finger in sacrifice if he thought it would move his uncle to confide to him the one detail of his life that would make them equal.

"Who did you murder, Uncle?" Caspar waited for an answer, but Godefroy started away from him. Caspar grabbed him by an arm. "Uncle, as if it would hurt to say."

"As you said, I don't require a witness, Caspar. My sins don't assist the family fortune."

"Just tell me! Why should you have privacy when I have none? Why should you get to avoid guilt and shame?"

Godefroy grabbed Caspar's wrist and yanked his hand off. "I don't! I don't, Caspar." They stared at each other. "Caspar! I don't," Godefroy insisted.

"Who, Uncle?" Caspar demanded.

"Aj! Damn it!" Godefroy released the wrist. He hesitated with his gaze fixed on someone walking on the sidewalk in front of the house. Then his attention reverted to Caspar. He leaned closer and breathed a name into his nephew's ear.

Caspar didn't experience the exultation of equality he'd thought to feel. He chortled with surprised mirth.

"Caspar!" Godefroy complained.

"Our Greek chauffeur? That's what happened to him? You didn't fire him? Why didn't you just fire him?"

126

"Aj! Aj!" Godefroy set loose a string of epithets, head rolling in frustration.

Caspar poked him in the flank. "Why?"

"Ow! Stop. He blackmailed me, the whore," Godefroy spat. Caspar chortled again. "It's not funny!" Godefroy cried.

"Stop whining. And yes, it is."

"Enough! And I don't whine! We have more important things to discuss, ja? Such as how to kill her. Bullets didn't work. A knife between the ribs didn't work."

"Fire? Beheading and then fire?"

"Blow up a gas stove while she's trapped in a house?" Godefroy said. Caspar chuckled. Together, both smirking, Caspar feeling happier than he could remember, they moved away from the window, sat in armchairs and tossed suggestions back and forth until Mr. and Mrs. Tremblay walked in the front entrance not much later.

"Did I hear someone mention a mountain of grenades?" Tremblay said upon appearing in the library entrance. "A stack of TNT would be more efficient."

"Oh, yes, but we already called that one. Now we're on ridiculous methods," Caspar said, standing with his uncle to greet their host and hostess.

"And the method is to do away with what?" Tremblay inquired.

"A witch that won't die from a shot to the head or heart," Caspar replied.

"Ah. Yes."

"How was business today, Mr. Tremblay?"

"Great. Just great. My agent in New York has sold off most of my stocks, I have a businessman interested in buying out my half of the brokerage, and I'm looking into an opportunity. Cinema houses."

"That sounds interesting. And how was your society meeting, Mrs. Tremblay?"

"It was lovely, thank you. How were the girls?"

"I've upset both of them, and they're crying in their room," Caspar said.

"Ah. I shall see what I can do to calm them momentarily. Shall we have tea together after I've freshened up?"

"I'd like that, Mrs. Tremblay."

"Oh, yes, I've contacted my mother," Godefroy inserted. "She'll be along in a few days."

"We shall have a room ready," Mrs. Tremblay said. "And she is welcome as long as she wishes, just as you both are. It will be nice to have another woman in the house. Does she play bridge?"

"She's a fiend."

"Oh, how lovely. We're going to have so much fun." Mrs. Tremblay wandered out of view, and they listened to her light steps as she rose to the second floor.

"Which of my daughters pestered who today?" Tremblay asked, a cynical expression on his face.

"Both of them pestered both of us," Caspar said. "Not to worry. They'll keep their distance for a few days at least."

Tremblay shook his head while muttering something rude and went upstairs as well. Caspar glanced at his uncle and discovered him grinning.

"The poor man. I pity him," Godefroy said.

"But you're smiling, and why pity him? I'd shoot him, but Farideh might think badly of me."

"Isn't it obvious? He's a father. He was all set to chase unworthy men away from his daughters, but instead he's helping unworthy men chase his daughters away."

"You're not unworthy," Caspar said, "and stay away from Farideh."

"Aj! Caspar! Stop it with the warnings!"

"Just stay away!"

Godefroy hung his head and sighed heavily.

Chapter Seventeen

August 2, 1929. Queens, New York. Circumstances of suspicious synchronicity.

Jimmy stretched his arm toward the warmth he expected on the other half of the bed. The small motion became a longer search until he bolted upright, staring at the other pillow and suffering the starkest sense of abandonment in his life. She'd left him. She'd god damned walked out on him while he slept. Feelings of inadequacy trickled over the abandonment and started to sink in. If a soul could feel like it was being swamped by mud, his did. He'd had heaven in his arms for part of a day and one night and lost it by simply shutting his eyes.

"Damn it."

"Damn what?"

His torso twisted around. He gaped at the figure relaxing against the window frame. She wore his too large silk housecoat, his too big slippers, smoked one of his cigarettes. Her hair was messed up, her make up smeared beneath her eyes. He'd never seen anyone more beautiful.

"I thought you left."

She laughed, inhaled a drag and looked out the window again, down at the traffic in the street below. When she puffed out, information arrived that he didn't like hearing. Her eyes lifted to survey the grey stone apartment block across from Jimmy's. "There's a man in the opposite building. He's been watching us."

"What the hell?"

Another tinkling laugh burst from her throat. "I've been making eyes at him to see how far he'd go. Right now he's masturbating."

"Son of a bitch!" He threw off the sheets and covers.

"If you're going to come over here, why don't you bring your gun and shoot him," she suggested.

"I am!"

Laughing yet again, she casually shut the curtains before he arrived. Naked, with gun in hand, he tried to yank one side open. She placed soft fingers on his wrist. "Mmm, no. Not worth it. Do it later when no one will notice."

Jimmy hesitated. He released the material fisted in his hand. "You're a different sort of dame, Talya," he said.

"How so?"

"You don't seem to mind that I'm going to kill him."

"Didn't I just tell you to?"

"Yeah, that's what I mean. You don't mind. You understand."

"Of course I do," she said, moving off to sit on the end of his bed. She eased back onto one elbow, spread her legs a little. "You're a deep sleeper, Jimmy. Not good. I was bored. Come here and entertain me." Her legs spread just a little further apart. The cigarette lost more length with another long drag that she inhaled and exhaled, watching him with sexy, half-lidded eyes. "Come on, Jimmy," she prodded. "You know where I want your angry mouth. Put your gun on my belly. Let me feel how cold it is."

"Thank you, God," Jimmy breathed. He approached, knelt on the floor, pressed his face between her legs and set the gun on her belly. He licked like a ravenous beggar. After only a few minutes, she was panting and staring with an animal expression. He loved that expression. He loved her.

"Mmm! Stop a moment. Take this cigarette butt. It's starting to burn."

He grabbed the short stub from her hand and threw it randomly toward the ash tray on the bedside table. He burned his fingers. The butt landed on the rug. He didn't care. His face went back between her legs.

She laughed and pulled him up by his hair. "Jimmy! The rug is going to catch fire. Go put it out."

"Damn it. Let the entire building burn around us." All the same, he lurched up and hurried to put the cigarette out.

"You want to kill someone in front of me, Jimmy?" she said. "You want to watch them die while you touch me?"

He looked into her eyes, her gorgeous, vivid, evil eyes. "Yes! Hell, yes!"

"Tell me who? You're wicked, Jimmy, aren't you? Tell me who you'd like to kill most in the world while I watch. And don't say the man across the street."

"Why not the man across the street?" Jimmy complained, moving to kneel between her legs again.

130

"Because we both know he's nothing to you. And he's nothing to me. You want me to enjoy myself, Jimmy? Then don't waste my time on meaningless murders."

Damn, Jimmy thought, lips brushing creamy skin on an inner thigh. Damn but she was perfect. He gave her an answer, a murder that would make him happier than every murder before and after, a murder that he'd remember and relish for a lifetime. "That little fucker!" he said. "That skinny, curly-haired kid who kidnapped that pervert Judge Brown from The Plaza! I want to kill him and his German father who looks like him! I want to shoot them both while you watch!"

He looked up and found her staring with an expression that suggested a disinterest in finishing their late morning fun. His feeling of inadequacy from earlier returned. "Talya, baby? Sorry, I'll pay more attention." He lowered his head, but she grabbed him by the forelocks.

"Describe this boy," she said.

"What?" he said, frowning in confusion.

"The boy. Describe him better. His eyes? What did they look like?"

"Brown, I think."

"Hair?"

"Brown, I guess. A little golden too. He had an accent I couldn't place. Sounded American, but not any sort of American I've met before. Must have been the German ancestry."

She released his hair. "Jimmy?" she said.

"Yeah?"

"I'll help you kill him."

"Yeah…? What? Really?"

"I think I know where he is."

"How would you know something like that?"

"I saw him on a train, I think, a boy whose accent wasn't the usual sort of American, a boy who knows German and French. The train was destined for Canada."

"He's Canadian?"

"Yes, he probably is. Jimmy, you don't happen to have something of his, do you, or something he touched recently?"

"Yeah. I've got his suit. He traded it for a bellhop outfit and wore the outfit to trick and kidnap Judge Brown. I killed the cretino bellhop and took the suit from him. Why?"

"I'm a witch, Jimmy. I'll do a reading on the suit."

"A witch?"

"Hmm. Yes. You scared, Jimmy?"

"No, I'm hard again. You're like a fortune teller? You're going to use the suit to tell my fortune?"

"Not exactly. Get the suit after, Jimmy." Once more her fingers grasped his forelock, but now she pushed his face down.

"Yeah, sure. Sure." He wasn't the type to let a woman boss him about usually, but this sort of submission? He liked it.

Chapter Eighteen

August 3, 1929. Mrs. Grace arrives.

"We're always looking out windows," Farideh said. "Did you notice? Women exist to look out windows."

Ara altered the complaint to a statement. "Windows exist for us to look out of them."

"But don't you see? This is what we're reduced to! We're the ones who have to smile and wait, and smile and wait, and look out the darned windows!"

"Fairy!" Ara cried. "I know you don't like waiting, but it won't be much longer. I'm sure Godefroy is just driving carefully. She must be very old, his mother, like Grand-maman."

"Then they should have let our driver drive," Farideh said. "He at least gets everywhere on time. They're over an hour late coming back! Even an old grand-maman doesn't account for that!" Frustrated, tired of stomping back and forth without the recourse of destroying another doll—because all hers were busted or bald, and only Ara's collection remained—Farideh flounced onto the window seat next to Ara. "I hate waiting."

"Careful. Don't ruin your dress snagging it on something," Ara said.

"I don't care if I ruin it." Even so, Farideh plucked the frilly skirt away from the only part of the seat that mattered, the chipped section where she'd smashed a visiting boy's toy fire truck at the end of a high-speed chase through the air, because it had been a flying fire truck, much less boring than a regular old fire truck, and the crash had been spectacular. The boy had gone home crying, and her father had been forced to bribe the parents with a brand new toy and a bottle of Cognac. The boy hadn't returned for another visit, and the chipped section still wasn't entirely smooth despite sanding, because Farideh absently picked at it whenever she sat on the seat.

"Perhaps they're giving her a tour of the city?" Ara suggested.

"Then they're purposely rude, making us wait."

"You've been in a horrible mood for days now," Ara said. "Please stop being angry with me at least. You know I'm not the one being mean."

Yes, Farideh knew her sister wasn't the mean one. Caspar was the mean one. His actions on the staircase had been a clear warning to stay away from his uncle, but that kiss had been more than a warning. It had been a promise of consequences. It had been an enticement. Despite her fear of Caspar, Farideh couldn't stop thinking of his mouth on hers and the hard bump he had pressed against her pelvis. She'd started to have aching dreams that left her restless and irritable in the morning. Worse yet, some of the dreams had both Caspar and Godefroy on the staircase with her. And all the while, Ara suffered unrequited love for the boy who wouldn't notice her if she were on fire. Ara's words. She'd said that yesterday.

"I'm sorry," Farideh said, but seconds later she jumped to her feet again. "Why can't he see that it's perfect if you have him and I have Godefroy? Why?"

"I don't know," Ara said, her voice subdued. "Please don't make me cry again. I don't have time to put ice packs over my eyes to bring down the swelling."

Farideh slumped onto the seat a second time. "I'm sorry."

"Oh! Isn't that the Cadillac?"

Farideh twisted toward the mullion window until she was on her knees like Ara, both hands plastered to glass and her left cheek as well. "That is just not how anyone drives carefully," Farideh said.

The family Cadillac careened around a slower car and narrowly missed an oncoming sedan. Horns beeped, audible even from the distance and despite that their window was shut.

"Oh, but ...! But Godefroy wouldn't drive like that? Would he?" Ara said.

"No," Farideh agreed. "But Caspar would."

"Oh, no! He didn't let Caspar drive?"

"I doubt Caspar gave him a choice," Farideh muttered as the Cadillac shrieked to a near halt on the opposite side of the street and then almost spun on the front wheels toward the curb on their side. Pedestrians yelped and pressed to the edge of the sidewalk. Some skipped onto the verge of lawns. One man toppled over a low hedge.

A slower vehicle to the rear halted, and the driver stepped out to shout at Caspar, who neatly parked the sedan with the passenger doors directly in front of the walkway of their residence, proving to

134

anyone with a brain that he'd known exactly what he was doing as he terrorized everyone on the 'stuffy suburban block', as he called their upper class neighbourhood.

"Oh, no. Papa is going to shout at him again," Ara said.

"He won't care."

"No, I suppose not. Oh, look. Godefroy is yelling at him already."

"That's to be expected."

Caspar stepped out of the car, grinning despite the focused public disapproval and Godefroy's bilingual remonstrations. Ara hurried to get one side of their window open to hear them better. It turned out that Godefroy didn't care the least what the neighbours thought of Caspar's harrowing parking skills.

"Your grandmother is sixty-three! Sixty-three! Have the courtesy not to smash her against either side of the car when you make a turn!"

"She was laughing," Caspar said. "Don't fuss." He moved to the rear, where a huge trunk had been roped to the back, replacing the fitted one belonging to the car. This trunk was so massive and heavy, the sedan's folding rack was in danger of scraping the asphalt. Instead of untying the rope that kept everything in place, Caspar pulled out a nasty-looking switchblade and cut through the multiple zigzagging lines.

"I am amazed that didn't fall off the Cadillac, the way he drives," Farideh said.

"He must really know how to tie knots," Ara said with a dreamy voice. "Doesn't he look beautiful in his new suit? I think dove grey is wonderful on him. He looks like an angel."

"Angel's wear white, Ara," Farideh said dryly.

"Not the angel of death."

Farideh gave her a leery glance and pinned her gaze on Godefroy. Godefroy had a new suit as well, a slate grey ensemble. Farideh thought Godefroy looked more like an angel of death in his darker outfit than Caspar did in his smoky one, but Godefroy didn't have the nasty disposition to go with the title.

Godefroy arrived at the rear of the car to stop the trunk from smashing Caspar's feet flat. Caspar had yanked it toward himself and staggered under the load.

"Careful, Caspar! It's too heavy," Godefroy said, catching a corner and lifting it for balance.

"Fine. You take it." Caspar abandoned him and headed for the passenger door.

"Aj! Caspar!" Godefroy cursed in Scandinavian and shoved the trunk back onto the luggage platform, grunting with the effort. The car bobbed up and down, and the frame sagged at the rear again. "Aj, Aj! Why this boy?"

"Papa will be angry with Godefroy if that huge thing scratches the car," Ara said.

"Godefroy appreciates objects of value," Farideh said. "See? There's a blanket under the trunk and cardboard packed against the back of the car."

"Oh. Yes. But then why did he let Caspar drive?" Ara said. Farideh sniggered, and then Ara did as well. "Yes, I know. Caspar probably didn't give him a choice."

"Hey!" the driver of the slow vehicle shouted. "What do you think you're doing letting a kid like that drive a car?"

"I beg your pardon? Are you the licensing board of the City of Toronto?" Godefroy said, facing the offended gentleman.

"That has nothing to do with it!"

"I think it does." Godefroy coolly walked away and opened the rear door.

"Hey! I'm talking to you!"

"Isn't it wonderful how Godefroy is so protective?" Farideh said dreamily. "He'll make a wonderful father."

"Here, Mamma." Godefroy lowered a hand to help his mother off the passenger seat. "I'll walk you up to the house while Caspar deals with the many people who admire his driving."

Ara sniggered alone this time, while Farideh reddened with mortification.

"Ha, ha, ha!" the most amazingly tiny elderly woman uttered, at last coming into view of the inhabitants of the house. "And for your information Caspar, I wasn't laughing. My dog was yelping in panic."

"Oh. Sorry, Grandmamma. Is it dead?"

Caspar's Grandmamma smacked him a good one with her purse, which appeared heavy, because he staggered back a foot. Godefroy laughed and offered the old woman his arm, and Caspar rubbed his nose, grinning again, but ruefully.

"Is she a midget?" Farideh said.

"Farideh! Shh! Oh, look at the beautiful fur bolero. It must be ermine."

136

"How did she give birth to Godefroy and a twin?" Farideh asked.

"Farideh! They were babies! Not grown men. Don't be silly."

"Still, how did she? She's a midget."

"She's not a midget! She's just short. You've been to Europe. Some places are full of short people."

Godefroy led his diminutive mother up the walkway, and down at the curb, the complaining driver hurried into his car and roared off. His decision likely had something to do with how Caspar rested one upper arm on the roof of Cadillac while clutching the open switchblade, but Farideh suspected Caspar's expression had speeded the driver's reaction. She couldn't see Caspar's face just then, but she could imagine it: grin vanished, eyes hard and soulless. Only a fool wouldn't run.

Caspar folded and shoved his switchblade out of sight and moved to close the car door.

"Cici! Come!" the old woman called.

A white mop on legs leapt out of the car and barked at Caspar, who halted with a spellbound stare. The mop charged, backed off, charged and backed off again, all the while issuing the high-pitched challenge.

"Oh, he does not like the dog," Ara breathed, "and the dog does not like him."

"That's a dog?" Farideh said. "Oh, wait. Yes, I see the head now."

"Cici! Come!" Mrs. Grace called again.

"We should hurry down," Ara said.

"Yes," Farideh agreed.

Ara slipped off the window seat and headed for the bedroom door. Farideh cast another glance outside. Caspar had shut the car door and started toward the house. He didn't seem concerned about getting the trunk in the house. Then again, if he tried to lift it without help, it might just crush him flat. Godefroy had braced his entire body to get it back on the car. What was in that thing? It couldn't be just clothes.

Caspar skipped up the different multiple staircases, clearing two or three steps at a time, and caught up with his uncle and grandmother. Farideh scrambled off the seat and rushed after Ara. They descended almost to the bottom and halted on the stairway, Farideh just a step up from her sister.

Their father already had the front door open, and yes, he was furious but holding his emotions in. Their mother had her most soothing smile ready, not that it was helping with Papa. Farideh hoped he wouldn't yell at Caspar in front of the neighbourhood, because virtually everyone would be spying through windows right now, if not issuing out into their yards to gossip across rosebushes, hedges and fences. Caspar's grandstanding had gathered a block-wide audience. Godefroy really needed to speak with him. Murderers should be quiet and unassuming if they wanted to remain undiscovered.

Godefroy appeared on the porch with his mother. "Mamma, this is David Tremblay and his lovely wife Deena, who is apparently my distant cousin."

Mrs. Grace had a clipped way of speaking, very precise and sharp. She betrayed her foreign heritage further with a tendency to start on a high tone and slowly end lower. This manner of vocalisation made her response to Godefroy's introduction all the more alarming, because it didn't sound like a joke, not even a bad one.

"If that's true, why aren't they dead?" she said.

"The branch of the tree is too distant, I suspect," Godefroy said, a pained half smile forming and disappearing as his attention lifted to Farideh's father. "Uh … sorry, Tremblay. My mother's sense of humour can be alarming." He laughed weakly, no doubt because Farideh's Papa didn't look the least amused or appeased.

"Mrs. Grace, welcome to the house," David Tremblay said without a hint of welcome in his tone. He offered Mrs. Grace a hand. "Please come in."

Seeming undisturbed and unimpressed, the elderly woman placed her small fingers in his and stepped into the house. The dog entered at her heels. "Cici, sit," she said.

The dog sat, mouth open and panting. The old woman's gaze lifted to discover the twins on the staircase. Farideh stretched her lips into a smile. Darn it, but she was nervous meeting Godefroy's mother. Without looking, she knew Ara felt the same, but because this was Caspar's grandmother. Although Ara found Godefroy polite and amusing, she didn't really have much interest in him, therefore his relationship to Mrs. Grace was secondary in Ara's mind.

Tremblay released the old woman's hand. "Godefroy, you and I are having words. Now. I'll meet you in the garage out back."

138

"Oh, yes. I should have told Caspar not to untie the ropes so soon. I shall have to drive very carefully to keep the trunk from falling off."

"He didn't untie them. He cut them," David said stiffly, "with a switchblade, a four inch switchblade, Godefroy. This is a quiet neighbourhood. It doesn't need a resident thug terrorizing the citizens."

Godefroy tucked his hands in his pocket and looked for all the world as if he wasn't the least anxious or alert to the warning signals of his host. "Oh. Sorry. I suppose he should be more careful waving that around. It is a rather large specimen."

"Out back, Godefroy."

"Yes, of course. I'll just drive the ca—"

"I'll drive the car," David interrupted.

"Are these girls yours, Mr. Tremblay?" Mrs. Grace asked.

"Yes, these are our daughters," Deena said, stepping forward a pace and offering a warm smile. "Farideh and Ara."

The twins curtsied in unison, each with a hand on the stair rail to keep steady, and then the old woman staggered them and their parents.

"If you know what's good for you, lock chastity belts around them and your wife too, or put my son and grandson in chains. Better yet, kick us out now," Mrs. Grace said. "And if you want to do it fast, let Caspar keep the car."

"I don't want a clumsy tank," Caspar said.

Ara locked both arms around the rail to stay upright. Farideh froze in dismay. Godefroy pulled his hands from his pocket and gaped in disbelief at his mother.

"Mamma!"

"Mrs. Grace, I assure you that both your son and grandson have been the epitome of good manners, circumspection and morality," Deena said.

"Don't be a liar. Those girls are what? Eleven, twelve? The only reason they're still virgins is neither has had her first flow, and don't wait for it to happen either. The second they're ready, bloody warning or not, one of my boys will have either of your girls' skirt up and his pants down." She gave David Tremblay a scathing glance after this pronouncement and added, "Don't think for a second you'll be able to stop him. You'll be lucky if you can shoot him after."

"You can be certain I will," the twins' father said, pinning a murderous glance on Caspar.

"Just get a chastity belt for Farideh. She's the only one who needs it," Caspar said.

Farideh blushed bright red. Ara sobbed and scrambled up the stairs, twice catching herself by one hand after stumbling. The sound of her hem ripping occurred on the second stumble.

"Godefroy, you still have the car keys. Off you go," David said. "Nice meeting you, Mrs. Grace. The advice was much appreciated." He guided her by the elbow out the door. The dog growled at him.

"David! David, we can't!" Deena said. "We can't! She's hunting them! Do you want Farideh to die? Do you want this to go on forever, for Ara's daughters to suffer the same fate?"

Tremblay stared out the door at the three Graces and then slowly turned to his wife. "We'll find a way to protect them."

"You can't!" Deena spat. "When will you understand? You couldn't kill her! You shot her four times, David! You aren't the right murderer!"

"Oh, this is interesting," Mrs. Grace said. "What's happening here, Godefroy?"

"I did say I would explain, Mamma! Deena, her little girls, they really are distant cousins. You shouldn't have said these embarrassing things about their virtue."

"Someone had to say it, and you weren't going to, were you? So the witch cursed these women? It's a curse on the female side? Twins? Is it always twins?"

"I don't know all the details, but they have a prophecy about breaking the spell, and we're involved."

"Cici, in the house," Mrs. Grace said. She stepped back in without waiting for a new invitation. "I like my bedroom window facing a sunny side, Deena."

"Yes, of course, Mrs. Grace. I have a room arranged. Would you like to see it?"

"Yes, I would. Do you play bridge by any chance?"

"I'm a fiend."

"How lovely. We're going to have so much fun."

Standing in the doorway, confronting Godefroy and Caspar, who stared back with eyes that did indeed belong to murderers, David Tremblay's shoulders sagged in defeat.

"Godefroy."

140

"Yes, David?"

"You drive the car out back to the garage."

"It will be my pleasure." Godefroy started back to the Cadillac. "Come along Caspar. Knot as many parts of that rope together as you can."

"Yes, Uncle." Caspar tossed him the keys. "When did the dealer say my Cadillac coupe would be ready?"

"A few days. It takes time to personalize a car, and don't forget the bank draft must go through."

"Yes, fine, but I didn't want the same colour as yours."

"Of course not. Red is not my thing."

"Then I'm surprised you didn't ask for white."

Godefroy spun around and fixed an indignant glare on his nephew. Caspar laughed and passed him by, no fear of reprisal in his bearing.

"Aj! Why this boy? Why?" Godefroy said and followed after him.

David stepped back and slammed the front door shut. His forehead landed with a thump on the back panels. "Damn it," he said.

"Papa?"

"Go to your room, Farideh."

"I'm sorry, Papa."

"Just go, princess. All right?"

"Yes, Papa."

Farideh ascended the stairs, weeping quietly all the way up. Right then, she felt more unworthy and sallow than a month of having Sylvie verbally abuse her without any protective Sister Thérèse present.

"Mrs. Grace, may I ask why you said those horrific things about your son's honour?" she heard her mother ask. Farideh stalled in the upstairs hallway to listen.

"You don't mention my grandson's honour, Deena? You think he has none?"

A delay indicated Farideh's mother had decided not to answer.

"Caspar has more honour than you think. At least he's not a liar like my son."

"A liar, Mrs. Grace?"

"Yes, a consummate one. Be warned. You might think Caspar is the dangerous one, but he's not the worst of the pair."

"And the reason for warning us to guard our daughters' virtue? Why would you say this about your son and grandson?"

"Well, they're cursed, aren't they?" This response sounded impatient, as if Mrs. Grace expected Deena to be aware of the reason already.

"I'm sorry, Mrs. Grace, but how are they cursed exactly?"

"They haven't said?" The old woman chortled. "Oh, but that just like Godefroy, slipping right past the household guards without giving his full credentials. He's as good as waiting in the boudoir already."

"Mrs. Grace, please tell me how they are cursed," Deena begged.

"No. If Godefroy hasn't said it, it's because you also haven't said things. My side has as much to lose as yours, perhaps more. Give him your full history if you want to rid your daughters of this curse. Give him something to work with. Give him some hope. Just give him what he wants to make it worth his while. Cici, come and see this nice cushion for you, my lovely boy. Come. Come. Oh, there's a darling, darling boy."

Farideh's mother appeared in the bedroom doorway. She looked at Farideh, shook her head and indicated her daughter should continue to her room. Farideh started past her.

"There's another large trunk on the way, Deena, and my personal suitcases as well. Godefroy arranged for a station employee to deliver them."

"I shall have someone watch for the truck, Mrs. Grace. Tea will be served shortly."

"I'd like to have it up here, if you don't mind. I need some quiet. Lugging a purse full of gold all day is tiring."

"Gold, Mrs. Grace?" Deena said with an inquisitive frown.

"Yes, that's what I said."

"Would you like to lock it in the household safe, Mrs. Grace?"

"No point. No bad luck coming my way for a few years. Off you go, dear."

"Yes, of course." Deena shut the door. Farideh paused outside her room. Her mother approached and pulled her into her arms. A huge, gulping sob broke from Farideh.

"Shh, shh," Deena whispered.

"I'm not a bad girl!"

"I know, my baby. I know."

"They make me feel like a bad girl!"

142

"Shh." Her mother let her cry for a bit, but then asked, "Even Godefroy? Does he make you feel bad?"

"No," Farideh said. "He makes me feel like a girl who can make him laugh."

Deena pulled way from her and gazed intently into her eyes. Hands on Farideh's shoulders, she said, "Remember that. Remember that feeling, Farideh. Remember who doesn't make you feel bad."

Farideh gathered in enough of a shaky breath to say, "Yes, Maman."

"There, my princess. You'll be all right. Godefroy will make sure of it."

"She said he was worse than Caspar."

"Yes, this may be true, but if he's the right man, if he's the man of the prophecy, then worse is better. It is no simple thing to hunt this witch."

"Yes, Maman."

"In you go. I'll bring up tea. We'll have a little tea party together, the three of us."

Farideh nodded and entered her room. Her mother shut the door, and Farideh, with her back against the door, listened to her soft tread retreating back downstairs. Farideh stared across the room at Ara, who wept on the window seat, alone, forlorn, inconsolable. Farideh had no words to comfort her, no words that would be true. Though Godefroy was forever gentle and polite with Ara, she didn't love him, and Caspar was consistently rude and cold. Neither of the Grace men made Ara feel better.

Chapter Nineteen

August 4, 1929. In church with the three Graces.

Farideh listened to the priest drone Latin words, grew bored and angled forward. Again.

Before she managed a decent glimpse of Godefroy, who stood between his nephew and diminutive mother, her father's hand fell on her shoulder and tilted her back into position. She sighed heavily and waited for the interminable Latin to end. The sermons were always better, not just because they were in English. Father Peter inevitably chose a saint of the Roman Catholic Church and expounded upon the sacrifice, the bloody and excruciating sacrifice of the martyr of choice each Sunday. She and Ara had a game of counting how many times he used the word 'sacrifice' and its derivatives. They also counted the word 'suffered', just 'suffered', because Father Peter most often used the word in the phrase 'and he suffered.'

But today Farideh didn't think she and her sister had the concentration to tally any of their favourite terms and phrases, not after Mrs. Grace's shocking pronouncement yesterday. Ara had been as mortified as Farideh, and now she hid beyond their father, the furthest away from Mrs. Grace as she could get. Farideh eased backward to catch a view of her sister and discovered Ara tilting back as well, but to look further down the aisle at Caspar.

Their father's hands settled on a shoulder each and jerked them back in place. An audible unhappy sigh escaped from Ara and whispered over into Farideh's ears. She sighed too. She wondered how uncomfortable the chastity belt would be, because she was certain her father would put her in one. She knew this predicament was partially her fault, but she couldn't stop herself. Truly she was worse than Ara; she tilted as often to stare at Caspar as Godefroy.

To make it all worse, she never caught them looking at her. The Grace's, all three of them, had been the epitome of cultured frost after the disastrous introduction of Grandmamma Grace. They'd proved for the entire evening and early morning that they could outdo royalty for proper manners. The Grace men were polite, but as forthcoming as aloof tomcats. Godefroy, who usually made efforts to smooth any awkward atmosphere, had been as distant as Caspar, and he didn't look at Farideh if he could help it.

Farideh had more than once overheard her father mutter bad things in concert with the words 'patrician, old world snobs.' He thought the worst of the Grace men, but Farideh didn't believe they intended to be dishonourable. Caspar's actions on the staircase those few days ago had been a clear warning to stay away from him and his uncle—if she could—and Godefroy avoided being alone with her in any case. Godefroy's behaviour had been commendable throughout.

But why had Mrs. Grace said such a horrific thing about her son and grandson? What had she meant by them being cursed? And why the interest in twins? Did Caspar have a twin who had died? Did Godefroy?

It was very frustrating. Farideh thought she should know these things—they were cousins, after all, even if distantly related, and one of the Graces would become her husband if the prophecy was true— but Godefroy consistently avoided speaking of his past and Caspar followed his lead. No matter how hard she tried, somehow conversations always ended up on a less personal topic.

She didn't dare ask her parents if they knew more about their house guests. Papa would burst a blood vessel for certain, and her mother had suggested she behave in a more subdued manner, which meant don't pry. But since her parents had decided to let the Graces reveal their secrets in their own time, which wouldn't likely occur until after they'd stopped being offended, Farideh intended to be more direct and ask Mrs. Grace herself at the earliest opportunity. Mrs. Grace owed her for upsetting Ara.

Many tilts and corrections later, Farideh's alertness won her the chance. The sermon ended, church services concluded, and the congregation began the quiet mass shuffle out from between pews and toward the double doors. Halfway to the end of the central aisle, Mrs. Grace realized she had left her handkerchief behind on their pew. Farideh volunteered to go back for it. When she returned, everyone else already stood outside chatting with nosy parishioners angling to know more about the Graces. Farideh found herself alone with the old lady except for the remaining few people moving past.

"Mrs. Grace?" Farideh said as she handed the dropped item over.

"Yes, dear?"

"Do you speak French?"

"Yes, dear."

Farideh rattled off her question as rapidly as she could while keeping her voice low. Some of the parishioners were as bilingual as the Tremblays, and voices carried in an empty, quiet church. "Quelle est la malédiction de votre fils et petit-fils?" *What is the curse of your son and grandson?*

"Why don't you ask, Godefroy, dear?"

"He avoids answering questions."

"Yes, he is a monster that way." Mrs. Grace gave her a light pat on the cheek. "Just keep your legs closed, dear, until he gives up and answers." Mrs. Grace turned away and meandered out into the sunlight, while Farideh remained in place, skin burning from her crown to well below her neckline.

Her mother stepped back into the church. "Farideh?" she called. "Come along. There are young people out here who'd like to meet your cousin Caspar. Why don't you help Ara introduce him?"

"Yes, Maman." Farideh reluctantly travelled up the aisle and closer to the formidable Mrs. Grace, who smirked at Farideh and then greeted a neighbour Farideh's father had introduced.

"Something the matter, my princess?"

"No, Maman."

Her mother patently didn't believe her, because she touched her forehead to check for a fever. "Farideh, what happened?"

"I asked Mrs. Grace about their curse."

"Yes, and?" her mother asked, hand lowering.

"She didn't say."

"Oh. What did she say, then?"

Farideh avoided her mother's gaze. "Advice."

"Advice? What sort of advice?"

Farideh leaned in and told her in a low voice. "To keep my legs shut until Godefroy gives up and answers my questions."

Farideh waited for her mother to be offended and protective, but instead, she nodded and said, "Hmm. Yes, do that."

"Maman!"

"Farideh. It works. Just do it."

Her mother, with the usual sweet smile, returned to her husband's side, and Farideh pouted in her wake. Yes, she'd forgotten. Her mother hadn't been a typical virgin at her wedding, but a highly skilled courtesan spy with a casual acceptance of the more sordid aspects of life. Given the doom she had to avoid, Farideh supposed knowledge was better protection than innocence, but still! Who wanted to be told to keep their legs shut just to manipulate a man? There had to be a more respectable way to beat this game of secrets.

Oh, yes! Farideh stalled ten feet from the entrance. "Maman?" she called.

"Yes, dear?"

Farideh waited with a fake embarrassed smile until her mother approached.

"Yes, Farideh?"

"You still haven't said what my doom is," Farideh whispered.

"Later, Farideh."

"You said that last time!"

"We're in church now."

"Yes, but when? I need to know! The fortune teller said so."

"All right. Today at tea."

"Good," Farideh said, pleased and eager for later. "I'll use it to get Godefroy to speak. He'll trade with me."

"Do you really think so?"

"Why wouldn't he? I don't believe what that old lady said about him being a liar."

"Your father says he's the best confidence man he's ever met, Farideh. Be careful."

"But he hasn't tricked any of us," Farideh protested.

"Yet."

"How would Papa know?"

"Farideh! He's the best confidence man I've ever met. All the best handlers are. An active agent needs decent support."

"Oh. Yes, I forgot."

"Now," her mother said, taking her shoulders and directing her toward the doorway. "Outside with Ara." She leaned a little closer from behind. "And stop reading my war diary."

Farideh blushed to her roots again. Her mother laughed and gave her a light push toward Ara, and Farideh walked away to join her sister.

Chapter Twenty

Fate rather than synchronicity.

"That's him! That's the little bastard!" Jimmy said. "That little son of a bitch! He's got a new suit, and he's with the bella bambina! Damn him! That's my style of hat!"

"It's a Borsalino, Jimmy. Lot's of men wear Borsalinos."

"I'm gonna kill him, the little bastard!"

"Jimmy."

"Figlio di puttana bastardo! Io lo ucciderà! Io lo ucciderà!" *Son of a bitch bastard! I will kill him! I will kill him!*

"Jimmy!"

"What?" Reluctantly he looked away from his target and toward the woman on the passenger seat of the borrowed Cadillac.

"You can't do a drive-by shooting. Not here," she said.

"That's a church! I wouldn't shoot anyone at a church! I ain't going to hell!" He realized how stupid he sounded and was glad she didn't laugh. Him, a murderer who thought he'd avoid hell if he didn't shoot outside a church. Yeah, it was laughable.

"Dannazione." *Dammit.* "I gotta go to confession and donate," he muttered. He couldn't remember the last time he'd done either. How did anyone confess the things he did? In bed and on the job?

"Jimmy, that's not the reason," she said. "He's with my relatives. You can't hurt my relatives, even by accident. You'd be hurting me."

"Yeah. Right. Sorry. Why is he with your relatives?"

"I don't know," she said, staring at the yard in front of the church. "I thought it was random, this boy being on the train with them."

"So it's not random?" Jimmy asked. She didn't answer. "Baby? Is it random or not? What is this?"

"I don't know!" she snapped.

"Hey! Sorry. Don't be mad at me. Baby? Come on! You know I won't hurt you or your family."

She wasn't listening. "That man ...?" she muttered.

"Who, the kid's father?" That bastard had a spiffy suit too, dark grey instead of smoke, and yes, a Borsalino that he currently held in his hand. The fedora didn't match the suit. It was black. The son of a bitch had a crowd of women around him. "Look at him smiling. Ain't he slick? Who does he think he is? He can't take time to comb all his hair back? He has to leave that curly shank hanging down like he's some famous Hollywood actor?"

"Jimmy!" Talya complained.

"He the one you mean, baby?" Jimmy asked. "The kid's father?"

"Yes, him," Talya said.

Jimmy scowled. That bastard, acting so easy around that many women. Jimmy decided to cut the man's suave smile off before he was dead. "What about him? You like his looks? Is that it? You like his looks?"

"Don't be like that. He reminds me of someone."

"Who?" Jimmy asked, because after some vengeful mutilation, he'd kill the kid's father and the guy Talya remembered as well. No man was allowed to be in her thoughts but him.

"It was a long time ago. He's dead and gone."

"Well, this guy is dead too, whoever he reminds you of."

"He can't be closely related to the boy," she said. She felt around her head to make sure the red kerchief was in place. "We can't be seen now, Jimmy. Let's go."

"Why can't he be closely related?" Jimmy asked.

"There's never two of them at once, not with that face."

"What? There's two of them now, the kid and the father."

"No, it'll skip a generation. That man must be a cousin or something, a spare from a branch family in case the current line fails. That boy has a brother somewhere about, but he won't look exactly the same. See if you can spot him."

"I don't get it. Why would a face skip a generation? And why would that make the kid's father a spare? A spare for what?"

She heaved a frustrated breath. "He's not his father! Never mind. Jimmy, we need to leave. Now! I can't be seen."

"Didn't you just want me to spot the kid's brother."

"I've changed my mind. Let's go."

"Why? They're your relatives, the woman and girl."

"I'll see them later. Do you want that boy to spot you? He's only a few dozen yards in front of us, Jimmy!"

"Well, it's a really crowded lawn."

"Jimmy!"

150

"Right. Fine. Let's go find a hotel and rest a little," Jimmy suggested.

"Not yet."

He reached for her hand. "Hey, why not? Come on, baby. I need you."

"We need to follow them and find out where they live."

Her fingers were unresponsive in his grasp. He let her hand go. "You just said we can't be seen."

"We can't be seen by those men! Just move the car somewhere quiet and put the top up. Wear your hat and put your Foster Grants on. You won't be so exposed."

"Why don't you wear them if you're so worried about being seen with me?" he said.

"Fine. I will." She grabbed the sunglasses he'd tossed onto the seat earlier, slipped the arms beneath her kerchief and settled the bridge over her nose. "Now move this car and put the top up."

Jimmy's grip on the steering wheel tightened. He had the distinct impression she was the one who wanted to hide. She couldn't care less if someone saw him, so long as no one saw her. "You can use the kid's suit to find where he lives later. We don't need to follow him now. Let's wait until dark."

"Jimmy—" she began.

He cut her off. "You don't want to be seen with me. Fine. I get it. You're slumming. But you listen to me when it comes to dodging spotters. You don't wear bright red kerchiefs on a job, and you don't follow in cars that attract attention, and my cousin Ritchie's Cadillac will attract attention. It's top of the line."

"Oh, really? Then what do you think of the one the boy intends to drive?" she said dryly.

Jimmy's head whipped around to look out the windshield again, but he didn't see the skinny bastard in front of the church any longer. Jimmy scanned forward. Along with a crowd of teenagers, his target had crossed the street in front of the church. They stood in a knot near a vehicle and slowed traffic trying to leave the area, not that they seemed to care, damned bunch of rich kids. Jimmy craned out the driver's side window to see better. The bastard had opened the door of a classy Cadillac sedan that rivalled cousin Ritchie's coupe. It was a gorgeous buttery yellow with shiny metal trim.

"That's a family car," Jimmy dismissed it. Damn that kid!

"He's still going to drive it. That's not the passenger door. This car won't attract any attention. Look at the cars parked on this street. They're all top of the line."

"We're not following now," Jimmy said and ignored her exasperated hiss. He squinted, trying to see between the crowd of boys.

The arrival of a diminutive old woman parted the gang of eager adolescents. "What the hell? There are two bella bambinas!" And one of them was jumping at the skinny bastard, trying to take something from his raised hands.

"My cousin has twins," Talya said.

"That woman's husband must want to commit murder every day. Look at those boys trying to get in good with the girls."

"Yes, I'm sure they have each and every one wrapped around their little fingers," Talya said.

Jimmy ignored her warning tone and agreed. "I bet." Two bella bambinas. He was getting a stiff thinking about the possibilities.

Talya pinched his thigh.

"Ow! Hey! Watch it!"

"Do not get ideas about those girls. Do you hear me, Jimmy? You make me happy, we'll talk about girls later. Maybe we'll talk about one of those girls. Hmm? You like that, Jimmy?"

He stared at her, riveted, in love all over again. "Yeah. Yeah, I like that."

"Then quit arguing with me about following the boy. We need to see where he lives if we're going to plan for later."

"Yeah, sure. No problem." He started the car, but then stretched to give her a quick kiss.

"Jimmy! People may see."

"And they'll see a red flag. Take that red kerchief off," he said. He kissed her again.

"Stop it! Fine. I'll put my hat on. Just don't drive fast until we get the top up. I'll murder you if my hair blows into a bird's nest." She tugged the kerchief off from the back, dropped the sun glasses on the seat, and patted her hair in place around her head.

"Your hat is red too," Jimmy said, grinning.

"I don't care!"

Jimmy laughed, put the car in gear and pulled a U-turn. Those rich kids had stalled enough oncoming traffic it was easy. "Talya, baby. You are definitely the perfect woman," he said.

152

"I know."

He laughed. Modesty had no place on his baby, and he liked that fine.

He had to back up a little to avoid hitting another parked car, but then he drove around the next corner and stopped a little beyond the church rectory, where they weren't in view of the crowd in front of the church. He stepped out to get the roof up, and Talya opened the overnight bag tucked near her feet. He paused to admire her gorgeous curves. She had a way of folding her body that made him want to squeeze her senseless while banging her hard. He still wished she'd go to a hotel with him.

She straightened with her hat in hand and gave her luggage a shove with her toe to get it out of the way again. Everything in the elegant carpetbag was new. Back in New York, Talya had gone into the women's department at Macy's and returned wearing a new dress, stockings, shoes, sweater and hat. A store clerk, with an obsequious smile and well wishes for the road trip gushing from it, had walked in Talya's train and handed over the full bag at the door. Jimmy figured Talya either had an account at Macy's or a hell of a good reputation and no problem using personal cheques.

His baby had to be a rich lady. Yeah. Really rich. One wave of a fancy bit of signed paper and clerks would bend over to get spanked if she asked. The idea was damned sexy, his baby smacking some groaning dame's naked bottom, maybe in the lingerie department. He could just picture it, a line-up of female clerks with their skirts up, drawers down, high heels spread, and all of them bent over and waiting. Ten bucks for you. Ten bucks for you. Ten bucks ....

Jimmy hastily passed a hand over his mouth. Damn, he was drooling.

"Jimmy! Don't just stand there!"

"Yeah, sure, baby." Still grinning, he got to work. He was just securing the top of the coupe when a vehicle screeched around the same street corner and came roaring directly toward them. Jimmy had a few seconds to recognise the butter yellow paint, and then he jumped over the hood of the coupe to avoid getting run down.

Chapter Twenty-One

Introductions and an incident.

"Papa won't let you drive again," Farideh said.

"Yes, he will." Caspar idly looked away from her and smiled at a pretty girl nearby. Ara had introduced the brunette in the blue and white dress, but Caspar had already forgotten her name, not that he cared to remember. He just wanted Farideh to fry the braids off her head from jealousy. Petty, yes, but after how many times she'd peeked at Godefroy while in the Blessed Sacrament, he was really irritated.

The pretty girl blushed and smiled shyly back. Caspar changed his mind. Maybe he did care what her name was. She was taller than Farideh. She had sweet baby cheeks and bigger breasts. She looked thirteen, maybe fourteen. Thirteen was better than twelve. He could just bite those cute cheeks. Interested now, he straightened away from his slouch on the passenger door. The girl's blush heightened. Her gaze flitted away and returned.

Next to her, Ara scowled, but Caspar pretended not to notice. He'd get to Ara later. Someday. Maybe. When she stopped being useless and neurotic. If ever. He'd never seen anyone cry so easily. She had no gumption whatsoever.

"No, he won't. He won't give you the keys," Farideh said. She shoved Caspar in the chest with a palm. "Stop embarrassing my friend."

Caspar pulled his hand from his suit pocket and jingled the keys at her while still smiling at the other girl. Seemed to him, Farideh's jealousy had heightened the second he'd become interested in someone else. Well, fine. "How exactly am I embarrassing your friend? We're only smiling at each other. She has a really nice smile. Yours is always fake, dear little cousin."

"How did you get those?" Farideh demanded. "And my smiles are never fake!"

He laughed. "Yes, they are. Always. Your father gave me the keys straight from out of his pocket. We were squished together while walking out of the church. My hand. His pocket. It was confusing."

Some of the boys in the accompanying group of young people laughed, but others scowled disapprovingly, the ones who thought they might have a chance with either twin. Caspar ignored them. They didn't have a chance. They'd be dead before that. He already knew where some of them lived. He might not be good with names, but he was great with addresses.

"You thief! Give those back!" Farideh attempted a grab. He lifted them higher. She jumped for them. Her body bumped into his. Caspar's teeth clenched. Agony how much he wanted to do something very heinous right now.

"Give them back!" Farideh shouted, and despite her noise and the bounce of her body against his, his attention shifted toward his left. A car had just started.

"Caspar! Stop teasing, Farideh!" his grandmother said. She barged through the young people surrounding the Farideh twins. Farideh stopped joggling against Caspar's body and scurried behind him.

"Grandmamma, why aren't you suffering through the tedious introductions with my uncle?" Caspar asked.

"Because they're tedious. I'm old. I'm cranky. I'm rich. I don't need an excuse. I'm sitting down. If anyone wants to be introduced, they can visit my golden chariot."

Grinning, Caspar opened the chariot door and helped his grandmother step inside. When he shut the door and turned to confront Farideh, he found her on the driver's seat.

"I'm not budging from here until Papa comes," she said, fingers locked around the steering wheel.

"So you want to drive. Sure, I'll teach you."

"I do not want to drive! Oh! You're impossible!"

"Driving is very possible. Let's see how well you can use those nice ankles of yours. Nice stockings, by the way. Are they silk?"

She blushed, and he had to admit a blush on her looked better than on the other girl. Farideh's blushes were like rose petals under creamy hot coffee.

"I'm watching you, boy," his grandmother said.

"Yeah, good thing."

"I know."

Smiling wryly, Caspar rotated away from Farideh. So his grandmother had skipped socializing for his sake. He didn't need an heir, not now, not so soon, but he had a bad case of not grateful. The frustration of being stopped almost overshadowed good sense.

156

Damn the curse. He didn't think girls had their periods so young. Why did they have them so young?

His attention skittered further off. A car had turned from out of a parking space down the street behind them. The driver conducted an unusual U-turn rather than going forward. Caspar's gaze narrowed first on the driver, who seemed familiar, and then on the woman who came into view. He couldn't see her face because she was patting her hair down. Against the dark hair and red dress, her hands were a lovely coffee cream.

This information wasn't very significant. Lots of women in Canada were the daughters of old world parents. Many had similar colouration, but Caspar had a reaction while looking at her hands. His spine prickled with energy. His fingers tingled. His senses heightened, but he stopped hearing the voices of the teenagers speaking around him. He heard the Cadillac coupe escaping. He heard his heart beating with increasing rapidity, and then he had nothing left in his mind, nothing but this undeniable urge, this yearning to get closer to the woman in the black coupe.

"Move over, Farideh!"

"What? No, I won't m—! Ow!"

He shoved hard enough to send her upper body sprawling across the seat and jammed himself in next to her bottom, which he normally wouldn't have ignored. He slammed the car door shut, started the ignition, shifted gears and roared into the crowded street, scattering teenagers and adults. Car horns honked. People shouted. He made a brake-shrieking entrance onto the three way intersection at Yonge Street. Farideh screamed in terror. Cars careened to avoid the Cadillac. He pulled a skidding U-turn and roared back onto Cheritan Avenue, this time heading the opposite direction.

"Caspar!" Farideh cried. "Caspar, stop!"

"Damn it, boy! What are you doing?" a voice from the rear seat demanded.

"Farideh! Farideh!" a distant voice screamed. Caspar vaguely recalled a boring girl with no gumption; then he focused on avoiding a collision. The oncoming driver swerved and went up the curb. Caspar corrected the Cadillac's direction and sped up.

"You monster!" a man shouted. "Get out of that car!"

"Caspar!"

"Uncle …!"

He didn't have time to stop. Somehow his uncle would have to catch up. He turned the corner onto Cortland, and there it was, the black coupe. The driver stood just at the side, shoving the top into place. Caspar smiled a toothy devil's grin of intended murder and jammed his foot on the fuel pedal.

"Caspar! Don't run anyone down! Please don't!" Farideh shrieked.

His victim spotted him and launched over the hood of his car to safety. Caspar rammed the brake pedal down. The Cadillac halted after several small swerves to either side.

Farideh continued screaming until she yelped, "Ouch! Grandmamma Grace! My braid!"

"I'll yank it again if you don't be quiet! My ears!"

"He's trying to murder someone!"

"So?"

"But I don't like hit and runs!"

"Don't be fussy."

Caspar reversed and pulled level with the other vehicle. His target had tumbled off the hood onto the sidewalk. In the passenger seat, the mysterious female stared at Caspar with a riveted, blank expression.

"Hey," Caspar said, leaning forward to see past Farideh, who had frozen while looking at the woman. "What do you see in that clumsy guy?"

The woman blinked. Caspar's gaze narrowed. At last he grasped the significance of her eye colour. The irises were the distinctive blue of Farideh's lineage. His evil smile returned. "Oh, it's you. Now I know why I had to chase you. Your body felt really good when I held it that night on the train. Why don't you trade places with this girl and come with me? I won't stab you with metal this time."

"Figlio di puttana!" *Son of a bitch!* Caspar's rival lurched to a stand without his hat. He shoved a hand beneath his coat and pulled out a pistol. Farideh shrieked and jammed herself into the leg space in front of the seat. The man aimed at Caspar and pulled the trigger. Caspar glanced at the muzzle. The shooter pulled the trigger again and then again. Disbelief washed away the man's angry expression.

Caspar's nose scrunched in disgust. "You call that a weapon? It's defective. Don't you know how to take care of firearms?"

Farideh peeked up to see what was happening.

158

"Wait a minute? Aren't you Jimmy Russo?" Caspar asked. "Hey, how's your brother? He still alive? Or is he in hell with Judge Brown?"

"Son of a bitch!" the man roared. He pulled out a switchblade with his left hand and charged the sedan.

Farideh shrieked and almost ducked again, but Caspar's uncle sped at the attacker from behind and yanked him back by the collar. Godefroy's knee slammed into the gangster's kidneys. The gangster toppled backward onto the street. The gun swung toward Godefroy. Godefroy rammed it down with a foot. The gun fired, and a bullet slammed into asphalt. Farideh jumped in shock.

"Puttana!" *Whore!*

The gangster yanked his arm free and tried to aim again, but Godefroy held his wrist away and hit him multiple times with a fist. The knife waved in Godefroy's direction. He grabbed that wrist as well and pressed a knee on his victim's neck. The gangster choked. A strangled gasp of pain sounded, the fingers of the right hand opened, and the gun dropped to the asphalt. Godefroy grabbed it, darted away from the knife, and shot the gangster in the thigh.

"Fuck!" the man howled, rolling in agony. Godefroy kicked the dropped knife away. It clattered into a gutter. "Fuck! Fuck!"

"What the hell, Uncle? You missed!" Caspar said.

"I did not miss!" Godefroy gasped out. He staggered a little. "Damn it, boy! Witnesses!"

"Like I care."

A car engine roared. Wheels tore black marks into asphalt without changing space.

"No! No, baby! I'm in front of the car!"

Caspar looked at the coupe and found his female prey in the driver's seat. She finally managed to shift gears, and the car shot forward. Godefroy jumped aside. The car screeched off down the street, swerving twice before steadying, but a bad left turn had the coupe up over the curb and the headlights crumpled against a low stone wall.

On the ground, the gangster rolled away from the curb and sat up. "Baby!" he shouted. "Talya!" He tried to get up. Godefroy shot him in the other leg. "Yeaaaaaaagh!"

"Papa!" Farideh wailed.

"Farideh! Farideh!" The girl's father charged up and yanked open the car door.

Sounds of witnesses filtered into Caspar's consciousness at last. He tore his gaze from the woman backing the damaged coupe off the curb and cast to the side and behind. Men, women and children ran shouting and screaming toward cars or toward the church. Some people ran in his direction. Except for the teenaged boys, most had a seasoned air about them. Farideh's mother staggered with a ripped hem not far to the rear of the last rescuer. There were grass stains on her skirt. Ara hovered near the corner at the rectory, both hands clutched over her mouth.

Damn. No gumption at all.

"Farideh!" Tremblay scooped the girl out and carried her away, moving backward several steps. "Damn you, Caspar!"

"Mamma, please step out," Godefroy said. He approached and opened the back door. He still had the pistol in one hand.

"Hurry, Grandmamma," Caspar said.

"Oh, be quiet. Brat!" His grandmother placed her hand in Godefroy's waiting one and hefted herself out of the car. "He drives like a maniac."

"Of course he does," Godefroy said. "Tremblay, take the girls into the church and keep them there until we get back."

"The church? Why ...? Was that her again?"

"Damn, you're slow, Mr. Tremblay," Caspar called through the open passenger window. "Where the hell were you all this time?"

"I got tripped by some idiot kid when we turned around from Yonge Street. He was screaming he'd murder you when he collided with me."

"Bobby Miller? Burton Road? Thinks he's an athlete?" Caspar asked.

"Robby Miller. He's on my blacklist now."

Caspar chortled, Tremblay glowered, Farideh sobbed, and Godefroy sat on the passenger seat of the sedan. He barely had the door shut before Caspar pressed the gas pedal and roared off in pursuit of his prey. The coupe had already disappeared around the corner.

"Figli di puttane!" the gangster yelled after them. *Sons of whores!*

Caspar made a rude gesture out the car window and sped onward.

Chapter Twenty-Two

Trust the curse.

At the next three-way intersection, Caspar hesitated. "Uncle?"

"Use your instinct, Caspar. Ja?" Godefroy said. "You noticed her before any of us did."

His nephew revved the engine and turned right onto Chudleigh. Off in the distance, a black car swerved around a slower vehicle and sped back into the correct lane.

"That's her," Caspar said.

"Ja. How did you spot her at the church? The street was very crowded."

"I don't know. My attention just slammed onto her."

"Ja, I know this feeling," Godefroy muttered.

"With who?"

"It's the curse, Caspar. It's pushing you."

"I know it's pushing me! With who? Farideh? Is it Farideh?"

"What does it matter? I refuse! I refuse, Caspar!"

"Don't pretend it doesn't matter! You're not trying to kill her!" his nephew said.

"And you? This witch? Why weren't you out of this car trying to capture her?"

"You have the talisman!" Caspar said.

"Don't lie to me! The man you wanted to murder, but the woman, Caspar? She is the witch who has damned soul after soul of our people, and you and I are next! But you aren't chasing her to murder her!"

The boy's cheeks reddened. "I was getting to it."

Godefroy heaved a frustrated breath and endeavoured to steady his emotions. He dug for the tiny lump of chain and caged crystal inside his inner breast pocket. "You have to wear the talisman. Keep driving. I'll put it on you."

"Why aren't you wearing that? You're the one who can kill without me around to watch."

"I don't know that it's a good idea for me to wear it. It's like admitting Farideh gave it to me, isn't it?"

Caspar's mouth dropped open a fraction, and then he said, "Yeah, you're right. I'll wear it from now on, but it didn't help me kill the witch last time."

"You weren't wearing it." Godefroy slipped it over his nephew's neck, pulled loose Caspar's tie and top button, and tucked the little cage and glowing crystal out of sight next to his skin.

Caspar wriggled and flinched away from his fingers. "That tickles."

"Sorry." Godefroy pulled the tie straight without redoing the top button.

"She just turned left."

"That might be Greer," Godefroy said, shifting back to his side and clutching the frame of the door through the open window.

"What did you do? Study the entire map of Toronto?"

"Ja."

Caspar laughed. "All our escape routes are already planned, Uncle?"

"Ja! What? You want me to be lazy?"

His nephew threw a grin his way and performed a perfect turn onto Greer at the highest possible speed. In front of oncoming traffic of course. The combined organic and metallic noise of a crash sounded. Screams, rubber squealing, metal crunching. Godefroy looked back in time to see a second collision after the first. A body shot forward through a car windshield and hit the vehicle in front. The death was messy. The body sprawled over the back of the other car, mangled, bloody, twisted, broken glass everywhere.

"You know, Caspar. I think cars need some sort of safety harness for the passengers," Godefroy mentioned.

"And how annoying would that be?" Caspar said derisively. "Did I just have a kill?"

"One or two. Feels like ... two, but I didn't see the first."

"Won't count for much, then. We don't have time to claim the body for the curse."

"No. Too bad."

"Maybe I should make cars my weapon," Caspar said.

"Too clumsy. You can't put a car in your pocket."

Caspar laughed again, but then grew serious and drove while looking for signs of his prey. They arrived at the Chatsworth intersection.

"I think I should have turned earlier," Caspar said.

162

"Follow your instincts," Godefroy insisted. "You just had kills. Trust the curse. There will be good luck."

"God, that sounds so stupid. Trust it and hate it and fear it."

"Ja, but this is what it is."

Grimacing, Caspar turned left again, but this time did it legally. He signalled, waited on the other traffic, and didn't kill anyone with reckless driving when he passed through the intersection. "Why would the curse help us against her?" he asked.

"I don't know. It may have something to do with the girls."

"You haven't gotten that information yet?"

"No. The girls have been reticent since their father hushed them on the train."

"He's being stupid."

"Ja, I know. I'll work on it tonight. Farideh looks as if she's willing to trade secrets."

"Not with Farideh!"

"Aj! Damn it, Caspar! Give it a rest! I have to take the information from the available informant, and she's it!"

"Then I'll be with you."

"Fine, fine."

The hunt continued in silence until they reached Yonge Street. Stopped at the intersection behind traffic, they watched with bored expressions as the damaged black coupe suddenly roared south down Yonge.

Godefroy blinked and then laughed. "Is she lost?"

Caspar sniggered, but the amusement didn't last. "Why isn't she using her power to escape?"

"I don't know. You said she was shot four times, once in the head, and stabbed as well. Her power has perhaps ebbed. It takes energy to heal, ja? Even for a witch."

"If you say so, but maybe it has something to do with the girls."

"Ja, that too."

"She brought that man here for a reason," Caspar said.

"We'll discover it soon enough when we get back to Tremblay," Godefroy said.

"He can't possibly bribe everyone to forget what just happened, not this time."

"Ja, but tru—"

"Trust the curse," Caspar interrupted derisively. "Up until I have an heir."

163

"Ja."

Traffic flowed on Chatsworth again. Caspar turned right onto Yonge, but didn't speed after his quarry.

Godefroy slouched, head propped on a palm while resting his elbow on the car door. "Either the curse is making us lazy, or we have plenty of time."

"Yes, because she's lost."

Godefroy squinted ahead. "Or ready to abandon the car. Is that the coupe?"

"Yes, I do believe so. Why would she leave it?"

"It's damaged and attracting attention, and if she is lost, she may think she passed this way before."

"She should have brought her broomstick." Grinning, Caspar parked the car in the nearest available space, and they walked back to the coupe together. They looked inside. Sunglasses and a red kerchief lay abandoned in the middle of the seat. Caspar pocketed both.

"Hey, that's not your stuff!" a man said.

"Did you see the woman driving this car?" Godefroy asked, turning to face a middle-aged man in the cap and matching jacket of a postal worker. "She's my wife. She had an accident, and we think she's confused."

"Yeah, just look at what she did to that expensive car. Women, eh?"

"Did you see her? Please, it's very important."

"I saw her go up that little avenue between houses," the man said, pointing. "You better hurry. She looked pretty frantic. She took her carpetbag with her. Did she get into a fight with you?"

Godefroy ignored the rude inquisitiveness. "Thank you. Your help is much appreciated. Caspar, bring the keys."

"Got them already." Caspar shut the car door and followed Godefroy into the alley.

"Catch her quick!" the postman called. "A pretty woman like that doesn't stay lonely for long!" He cackled after.

"Give me the gun, Uncle."

Godefroy pulled it from out of his belt and handed it over. One shot, no screams. The sarcastic postman died with his brains splattered out the back of his head. Letters from his mail bag scattered to his side. Godefroy received the pistol back and started walking again. "Why'd you give it back?"

"In case you need to shoot her from a distance," Caspar said.

164

"Right. Let's move. There's noise from the houses now."

"Yeah, I hear it."

They walked at a brisk pace through a narrow lane between sides of buildings and fenced-in backyards, and then on to another street sidewalk, where they stepped out of view of the alley entrance. Shocked citizens at the other end had begun to surround the body on the sidewalk.

"Uncle?"

"Yes?"

"This many kills, I'm not clear on the rules. It's not exactly cumulative, the effects, is it?"

"Not really. The judge gave us little more than a year, if that. He had a soiled heart. The pair on the train gave us seven years roughly, because you murdered them together and because they weren't young or very innocent. Another few years for the car crash, simply for the cruelty of your intentions in causing it, whatever the state of the victims' souls, but the postman, he may give you a few months of extraordinary luck. The curse isn't very hungry now."

"Me? The postman will give me the luck?"

"Ja. Around now, incidental murders give you the luck, not the family. The limit is around nine to eleven years of familial fortune before the curse starts burping the excess of good fate at you while still farting over the rest of us."

Caspar laughed. "Oh, good, because I survived three misfires from that pistol. I probably used up my personal luck right there."

Godefroy grimaced at him. "Ja, Caspar, I saw that. My heart doesn't thank you for the fright. Don't do it again. Remember what I said about wheelchairs. You can still father the heirs without a mind to know you're doing it. Now which way are we going?" He looked to the left and right, but didn't see a woman in a red dress anywhere. Caspar's silence brought his attention back to his nephew. The boy had a disturbed countenance. "What?"

" … nothing. I just …."

"You thought about how you'd father a child as a mindless, drooling idiot, and then die in your pissy sickbed with shit all over your ass and legs?"

"Shut up, Uncle!"

"No! You remember that image! No more stupid risks!"

Caspar attempted to avoid complete capitulation. "Fine, I'll be more careful about the driving."

Godefroy could have punched a board through a wall from sheer frustration. He leaned forward, forcing his nephew to angle back. "This isn't just about the driving. You asked for a longer run, Caspar. With that attitude, do you really expect me to take you seriously? Do not dare the curse to smite you again!"

The boy's gaze lowered. "I'm sorry, Uncle. I'll be more careful."

Godefroy shrugged straight, inhaled deeply and endeavoured for calm. "Which way?" he asked.

"Across the street."

"Fine. Lead."

Caspar navigated through the traffic, and Godefroy followed him to another lane with a wooded pedestrian park beyond it.

Chapter Twenty-Three

An instinct for deception.

Caspar's spine tingled. Anxiety. He didn't feel this emotion often. He'd suffered it during the kidnapping of Judge Brown. The murder hadn't bothered him, but catching his victim and carting the living body off to somewhere quiet—where he could torture as he wished, provoke screams, induce begging, get answers—that had made him nervous. He hadn't wanted to fail.

He didn't want to fail his uncle. Godefroy … for a brief instant, back there at the end of the other alley, Godefroy had frightened him. Caspar wasn't accustomed to feeling fear. His uncle was his rock, his single stable brick in a world with a shaky foundation. He didn't like how his entire being had rattled when Godefroy had hovered over him.

"Caspar?" his uncle said. "Caspar, why do you stop?"

Caspar realized he'd faltered before the end of the lane. "Nothing, Uncle. Just thinking." He started forward again. Godefroy clasped Caspar's upper arm and halted him.

"The curse has been fed, Caspar. You need to brace yourself."

"What?" Caspar raised his eyes, found the man he needed to see, the concerned man who'd raised him even while his father had still lived. Of the last remaining members of his family, only Godefroy had ever really cared. Caspar's father had been morbidly depressed and grim. His grandmother always watched for signs of temper and madness. Caspar never felt comfortable around her. But he did with Godefroy. Until now.

"The curse is satiated," Godefroy said. "Everything you never had to worry about, you have to worry about now."

"But you said I'd have good luck."

"It's not about the luck. The curse feels no need to push you. You feel things now, ja? Things you never did before. I can see it."

"Fear," Caspar said. "Fear and torment."

"Ja, the other half of the curse," Godefroy said. He lifted a hand toward Caspar's shoulder. The boy smashed it away.

"I'm going to end up like my father? A pasty wreck who never wants to get up out of bed?" Caspar demanded.

"I'm sorry. You must have read this in the archives."

"I concentrated on learning how to make quick kills. I skimmed a lot of stuff. I don't want to be like my father!"

The hand rose again. This time Caspar let it clasp a shoulder. His uncle's head lowered. Lips settled on Caspar's forehead. Words were breathed on his skin. "Then don't, Caspar. Get up despite depression. Live despite fear."

"How much of me is this curse, Uncle?" Caspar demanded. "Who am I really? How can I ever know?"

Godefroy's arms wrapped around him, and his chin rested lightly on Caspar's crown. "Break the curse, Caspar. Break it no matter what."

Caspar clutched the back of Godefroy's suit jacket with one hand, heart beating too fast, stomach unsettled, the energy in his spine a torment he hated. "I don't know how."

"There is something at work here other than the curse. If you can't trust yourself, then trust it." His uncle's head shifted. "She's close, Caspar," Godefroy breathed into his ear.

Caspar looked up. "The air?"

"Ja. It feels heavy." Godefroy pulled back. "Look there."

Caspar squinted in the direction his uncle indicated. In the small park, beneath the trees, dead birds were scattered everywhere. A small flock of starlings decorated the earth near a garbage bin. The plump bodies of dozens of pigeons surrounded an occupied bench. An old man sat there, his torso slumped over his lap. A bag of bird seed had fallen at his feet. Grains speckled the dirt path. A lifeless squirrel sprawled in the centre of the spill.

Caspar stepped away from his uncle, but trailed one hand around his flank and grasped the suit from the front. He scanned closer to their position and found a dead bird only feet away. "Uncle?"

"I can't follow you. Whatever you do now, I can't witness, not until you break whatever spell she casts here. I think the only reason I'm not dead now …." He paused to inhale and struggled with the air like it was some viscous fluid that would smother him.

"Is because you are my witness," Caspar ended for him. He pushed Godefroy backward up the alley, until his breathing wasn't as laboured. "I'm going. Stay distant until you feel the air change."

"Ja."

168

Caspar started down the path to the centre of the park, and the tormenting prickle in his spine was gone, the hesitation vanished. The guilt, the anxiety; he didn't give a damn for either. His uncle meant everything to him. This renewed sense of determination lasted for the three minutes he searched, and then he saw her, and that purpose-blurring slam of attention tore all thoughts from his head again.

She sat on a bench off the main path, almost hidden by trees except for the too-vivid red dress and brimless cloche hat. She had a handkerchief to her face. Tears wetted her cheeks, but the expression, what he could see of it, wasn't fearful or sad. It was angry, frustrated, confused.

Caspar turned down the side path and rounded the trees into her view. Her head lifted. She froze with wide eyes. Hands in his suit pockets, Caspar slouched onto the bench at her side. "Weird weather. It's raining dead birds and squirrels. And old men."

Her torso angled in his direction while at the same time shifting away.

"Don't run again. Are you really that boring?"

Apparently she was, because she darted up, carpetbag in her grip, and dashed down the path. Caspar chased her, spun her about and slammed her into a tree. She held the bag in front of her as he pressed in. He set both hands on the bole and leaned down to bite a cheek.

"Ah!"

He lifted his head. "Sorry, but those are cute, your cheeks. Cheeks look better blushing. But you weren't blushing, so I had to bite."

"Who are you?"

"Are we back to that again? Does it matter? Turn a little. I need to bite the other one."

"Get away from me!"

"Mmm, no." He pursued her face and almost bit the other cheek. She shoved him back. He lunged forward, grabbed the loose arm and pinned it over her head. A kick in the shin changed the battle from a melee against a tree to a struggle on the woodland ground as Caspar forced her off balance and fell on top of her. The bag tumbled to the side. He wedged his body between her legs, caught her wrists, rocked his pelvis against the softness he'd been remembering since the train.

"Your lingerie? What colour is it today? Is it red?"

Persian profanities heated the air around his ears. He laughed and kissed her, reared away before her teeth latched on, kissed her again. Instinct provoked a second thrust of his pelvis against her fork. For a brief moment, she didn't struggle, let him kiss, pressed with equal intensity against his crotch, but then she jerked a hand free and scratched him down one side of his face. She almost snagged his eye out.

"God! Fuck! Fuck! Stop fighting me! I love you!"

His blood dripped onto her face, into her mouth. He struggled to seize her wrist again. She smashed at his ears, his throat, caught her fingers in the chain and yanked the caged crystal into the open.

The fighting ceased. She opened her bloodied mouth and shrieked a high-pitched cry of terror. In the silence that followed, with his breath gasping in and out from excitement and hers from terror, her eyes lifted to meet his.

"No," she whispered. "No."

"Let me put it this way," Caspar said. "Fuck me and I'll let you live. Kill me after. I don't care. Just fuck me." He lowered to kiss her again.

"No!" The battle recommenced. She gouged at his neck. He dragged her hand off. The talisman hit her face near an eye. She flinched away from it. The cage and chain dragged along her cheek. Caspar followed the trajectory, lowered his face against her neck and bit a shoulder. She shrieked a second time. The cry broke off with a shocked inhalation.

Caspar raised his head. The muzzle of a gun pressed against her brow. He remembered he had family, an uncle, a purpose. He still thrust the gun away. "Uncle! Don't!"

"Caspar—"

"You're his witness?" the woman said. "You …?"

"Uncle, don't shoot her until after we fuck," Caspar said. "I don't want her ugly while I do it. We'll kidnap her after, while she's senseless from a bullet in her brain."

"Caspar, you'll father the heirs on her."

She struggled again. Caspar laughed and shoved her down. "Fine. I'll father the heirs on her."

"Caspar, stop!"

"No!" Caspar caught both her wrists together and reached under her dress. "We can't kill her, Uncle. So just let me fuck her. That's all she's good for."

170

"Your uncle is your witness?" she grunted, digging in her heels and trying to creep out from beneath him.

"Yeah, so?" Caspar snatched her lingerie and yanked.

"So you're fine with that? You don't care that he abandoned your father to die alone, without the one person on earth who could have brought him peace during his final moment?"

Caspar stilled. "What?"

"And your twin? You're fine with not having your brother to live and die at your side? You're fine that your uncle stole his life from you, tore away the sibling who would have made you feel whole?"

"My father ...! My father did that!"

"Your father?" Her laughter scorned him. "If he's the witness, then your father was the slayer! The slayer can't touch his own family!"

He stared at her, his soul freezing, congealing his insides, smothering the fire in his crotch, the madness in his mind. "Uncle ...?"

"Yes, that's right," she spat. "That's how it works. You can't kill your heir or the witness, but the witness can kill as many of his heirs as he wants until the curse gets the best of him." She laughed again. "You didn't know? You're a fool. A stupid, young fool. He doesn't have to care if you live or die, just that he never has an heir to succeed him."

Caspar lurched away from her. She scrambled backward, snatched the carpetbag and hesitated with her attention fixed on Godefroy. Caspar pulled out his switchblade. She glanced at him, but focused on Godefroy again. Godefroy remained crouched on one knee, his impenetrable gaze on Caspar and the gun pointed earthward. The witch scrabbled further back, staggered upright and ran down the path. Caspar and Godefroy remained as they were.

"You did it," Caspar said. "My brother. My mother."

"Ja."

"You destroyed records about witnesses killing heirs."

"Some. Some I altered."

"The diary ...? You planted it for me to read. Is anything in it true?"

"Some things."

"When my father was in the coma? It's because you tried to kill him too?"

"Ja."

A wave of dizziness washed over Caspar. He dropped the switchblade, realized it, and lifted his numb fingers. "I can't," he whispered, staring at them. "I can't even want to."

"Break the curse, and you can murder me if you want. I'll let you."

Caspar curled against the loamy earth and howled in despair. His uncle's hands slid over his back, clutched his flanks, pulled him up into his arms. Godefroy muffled Caspar's next howl against his chest. Caspar couldn't struggle, couldn't hate his uncle, couldn't want his death. He could only grieve. His rock had shattered. He had no foundation.

"Caspar, this isn't how she made it look."

"How can I believe you? How can I believe anything you say?" Caspar wept. "Why am I still clutching at you like some stupid child? Why? I mean nothing to you!"

"This is not true. I love you! I do love you! That witch, she didn't say the full truth. She doesn't know the truth!"

"And what's that? Yes? What is it? That I'm just another slayer you must accompany? Is this your long run, Uncle? Are you planning to murder the next witness too? Are you aiming for immortality like her?"

"Your father was there! It was his plan! But I failed!"

Caspar gulped, sucked in a shuddering breath, and waited for more.

"I failed him. I didn't hit hard enough with the stone, and ...." His uncle inhaled shakily, and Caspar looked up to see him weeping as well. "He woke up. He woke up to live his accursed life with one child dead, his wife dead, to live with a brother who hadn't been strong enough to end this everlasting torment. I killed a little boy! I killed ...!"

His uncle's eyes scrunched shut. Caspar waited out his misery, fascinated. Was it real? Could it be real? It felt real. "Did he watch you do it?"

Godefroy opened his eyes, looked down, met Caspar's gaze. "No. I had to do him first. He would have been compelled to stop me."

"Then why didn't you shoot him?"

Horror and revulsion played over his uncle's face. He struggled for control and banished the emotions. "I couldn't do that to him."

"Why?"

"I would have collapsed. I can't .... I couldn't ...."

172

"You couldn't splatter his brains all over the place? Squeamishness is useless in a witness."

"He was my brother!" Again Godefroy struggled for calm. "It was hard enough to lift the stone. I drank. I drank for hours before. He shouted at me. He begged. He …!"

"He what?"

"I can't. I can't say it."

"He what, Uncle?" Caspar wrenched himself upright, grasped his uncle's lapels and shook him. "He what?"

"He mutilated himself."

Caspar released him. He didn't want to know more. Even if his uncle lied, he didn't want to know, except …. "Why did you fail to kill me?"

"Because the curse was stronger. It has forever been stronger. I am not the first witness who has tried to assassinate the slayer's heir."

"What happened to you, Uncle?"

"I fainted. You woke me up. You wanted help to wake up Helge." Godefroy's tears began anew. "We couldn't, and I said …. I said your brother had begun the enchanted sleep and that you would free him from it one day. I wiped away your tears. I fed you. I put you down for a nap in my brother's bed. I laid Edvard next to you, and I went outside to dig your mother's grave, and I put … and I put little Helge in her arms." He lifted a hand over his eyes to hide his misery.

Caspar yanked his wrist down. "Is that true? Is any of it true?"

Godefroy sobbed and bent over the earth without answering. "Gud! Gud hjälpe mig!" *God! God help me!* "Aaah, aaah!"

Caspar stared at him. Slowly he reached out and placed a hand on his uncle's head. His uncle clutched it and wept.

Caspar's mind cleared. There was only one truth that mattered. They were cursed.

Chapter Twenty-Four

The art of confidence.

Beneath a blanket that had been loaned to them, Farideh and Ara huddled on a pew near the front of the church. Farideh had become dizzy and faint not long after their father had pulled her from the sedan. Police officers had arrived and attempted to question her, but she'd stammered and forgotten words, mixed up languages, shivered and stared in incomprehension at the uniforms and the mouths moving in unfamiliar faces.

The demanding noises, the frustrated eyes, it all became more and more unreal until Father Peter had arrived with the blanket. He'd helped her father force the police officers to back off, and they'd given her some quiet. Ara had arrived to cuddle next to her. The world had become real again, but they hadn't spoken. The police waited for Farideh to show signs she was able to talk, but she didn't want to tell them anything. She didn't like their ugly behaviour, the accusative pushiness of their questions, the way their expressions questioned the validity of even the simplest response.

"You say your sedan is yellow?" an officer said.

"That's right. You've asked this already."

Farideh peeked over the back of the pew. Her father and mother stood near the centre of the church. Two officers faced them. Father Peter sat on a pew where he could observe all four. Grandmamma Grace had pleaded exhaustion and been conducted to the vestry where she rested on a small two-seat sofa. Father Peter had offered the vestry to the girls as well, but the police hadn't wanted to let Farideh out of view. The police had questioned her parent's more than once now. The sergeant left the church, came back, left and came back again. Always it was the same questions, but this time his ugly comportment was smug as well.

"There was a report about an accident over on Chudleigh and Greer," the police officer said. "Witnesses say a yellow car was involved."

"Is everyone all right?" Farideh's father asked.

"There were two deaths."

"Are you saying my cousins have died, officer?" her mother said.

"No, ma'am. I'm asking if you if your cousins were involved in that car accident, because if they were, they're murderers."

"How is she to know that?" Farideh's father demanded. "We've been waiting here all this time. Why aren't you sending men to find that kidnapper?"

"My men are out there investigating your claims and searching for your relatives. We don't have proof there's any kidnapper. What we have here are witnesses who watched this kid Caspar steal your car, almost run down dozens of pedestrians, and then his uncle shoots a man the kid tries to run over. And now I've got dozens of unhappy citizens scared of being murdered by your wife's cousins, and a visitor to Toronto is lying in the hospital with bullet wounds in both legs."

"That man is a kidnapper and a hardened criminal," Farideh's mother said. "He was stalking us in New York."

"So you say, but this isn't what witnesses saw. Now if your girl can talk, she can confirm she saw this woman kidnapper from your vacation. But she's not talking is she?"

"Ara already confirmed this. The woman on the train was in that black Cadillac coupe," David Tremblay said.

"Ara? Ara wasn't the one sitting in the car with this Caspar Grace, was she?"

"No, we've gone over this already."

The sergeant's antagonistic, smug attitude intensified. "Well, if she wasn't in the car staring right at this woman, she was pretty far away to recognise a supposed kidnapper."

"Farideh will talk later when she's not in shock," David said. "Look; call the number I gave you."

"We had another report as well, Tremblay. Just feet away from a parked black Cadillac coupe with a busted front end, a postman was murdered. Shot to death right in the head."

"Call the number, Sergeant," David repeated.

"This is a police investigation—"

"Call the number! Call it or lose your job!"

"Now, you listen here! You don't threaten me! I don't care who you are! You don't threat—!"

"Sergeant Pike," Father Peter interrupted. He indicated the church entrance. "They're here."

176

The sergeant and his underling faced the double doors. Caspar and Godefroy had entered the church.

Farideh and Ara twisted around until they knelt on the pew with arms resting on the back. Caspar had an unsightly scratch on the left side of his face. It ran from just above his eyebrow, skipped his eye and continued down to the middle of his cheek. Blood striated his neck as well, three long lines of it. Godefroy bore no sign of injury, but both Graces had a grim, defeated air that unsettled Farideh and had Ara clenching the wood of the pew until her fingers were white.

"Something very bad happened," Ara breathed.

"I know." Farideh waited for the police officer to spout accusations and arrest the Graces, but oddly he stared up at Godefroy and said nothing. Farideh thought he looked a little awed. "Why isn't he being mean and pushy like with Papa?"

"It's the archangel effect," Ara whispered.

"Huh?"

"It happened to you too, remember? You were stunned when you first saw him. I think it's a part of their curse."

"That doesn't seem like a curse to me," Farideh muttered—well, except that Caspar's stare could freeze a venomous snake, but even that didn't seem much of a curse.

"Shh!" Ara hissed.

"Oh, Caspar!" their mother cried. She pulled a fresh handkerchief from her purse and dabbed at blood on his cheek. "Oh, it's dried up and scabbing. We need water to clean this."

"We'll take him to the lavatory, Mrs. Tremblay," Father Peter said, rising to a stand.

"Before that, Caspar, the keys and kerchief, please" Godefroy said. His nephew dug both items from a pocket and handed them over. Godefroy offered them to the sergeant, who accepted them with the same numb stare. Deena and the priest paused to watch his reaction.

"Sergeant … uh …?" Godefroy prodded.

"Pike!" the police officer said, blinking and seeming to return to the present. He glanced down at the red kerchief with a puzzled frown.

"Sergeant Pike, we followed the female kidnapper to a park not far off Yonge Street. She abandoned the car. Those are the keys. She wore that kerchief before she fled. If you have blood hounds, I suggest you make use of them. She's a murderess. She shot a postman. She caused an accident on the corner of Chudleigh and Greer. I'm afraid there were deaths. She should be apprehended with all speed. This is a very dangerous woman."

"She caused the car accident?"

"Yes. I'm sure there were witnesses. They should be able to corroborate her presence. A damaged car making dangerous turns in heavy traffic is hard to miss."

"The reports were a yellow car made a squealing turn at that corner."

"Yes, but we had no time to stop and assist the injured, I'm afraid. We couldn't risk losing sight of her."

"You say she shot the postman?" Sergeant Pike asked.

"Yes, officer. He only wanted to offer the woman his assistance." Godefroy shrugged sadly. "What man wouldn't? The poor fellow. We were endeavouring to stop her when he interfered, thinking we were criminals assaulting a lady. He hit me with his letter bag. I dropped the gun. She picked it up and shot him. Fortunately, it misfired again after that or we wouldn't be here now. Caspar was lucky not to lose an eye during the initial struggle before she seized the gun."

"You say you were there where she parked the damaged coupe. Why didn't anyone see your vehicle?"

"Uh, yes, we parked it in a bad place and the landlord called for a tow." Godefroy smiled sheepishly. "We left it right in front of his driveway entrance, but he was very nice about it after we returned and drove us to the garage to fetch it."

Godefroy switched the subject back to the escaped murderess. "You should tell your people to be very cautious. We chased the woman down some walking lanes between houses, but we had to turn back at the park. We saw dead birds throughout the park and an old man slumped over a bench. We didn't dare approach closer. I believe this woman may be carrying some sort of toxic chemical in her carpetbag."

"Lord have mercy on us all!" Father Peter said. "This is horrendous! What sort of person does such a thing?"

"An international spy, I'm afraid. I'm sure Tremblay will need to contact his superiors immediately to alert them," Godefroy said. "You have done so, haven't you, Tremblay?"

Farideh's father stared at him with a hard expression.

Godefroy gave a small start and another chagrined grimace. "Oh, I'm sorry. I shouldn't have …."

178

"What is this?" Sergeant Pike demanded.

"Well, you have to keep it hush, Sergeant," Godefroy said. "Tremblay is a Canadian operative of great value to our government. This woman has more than once tried to harm his children to force secrets from him." Godefroy looked at Tremblay. "I'm sorry, David. It can't be helped. You'll have to confide in these men and call your superiors at once. I'm sure the sergeant and his junior will swear secrecy. And you will too, won't you, Father Peter? This is for Canada, after all."

"Oh, he's good," Ara whispered during the tumult of emphatic agreements.

"Yes," Farideh agreed. "How did he know Papa was a spy?"

"I think he's been everywhere in the house while we've been sleeping," Ara said.

Farideh ripped her gaze from Godefroy to stare at her sister. "What? How do you know?"

"Well, I haven't been sleeping well lately," Ara whispered, covering her mouth to make the words even less audible to anyone but Farideh, "and I saw him come out of the room where the safe is hidden, and he's been in Papa's office too."

"Why didn't you say anything?"

"He's either the angel of death or his handler. I didn't want to say anything. Papa wasn't talking. Godefroy had to get information from where he could. How can they protect us if they're ignorant? Well, Godefroy saw me, and I saw him. I smiled, he smiled, and we went back into our own rooms. It was just our funny little secret until now."

"Ara, you amaze me," Farideh said.

Ara smiled a tiny wicked smile, but then focused on the conversation again. Farideh boggled over the duplicity of her sister, a duplicity she apparently shared with Godefroy.

"He can't have found Maman's earlier diary," Farideh whispered, looking at him again, "or he wouldn't still be asking Papa about our curse."

"If he didn't find it, it's not in the house. Did you notice his accent, Fairy?" Ara whispered back. "It's practically vanished. He's brilliant."

"The best handler ever," Farideh breathed.

Ara gave her an offended glance. "Is not. I am. I'm far more subtle."

Farideh boggled again, this time over her sister's self-deception and conceit.

The group of adults split up. Their mother and the priest led Caspar to the lavatory to have his wounds cleaned. Godefroy continued his report to the police officers, adding more details as they required it. Their father was permitted to retreat to the vestry to use the church telephone.

"Godefroy must have ditched the gun," Ara said a bit later.

"Huh?"

"Fairy, you should rest. You aren't thinking all that quickly."

"I don't need to rest! What do you mean he ditched the gun?"

"Shh! Keep your voice down."

"Sorry." She lowered her voice, blushing a little because Godefroy had glanced her way. "So what did you mean?"

"As if they would let that woman get it," Ara whispered. "Caspar shot that postman for whatever reason, but Godefroy blamed the witch, so they can't be found with the murder weapon on their persons, can they?"

"Oh. I can see your love of The Hardy Boys has its uses after all."

"Do not start with me on that again."

"You've switched from an imaginary boyfriend to the imaginary boyfriend's ultimate criminal rival."

"Fairy!"

Farideh laughed at Ara's severe expression, but stopped when Caspar arrived at their pew and sat facing the front of the church. He didn't look at them. His scratch had been cleaned, but it was still a nasty red gash.

"You fought with her again," Ara said. "Don't worry. Maman's poultice will make the scratch go away."

He offered no reaction. His expression didn't change, but the sensation of despair assailed Farideh again. She and Ara slid around until they sat properly on the pew, but their gazes remained on him.

"Caspar?" Ara tried again. "Caspar, I'm sure you won't fail next time. Don't be hard on your—"

Her breath shuddered inward. With a swift motion, he'd pulled the talisman from around his neck and dropped it on Ara's lap. He rose and departed without a word. Ara hunched over the abandoned artefact, covered her mouth and wept tears on it. Farideh gazed at the dull crystal and determined to get answers from Godefroy that night

180

no matter what. Something very bad had happened, bad enough to crush Caspar's spirit.

She half turned and searched the church. Caspar had collapsed on a pew closer to his uncle, but didn't look at either him or the officers still present. The sergeant exited the church for another consultation with his men outside. His aide gave them some privacy at last and departed as well. Neither exhibited the ugly comportment of before. Now they moved with an almost eager enthusiasm, like guard dogs about to win a reward from their master. Godefroy glanced at his nephew, lowered his gaze and shoved his hands in his trouser pockets.

Noise at the vestry door attracted Farideh's attention. Her father walked up the aisle. Godefroy's dejected stillness melted. He moved forward to meet David. They halted facing each other.

"The gun?" David asked, his voice low but not obscured enough to stop Farideh from hearing.

"I pitched it in a garbage bin without the bullets. I wiped it clean of prints and tossed some greasy rubbish over it. Here." Godefroy pulled several bullets from his pocket and handed them to Farideh's father. "Best if they're not on me."

"You're damn right about that," David said stiffly. "Why the postman?"

"He was rude."

"Fuck, Godefroy!"

Farideh hunched lower in the pew. She'd never heard her father swear like that before.

"Sorry," Godefroy said.

"You or the boy? Who shot?"

"Me."

David glowered. Godefroy bore up under the stare without looking away. "The car crash?" David asked.

"Caspar's doing, as you likely guessed."

"Damn it! How do you expect to the cops to believe what you said? There were witnesses!"

"And the cops will ask about the black coupe with the damaged front, plant the seeds of doubt, and the witnesses, in their attempts to be important, will remember events differently."

"You can't be sure of that."

"Yes, I can. I've done it before. It's easy. You know it's easy, Tremblay. You've done it too. The witnesses will be led. Sergeant

Pike is very eager to be a heroic accessory to your secret and exciting life."

"Fuck," her father said again.

Godefroy glanced at Farideh and looked away. "The deaths in the park were a form of smothering, not toxic gas," he said to her father. "The witch makes the air unbreathable when she's upset."

"We'll have to go with the toxic gas story."

"Ja."

"Watch it with the accent!"

"Sorry."

"You don't relax until you're off the job, Grace," her father said.

"Yes, fine. I've got it. Your superiors? Will they assist?"

"How the hell do you know anything about that?"

Godefroy shrugged. "One of your daughters mentioned a war diary. You strike me as a man who would be wasted at the front, Tremblay. You and your wife are still active, aren't you?"

"Are you a damned spy?"

Godefroy laughed. Farideh heard only bitterness. "No. I'm just very good at what I need to do."

"And what is that?" David demanded

"Keeping my nephew active," Godefroy said.

"As a murderer? Why?"

"Equivalent exchange works very nicely for me, Tremblay. Tell me about your wife's family curse."

David's lips thinned, and Farideh knew he still wasn't interested in telling Godefroy anything. So stubborn. He wanted all the Grace secrets before he decided to dole out any of his own, but Farideh believed her sister. Godefroy had already stolen any information he was interested in, except for the facts about her mother's family curse.

Godefroy stepped back a pace, his gaze hard. His hands went back into his pockets and he retreated to sit with his nephew. Farideh's father spat another bad word and glanced at Farideh. She huddled even lower in her pew.

"What have you decided?" her father unexpectedly asked.

"To tell him everything if I can get what I need to know from Maman," she said.

"Equivalent exchange, princess."

"Of course," she said.

His finger thrust toward her. "And don't let him touch you!"

182

Farideh blushed red and nodded. Her father thumped off to the vestry, very not happy. Farideh looked at the Graces. They were together, inches apart on the same bench, and yet Farideh had never witnessed so much distance between them until now.

Chapter Twenty-Five

Resolve.

"I'm going anyway," Farideh said. She peeked out the crack of the door, but then glanced back at her sister when Ara didn't answer. "Ara?"

Farideh shoved the door almost shut and squinted at the dim figure in the bed. The lights in the room were off. Officially she and her sister were asleep, but Farideh was about to take the risk of being discovered out of bed and where she did not belong under any circumstances except two: housecleaning or marriage. Housecleaning was a poor excuse this late in the evening and marriage out of the question at her age.

"Fine, but what's the use?" Ara said. "Wait until Maman gives us the full story tomorrow."

"She should have said it today. She promised."

"I know! But there was an attempt today. She has a migraine, Fairy! Papa is still furious with the whole mess."

"He's not here! He's off reporting to his superiors still. Now is as good a time as any. I have to give the crystal at least. If Caspar doesn't want it, fine. Godefroy will take it."

"Fine! Fine. Just don't let him touch you."

"Ara! He's not like …."

"Not like who? Caspar?" Ara demanded. "What has Caspar done to you?"

"Nothing," Farideh said, glad she was in the dark. Her overheated skin would have given her away worse than firing off a flare gun. "He scared me off, is all, by being a rude pig."

"He's mine!" Ara said.

"I know!" Farideh snapped, shaking both arms in frustration. The dim crystal rattled in its little cage.

"Shh!"

"You started yelling first!" Farideh said.

"I'm not yelling! Just go!"

"Fine!" Farideh yanked the door open. Faced with the dark corridor, her anger evaporated. It wasn't that she was afraid of the dark, but if Caspar were lurking out there ....

But he wouldn't be. He'd officially abandoned them, hadn't he? When he'd thrown the crystal onto Ara's lap.

Farideh glanced at his door and found no light beneath. Not very relieved, because it would be just like him to trick her and hide, she stepped out into the chill space and pulled her door ajar. Godefroy was still awake. A light shone from his room. She moved down the hall toward the warm glow.

She almost knocked, realized that would be stupid, and tried a light scratch. She won no response. She glanced at the keyhole, but it was black; therefore the privacy flap still covered it.

Well, she couldn't dither outside his door all night. One of her father's hired guns was bound to show up on patrol soon. She opted for opening the door just enough to peek within.

Praying it wasn't locked, she twisted the knob. She sent a silent thank you to heaven when the door opened with only a light push. She craned around the corner and discovered Godefroy slouched over his writing desk, his head resting on a forearm. His other hand sat in his lap with an open bottle of brown liquor.

Farideh stepped in and shut the door as softly as she could. She approached with the talisman raised. She thought to put it on the desk and leave before he awakened and discovered her, but she hesitated at his side. A diary lay open on the desk, and remnants of crisped paper sprinkled the bottom of a candle holder. The candle had burned three-quarters down, but it was no longer lit.

Farideh bent closer to the diary. More than one page had been torn from the gutter. Godefroy had destroyed multiple leaves in one section. Farideh straightened in disappointment. There was no use trying to read what remained. He'd used another language, probably Swedish.

His Borsalino was on the desk as well. It was upside down and cradled an open switchblade. At first she thought it must be Caspar's. She'd seen his weapon up close that morning. She'd snagged it from his pocket when he left the suit jacket hanging off the back of an armchair. She'd pushed the switch, shrieked in surprise, and dropped the knife point first into the floor mere inches from her toes. Godefroy had entered the room, pulled the weapon out of the wood, shushed her and hidden the filched knife before her father arrived to

186

check on her. Farideh had lied about being startled by a bee in the house, and Godefroy had kept his foot on the telltale hole in the floor until he and her father left the salon.

But this one couldn't be Caspar's blade. A closer examination revealed a different coloured handle. The wood texture was finer, darker. Farideh tilted the hat toward her. The name tag had been cut from the inside. Another inspection of the candle holder confirmed there were burned fibres scattered with the paper bits.

Puzzled, she glanced around the room and spotted the huge trunks the Graces had brought to the house, the one Godefroy had personally seen after and the one that had arrived later on a different vehicle. He'd placed them together on one side of the room. A heavy lid stood propped against the wall. Farideh approached to discover the contents of that trunk.

She found books and bundled letters. A lacquered box sat to one side of these. She lifted the lid. Scrolls were piled within. Some were in poor shape. They all looked very old. Cracked parchment suggested even a small touch might crumble them. She replaced the top.

Those books …? None had printed letters on the covers or spines. If they had any lettering, it was hand-written. On several, variants of the word grace were written in other languages, but always at the end of the title. All the books were of a size easily carried in one hand. Were these all personal memoirs?

She glanced at the other trunk. Could it be full of family memoirs as well? She didn't think she should take the risk of trying to open it. She might awaken Godefroy.

She returned to the desk, set the talisman on the open pages of his diary, and glanced at Godefroy. His suit coat was off and hanging from the back of the chair. He'd removed the vest as well. His tie was loose and the shirt undone. His suspenders hung at his waist.

He wouldn't like that alcohol spilling over his new trousers. She reached for the bottle, slowly pulled it from his lax grip, and placed it on the desk. She couldn't find the cap. After a brief delay, she moved the bottle further away in case he awakened groggy and inadvertently knocked it over.

Just as she put the bottle down, a warm arm wound around her hips. Farideh froze in trepidation. Flee? Stay and brazen this out? A pleasant tingle started in her spine and spread to wherever he touched her. The idea of brazening the situation out strengthened.

"Vad är det här? Vem är denna vackra houri i mitt sovrum?" he murmured.

His head lifted from his arm, and he blinked at Farideh's favourite sleeping outfit, a loose cotton undershirt with harem pants below. His attention focused on the undershirt. "Ser jag rätt? Är detta en harem pojke? Min sömn är förbannad också."

His forehead landed on her upper abdomen. "Aj! Rotten luck."

Farideh endeavoured not to disturb him even with her breathing, until his free hand rose and clasped the material over her right breast. She squeaked. He bolted straight in the chair and released her.

"Farideh!" His eyes bugged like a pair of owl's peepers. An owl on fire and panicking.

"Uh … sorry," she said. "I brought the talisman."

"What?" He glanced at the diary, discovered the necklace, looked again at her. "Another time would have been better? Ja?" One hand lifted over his heart. "Helvete. Mitt hjärta."

"But I need to know what's happening!" Farideh protested.

"You tell me."

Farideh bunched her fingers in frustration. "Maman got the migraine and hasn't said yet."

"Fine. Later, then. Get out."

"What did you say just now," she demanded, "while you were still sleepy?"

"Nothing!" he said. "Just leave."

"No, I will not! I want a translation. I won't leave without one. I won't!"

"Aj! I thought I was dreaming of a harem boy. All right?"

Farideh's face caught fire. She was vaguely surprised her head didn't explode. "Boy? Harem boy?"

"Ja, the undershirt threw me. But ja, my palm is burning now after touching proof you're not a boy." He flapped the guilty appendage near his head and looked away from her. "Please leave."

"I look like a boy?"

"I wasn't looking at your face!" he cried, now with the palm over his eyes. "Gud i himlen. Jag är i trubbel."

"What were you looking at?" she demanded.

"What …? Get out of my room, little girl!"

But Farideh had suffered enough of his distractions and evasions, and pushed for answers. "Why are you burning pages of your diary?"

188

"What does it matter why? It's just a stupid diary! They're all stupid and vain!"

"They are not vain! I keep one! Don't you care that your memoirs will be lost forever? Don't you care that your descendents will never get a chance to really know you?"

He lunged to a stand. Farideh squeaked again and leaned away from him, feeling very small and threatened, but certain naughty parts of her body tingled with increasing excitement.

"Those pages weren't worthy of my descendents!" he said. "They weren't worthy of my past!"

He slapped his hand on the diary and yanked out more pages. Along with the scraps, the talisman rose in his fisted hand. He caught sight of the happy shining crystal and staggered back. He almost fell over the desk chair. Farideh lurched forward and helped steady him on the seat. His breath ragged, he stared at the caged stone.

"Is it redemption? Why does it even like me?"

"Are you going to save us, Godefroy?"

Both Farideh and Godefroy looked toward the bedroom door.

"Ara?" Farideh said.

"Are you going to save us?" she repeated.

"Ja. What else is left for me?"

"Caspar will forgive you."

"You don't know."

"He'll forgive you." Ara approached the desk and confiscated the open bottle. "I like the dog," she said and returned to the corridor. "Farideh, you shall not stay in this room with him. You'll ruin Caspar's long run."

"What?" Confused, Farideh glanced at Godefroy. He was smiling, not a huge smile, just a small one, but with a hope to match the cheerful fire in the crystal he held. "Godefroy?" Farideh said.

"Ja, she's brilliant, your sister. Best go now before she finds a way to make you pay for disobedience."

"Huh?"

"She's your handler, isn't she?"

Farideh scowled. "I don't understand either of you!"

"No matter. You don't need to. You just need to let us take care of the little details."

"Aaaaah!" she hissed. "I hate this! It's like you and Ara are twins! You're both keeping secrets!"

He chortled. Farideh pushed him off his chair, ignored his startled yelp and the crash, and thumped from his room.

"Aj! Close the door!" she heard Godefroy say, but she refused to go back and continued to her room.

"I'll get you good later," she muttered to herself. "Just you wait. No more secrets!" She entered her room, heel kicked the door shut with a small thud and confronted her sister's dark figure. "What is going on with you and Godefroy?"

"Nothing, really. We're just agreeing on things."

"What things? What's this long run thing that Caspar is doing?"

"Oh, that's just something that fell into my ears out of the messy cloud."

"What messy cloud?"

"You know; the one that's been around us since the fortune teller's at Coney Island."

"But what does it mean?"

"That you're twelve."

Farideh's shoulders slumped. "Ara! Make sense," she pleaded.

"Stop trying to kiss Godefroy. Or Caspar."

Darn it. Not that sort of twelve again. "I'm not—!"

"Go to bed," Ara interrupted.

"Ara!"

"Go to bed! I'll start crying," Ara threatened.

Farideh gave up and went to bed. "Why does that witch think I'm the strong one?" she grumbled into her pillow.

Ara slipped into the bed on the other side and cuddled in close. "Yes, that was odd, wasn't it? No one appreciates guile, I suppose."

"Except Godefroy," Farideh sniped.

"Don't be jealous."

"I'm not!"

"Go to sleep."

Farideh huffed in frustration, but all the same, she shut her eyes and tried to sleep. Somehow she knew her sister was smiling into the darkness and found herself doing the same.

"Thank you," Farideh said.

"Hmm?"

"For making Godefroy happy again."

"You're welcome, Fairy."

Farideh sighed in contentment and at last fell asleep.

190

~~~

The story will continue in the second novel of *The Grace Murders*.

~~~

Translation of Godefroy's sleepy comments in the final chapter:

"Vad är det här? Vem är denna vackra houri i mitt sovrum?" *What is this? Who is this beautiful houri in my bedroom?*

"Ser jag rätt? Är detta en harem pojke? Min sömn är förbannad också." *Do I see right? Is this a harem boy? My sleep is cursed too.*

"Helvete. Mitt hjärta." *Damn it. My heart.*

"Gud i himlen. Jag är i trubbel." *God in heaven. I'm in trouble.*